THE GIRL DOWNSTAIRS

Tony Flower

An Authors OnLine Book

Text Copyright © Tony Flower 2014

Cover design by Tony Flower and Kelly Dempsey ©

British Library Cataloguing Publication Data.
A catalogue record for this book is available
from the British Library

ISBN 978-0-7552-0751-0

Authors OnLine Ltd
19 The Cinques
Gamlingay, Sandy
Bedfordshire SG19 3NU
England

*To the JBO, the Old Gits and
the Curry Nights Collaboration.*

Also by Tony Flower

That Bloody Book

Why?

www.tonyflower.net

Disclaimers and Acknowledgements

Before we embark upon this extraordinary journey, I would like to stress that this is entirely a work of fiction. I have no prejudice against or knowledge of corruption relating to any of the organisations or countries featured herein. All characters and the bodies that they represent are there purely to service the story and, if some are depicted in an unfavourable light, it is purely for dramatic or humorous effect; apart from the bits about pimps and politicians, in which case I mean every word. As usual, any resemblances to persons living or dead are purely coincidental.

A huge thanks to the many comedy writers and performers, whose works have not only enriched my life, but have also inspired some of the more bizarre passages.

I confess unashamedly to paraphrasing, or nicking the odd word or two, from some influential people; including, in no particular order, Morrissey, Ghandi, Billy Bragg, Laurel & Hardy, Tom Waits, Carter the Unstoppable Sex Machine, Otway, George Bernard Shaw, the Stray Cats, Jacques Brel and Pete Townshend.

Cheers to Joe Langfield for advice on the Dutch connection and to Dan Jones for his constructive criticism of the first draft. The book has been much improved as a result of your input (what was it like before? I hear you ask).

And finally, thanks to my long-suffering friends, from whom I have, again, stolen entire conversations, along with the occasional priceless witticism.

Apart from that, what's left is wholly my own work. I hope you enjoy reading it as much as I have enjoyed its creation.

The Prologue

She passed quickly by green bamboo hedges and fields of rice, the early morning sun warming the cracked ground beneath her hardened bare feet. The heavens were clear blue and birds and crickets competed noisily for sovereignty of a stunning landscape. The familiar walk to school in the next village was long and arduous; but better that than to hunch down in the paddy fields all day. Her family were poor, but insisted that she and her siblings attend school without fail; a good education was their only hope of escape. A home-made latanier hat kept her as cool as could be expected and she swatted flies as she walked proudly beside An Dung, her beloved older brother and protector. It was he who had saved her when the man had jumped from behind a bush and scared her; tried to take her away. The blow from the big stick had left the man unconscious and bleeding as they'd ran the rest of the way, anxious about the consequences. They had told no-one and the man had not returned; but her journey could never be carefree again.

Each Monday the school-day began with a salute to Ho Chi Minh and his picture hung in every school and house; then the song would be sung loud, in honour of their country. She would concentrate hard during lessons, hanging on every word uttered by her teacher; before an afternoon nap and the journey home beneath a burning sky. When her mother returned from the fields, she helped her to prepare a dinner of vegetables and rice, eaten gratefully by the extended family. Her

1

father would ask about her day and she'd tell of all the wonderful things she'd learnt, of a world beyond his wildest imagination. Unspoken filial obedience and respect ensured that her homework was completed before there was any opportunity to play; and finally, a little time to run through the village with her friends, a time to climb trees and swing on the tyre across the stream before bed, exhausted, and another early start the next day.

She was clever, everybody said it was so; her parents, schoolteachers and friends alike. Eight festivals ago, on her first birthday, the One Year Ceremony had foretold of a life commanding respect. When the traditional tray of objects had been held before her (each object with its own meaning associated with a child's future), she had chosen the pen without hesitation; a sign agreed by all present that this precocious toddler might one day become a teacher.

It was her home, this village, despite the poverty and lack of hope; a place of family, love and trust. Why should she ever wish to leave?

1.

It was turning into a good day for Sandra; the kind of day she lived for. Brushing an errant curl from her eyes, she made herself comfortable in her favoured position on the boat, overlooking the busy towpath. Some artists required solitude and silence, but Sandra relished the inspiration gained from passing strangers, the unwitting characters that populated her work. They wouldn't have recognised themselves, but a colour, an expression, a stance, was all she needed to set the creative juices flowing; and flowing they certainly were. She loved to paint and was thrilled that her work was beginning to receive acclaim in exalted circles; that the exclusive Galerie Vieleers had agreed to exhibit some of her recent abstracts.

In a previous life she'd used art as therapy, to escape from the stress of a high-pressure, responsible position; where she was required to make cold and impassive decisions on a daily basis. Like so many, she'd been carried along on a wave of ambition and social mountaineering. Thank God that was all behind her.

Now her creativity manifested itself as an extension of the rediscovered real Sandra; with all the warmth, passion, patience and humour of her long-lost youth. Surrounded by her conceptions – the brightly coloured kettles, pots and jugs in blues, reds and yellows that adorned their floating home – she no longer cared how she appeared to others. OK, so what if she was a little overweight? Her mop of brown hair was unkempt and she literally lived in those paint-splattered dungarees; in her late forties, she was finally happy and contented with her life.

She glanced at Pete, surrounded by his precious tools as he tinkered with something mechanical; probably that temperamental generator again. The sun glinted off his pate and what little hair was left hung lank, thin and grey on his shoulders. Why was she with him, when her friends were unanimous in the opinion that he was a waster, a dropout; bringing nothing to their relationship but a simple need to be loved and looked after? The bum in the boat, they called him, rather unfairly, Sandra thought.

Because it was a simple truth that she loved him; he was the kindest man she had ever met, barely a cross word with anyone, whether friend or stranger. She would never forget that Pete had been there to catch her when her world had fallen apart; the loss of her job in the City, her husband Ben's affair, their son Stephen leaving home at eighteen to travel the world (where was he now? Bangkok, the last she'd heard). All had occurred within the space of a year and Pete had helped her to pick up the pieces, to rebuild her life, to feel human and wanted again. Polar opposite to her ex-husband, Pete had seemed free and unconventional; for the first time she had encouragement to follow her heart and her art, a belief in her talent, a belief in herself.

Sandra smiled as she recalled how they'd met. She had always fancied a canal holiday and, in an effort to recuperate from recent reversals in her fortunes, had enlisted the company of her best friend Liz. After a brief demonstration, they'd been left in charge of a small, but fairly hefty barge (named *Onion Bargee*, for God's sake) and had nervously set about negotiating the Grand Union Canal. It was a midsummer's day and the sun blazed on their shoulders; the unheeded warning of the painful sunburn to follow. After a few miles of relaxing, traffic-free sailing, they'd started to chill-out. 'Hey, this isn't so hard,' Sandra had said, as she zigzagged across the water and took the first bend a little too tight, 'I could get used to this.' And there, their vessel's erratic progress had been halted; they were grounded and, no matter how hard she revved, it stubbornly refused to move.

Pete just happened by at the right time, a passing drifter in his boat named *The Drifter*, oozing confidence in his natural habitat; the canals were his home. A knight in not so shining armour, he'd towed them to safety and a hearty lunch at the local pub. Good ale and fine wine had assisted the conversation and, as he was travelling in the same direction, Pete had volunteered his services as a guide for the remainder of their holiday, Liz increasingly playing gooseberry as Sandra and he flirted relentlessly.

Mutually sympathetic ears had been offered as they exchanged their life-stories. His had been a similar epiphany to hers; he was just a hell of a lot further along the journey. In defiance of his affluent father's expectations, he'd simply opted out in his mid-twenties; decided that he didn't need all that crap. He would cultivate an easy-going eccentricity, live a solitary, simple life, travel the waterways and come and go as he pleased, stopping for easy conversation when and with whom he wished. He'd taught himself the nuts and bolts of barge maintenance and aspired to self-sufficiency, even to the extent of making some of his own clothes; he was particularly proud of a pair of indestructible denim jeans that would last forever, but never grace the catwalk. *The Drifter* was a floating testament to his resourcefulness, patched up and pock-marked, the toilet repaired with an old trombone, a lonely bachelor's paradise; aesthetically disagreeable, but perfectly functional and floating still. The odd casual job financed his lifestyle and treats were few and far between, but generally he had no regrets. He'd escaped from what many people would consider to be a decent prospective career, but to him it had felt like a prison. He didn't miss his BMW and the associated trappings of prosperity and was perfectly content that it was all long in the past; he would never go back.

'I've always had trouble with BMWs,' Sandra had said.

'You owned a BMW too?'

'No, but every time I drive on the motorway there's one right up my arse.'

After some months of learning how to date again – comfortable evenings in canal-side pubs, candlelit dinners in relaxing restaurants, long country walks – they had both agreed that their relationship was a good thing and had started to discuss a future together. Sandra, however, had grown used to a little more luxury than that afforded by Pete's somewhat modest accommodation. 'No offence, but there's not even enough room in there for my shoes; if we're going to live together, then we're going to need more space; we'll end up killing each other otherwise.'

'But this is my home,' Pete had protested, his outstretched arm taking in the vista of the green, algae-infested, stagnant canal and his flaking blue-painted boat. 'I love this life. Give it a chance; you'll get used to it and grow to love it too.'

'A barge was OK for a week's summer holiday,' argued Sandra, 'but I'm not sure if I could live like this permanently. It's cramped, uncomfortable, cold and damp. All seems very romantic on the surface, but the reality is different.'

'OK, how about a compromise then?' said Pete, thinking aloud.

'What kind of compromise?'

'A big compromise.'

'How big?'

'Another country kind of big.'

'Go on,' she said, her curiosity aroused.

'An old school friend of mine, Martin, was made redundant a few years ago. He would occasionally spend his holidays on the canal with me and he often spoke of buying his own barge. He'd travelled around Holland for work and always said he'd like to live there, so he spent his redundancy on a houseboat in Amsterdam. Now he has to come home for business reasons and he wants to rent out his boat long-term. He'd jump at the chance of having someone he knows look after it and it's pretty spacious and in a nice location; I visited him recently and had a great time. Only problem is, it's a static boat, so we'd be stuck in the same place, but I'm willing to give it a go if you are.'

Sandra thought about this unexpected proposition and at first thought no, I couldn't do that. But the more she considered it, the less apprehensive she became. What was there left to stay in England for? A few friends (most of whom were joint friends with her ex-husband); Liz was the only one she'd really miss and she could come and visit. Her son had flown the nest, adamant that he was big enough and ugly enough to look after himself and, the truth be told, he probably was. They'd always encouraged his independence and he could cook, wash, iron and clean; though in reality she knew he wouldn't bother using any of these valuable life skills. The house was sold, the proceeds split fifty/fifty; and any good memories were tarnished beyond repair.

She squinted and took another look at the rather eccentric-looking man before her. She couldn't deny that Pete made her laugh and, with his dry sense of humour and laid-back attitude, nothing seemed to faze him. Amsterdam? She'd never been there, nor considered it as a potential home, but sod it, she thought; why not take some risks for a change?

'OK, when can we go and see it?'

Pete looked shocked. 'Do you mean it; you really want to go and check it out?'

'Why not? I could do with a bit of adventure in my life; we'll go and book a flight tomorrow. You'd better let your friend know that we may be interested.'

'But we have tickets for Glastonbury in June,' said Pete, suddenly appearing unsure of his impulsive suggestion.

'We could still come home for that,' replied Sandra. 'What have we got to lose? Let's go and see if we like it first, before we start planning anything.'

It had been love at first sight when Sandra laid eyes on the

Christina; it really was luxurious, with sufficient fixtures, fittings and space to satisfy her desire for a little comfort. It had a three-piece suite, a dining room table, a fitted kitchen and a separate bedroom; this wasn't a boat, it was a floating house. A tour of the city made up her mind, with its feeling of freedom, culture, and art galleries aplenty. Yes, this could be the life for her; and Pete seemed keen too, not unhappy to be leaving behind his lonely freedom.

'It could do with a lick of paint,' said Martin, 'but I'm happy for you to do with it what you will. The way my business is going, it's likely to be long term. I may decide to retire here, but that's a long way off.'

And that's how their idyllic life in Holland had begun: Sandra relishing her new-found freedom and time to create; and Pete apparently contented being Pete, strumming his guitar, immersed in music, reading, tinkering with whatever required tinkering with, without a care in the world.

And, enveloped in their dream, they both chose to ignore and avoid the seedy, criminal, clandestine world just a few blocks away.

2.

There it was again from the flat downstairs. The noise kept Terry awake every night, the rhythmic creaking of the bed, the grunts, and the false-sounding cries of ecstasy; not real, just like some dodgy 1970s German porn movie. He pulled the sheets up around him and shivered in the damp-stained, musty room. The bed and covers weren't big enough for his six-foot, lanky frame, and he had to choose between its meagre warmth on his upper body or his feet; maybe he should have left his socks on. Surroundings of greater luxury were readily available to him, and the paper would have been happy to cover the expense, but that wasn't how he liked to work, preferring instead to aim at the very heart of the story and live amongst its characters; it aided the authenticity of his writing.

Once again his hand found its way beneath the covers, his thoughts drifting to the girl downstairs, and he wished he were the one beside her. The foreplay was the best bit: the anticipation, the location and circumstances, as myriad and adventurous as the spiralling depths of his wild, vivid imagination; then to the deed itself, over too quickly, sordid, vacuous and meaningless; and finally the inevitable damp, forlorn, uncomfortable emptiness of the aftermath.

The other bed in the room was empty, his unfortunate, diminutive, amiable colleague Barry hospitalised after the beating that had left him maimed, battered and bruised; his camera, the tool of his trade, his pride and joy, smashed beyond repair. They didn't like having their photo taken round here.

'If you don't want others to know what you're doing, then it's likely that you shouldn't be doing it in the first place,' was Barry's philosophy on investigative journalism and its pictorial bedfellow. Masquerading unconvincingly as a tourist, he'd insisted on taking his camera to the very fulcrum of the tale, unaccompanied; and there he'd been left, in a deserted, dank alleyway, his leg smashed and useless, until a kind passer-by had heard his cries and called the ambulance.

Terry had been apprehensive when told of his latest assignment. 'Haven't you got anything in Afghanistan or the Gaza Strip or somewhere?' he'd pleaded. 'I could do without being plunged into the midst of temptation at the moment.' His pleas had fallen on deaf ears; they were concerned only with the finished article and cared little about the fragile state of its scriber.

'We want to see the human side, the suffering of the victims of this tainted profession,' his Editor Chris had replied. 'We want a thorough investigation into the evil men who control their lives, their every move. This is a gripping story waiting to be written and I'm convinced you're the man for the job; take Barry with you to capture the visual element and we'll look forward to another one of your masterpieces.'

And Terry was good, one of the best in the business. He told it as it was and an unflinching honesty ran through both his work and his life. His reputation went before him; regular, informative columns written with sardonic humour, interspersed with cutting-edge features that got to the heart of the story without sentiment or spin. Little did his readers know of the man behind the words.

On the rebound, Terry's nerves were frayed and his emotions raw from the split with Gemma; he was distraught at his childhood sweetheart's betrayal and cruel preference for another. Nineteen years they'd been together, nineteen long and happy years since their eyes had met across the bedlam of an anarchic classroom. Balls of screwed-up paper had ricocheted off the walls around them, but their eyes had never strayed. Terry had written the note surreptitiously and lobbed it towards her with a quizzical look, his eyebrows raised in anticipation. "Meet me outside after school", she'd read, red-faced, and, ensuring no-one was looking, nodded her ascent; and there, by the school gates, their life together had begun. A life that he never questioned; not once feeling the desire of his peers, to sow his wild oats or to seek experience elsewhere; he was a contented man.

They'd been apart for a few years, their Universities at opposite ends of the country – he studying Communication and Media in Bristol, where he'd taken great pride in his thesis on British comedy; and she with her head in Law books in Lancaster – but they both knew that their paths would ultimately lead to the same destination. Marriage was an outdated institution and unnecessary, Gemma had argued; so they'd never cemented their relationship with a ring or a vow.

'You know why people wear wedding rings, don't you?' she'd said, after turning down his proposal.

'Go on, enlighten me,' he'd replied, feeling both deflated and foolish.

'It's because they're more comfortable than a ball and chain.'

In his naivety he still thought that mutual love and trust would be enough to keep them together.

His job had been the catalyst, increasingly taking him to the underbelly of the world's nastiest places, in search of stories to satisfy his Editor's and the public's seemingly insatiable appetite for the unpleasant, seedy side of life. Gemma had simply grown bored with being alone for long periods, weeks on end, sometimes months, and Sam had conveniently been there when Terry wasn't. The split was as amicable as it could have been; too much respect to allow their true feelings to show. 'I'm so sorry,' she'd sobbed, as Terry lugged the last of his cases into the car.

Fortunately, there were no children involved to make things messier, Gemma always insisting that they wait until she was in her thirties before starting a family. Now those kids wouldn't be his. Could a man ever recover from such heartbreak? Maybe Amsterdam was the very place to recuperate, to try something new, to escape from the constraints of the past and of a life that had seemed mapped-out and preordained.

She'd smiled at him as he passed her doorway yesterday, the girl downstairs with her radiant gleam enveloped in full ruby-red lips and those stunning almond eyes, embellished with wide round balls of chocolate brown. About 5' 5", her back arched against the door frame, the bronzed leg bent at the knee to taunt him as he nodded hello. That smile so inviting, that he wasn't naïve enough to think was just for him; but did it appear so genuine to every man that happened by? He closed his eyes again and pictured her face, eventually drifting off to a fitful slumber.

Terry awoke and sat up with a start, in a cold sweat, his covers mangled and twisted. Was that a scream from a dream or was it real? A bemused face stared back at him from the cracked mirror; the quiff of oily black hair that he often thought made him look like Elvis, collapsed over one eye. There it was again, a scream of fear so chilling as to induce a shudder of dread. It came from downstairs and his imagination ran riot with all kinds of shocking scenarios. Should he try to help, to rush to her rescue; but no, it would blow his cover and all of the time spent staying in character as a desperate man in search of solace in the sins of the flesh would be wasted; the story untold. In the last few days he'd felt the boundaries between reality and this act of deception blurring, merging; he was turning unconsciously into that desperate man.

Was it curiosity that got the better of him or a genuine desire to rescue a lady in trouble? Maybe he was simply doing his job, attempting to get behind the scenes and find a different angle for his story. Whatever the motive, he slowly descended the stairs without a thought for his own safety or for the tale he was there to tell. A deathly silence had followed the last cry and he crept apprehensively onto the street, fearing the worst. The door hung open, creaking in the breeze and, by the misty lamplight, he glimpsed two shady characters, retreating quickly through the alley opposite. The neighbourhood apparently deserted, he approached her door with trepidation, keeping to the shadows.

As he entered the sparsely lit room, a barely visible figure shrank back into the corner, whimpering and frightened, a sheet covering her body.

'Don't be scared, I'm here to help,' said Terry, trying to convey reassurance.

'Who are you?' she asked. 'What do you want?'

'I'm from the flat upstairs; heard you scream and figured you might need some assistance. Are you OK?'

'You should leave now. If they find you here they will kill you. I will be fine,' she sobbed in pain.

Terry attempted to place the strange inflections in her speech, the mixture of accents, part Oriental, part Eton English, part Dutch; he'd never heard anyone speak like this. It was convenient that, wherever he ventured in the world, the second language was his mother-tongue; a by-product of cruel colonialism, the fact that the English language bestrode the world was succour to the lazy country of his birth. Why should he bother to learn another language when the whole world spoke English and he could make himself understood in most places? A renowned wordsmith and proud of it, Terry felt shame when attempting to communicate with his fellow human beings abroad. Why should he automatically expect them to converse in his tongue?

Locating the light switch, he closed his eyes in the sudden brightness. Reopening them gradually, he fixed his gaze on the face from his fantasy, unblemished and beautiful, just as he'd pictured her. A hand shielding her eyes, she stared back and winced in pain as she sat up to greet this unwanted guest. Terry looked around the apartment: surprisingly luxurious for a room in the midst of the downmarket end of Amsterdam's Red Light District and a stark contrast to his own uncomfortable fleapit; then his gaze reverted to the vision before him.

'Ouch, they always go for the body,' she winced, 'so as not to leave any visible marks. Otherwise I could no longer earn them any money. Who would pay for a whore with a battered face?'

'Your English is very good,' observed Terry. 'How did you learn to speak it so well?'

'You ask too many questions; the less you know the better for you.'

'I want to know,' he replied, 'I want to know who you are and who would be so cruel as to do this to you.'

'Ha, I am just another whore. You don't really want to know me. My English is so good because I spent three years in London after they stole me from my family. An old gentleman who said his name was Higgins taught me your tongue to GCSE standard and said the exam would set me free; free to find a respectable job and to live by your culture. Only wanted company, never any sex; he promised to turn me into a lady; then the press discovered how he spent his evenings and I never saw him again. Ha, half of my customers are from your country; drunken fools, most of them, but my English helps me to understand them better. They are away from home and think they can do as they please; some of them can barely stand, but still they try to perform.'

Ah, the ambassadorial qualities of the Brit abroad, thought Terry. Whenever he'd ventured overseas he'd often been embarrassed by the behaviour of some of his fellow countrymen. He knew it was a tiny minority and that most of his compatriots were relatively civilised; but nevertheless, it was always the few that attracted the publicity and tarnished the name of his nation. In his current state of mind, though, Terry had to confess that he too had been sorely tempted by the copious array of flesh on display in this tawdry circus of copulation.

He vaguely remembered the scandal of the discredited

14

professor; plastered all over the *Evening Standard* one evening for his amusement as he'd made the familiar tube journey home. A man once esteemed for his philanthropic work across Africa and services to the English language, now notorious for something else entirely; his career and reputation in tatters. The warning bells rang in Terry's mind about how his own presence here could easily be misconstrued in the hands of a rival newspaper; still, he couldn't pull himself away.

'Can I get you a drink?' he asked. 'You look like you need one.'

'There is some whisky in the cupboard over there. Guess you better have one too if you insist on staying; but I will tell you now, if they come back they will hurt you too.'

'Nice place you got here,' said Terry, ignoring her warning as he handed her a generous tumbler, half-full of single malt; a good whisky and not cheap. 'How did you get to live in such luxury?'

'I spend most of my time behind a window, but they bring the important men here; the ones who cannot be seen walking the streets of Amsterdam window-shopping.'

Suddenly, she felt uncomfortable and wondered why she was opening up to this stranger; telling him so much. He seemed to care, to be genuinely interested in her as a person and not just as an object of desire; but why should she trust him when she had been betrayed by so many? She had seen this outsider around these past few weeks and had wondered what he was doing here; he looked out of place, like he did not belong. She had noticed that he looked at her each time he passed, a kindly, respectful face, not lustful or cruel like most of the men she encountered in her work.

Men – the very word made her sick; she thought she could read them like a book, but this man had her confused, her defences breached. Men – were they not all the same, ultimately demanding the same thing, whatever their methods? She wistfully recalled her home village, her family, her father and brother. They too were men, but bore no resemblance in outlook or culture to the bastards who had brought her here and destroyed her very spirit and soul. Would she ever see them again?

Her thoughts returned to the man in front of her and she saw compassion in his eyes. She invited him to sit down; what harm could it do to tell her story to a stranger, to share her burden? What were her secrets worth, when everything else was so worthless?

Terry listened, spellbound, as she recounted a sadly common tale of a simple Vietnamese childhood, cruelly stolen at the age of fifteen; inadvertently sold by her destitute family on the premise of a year's salary in advance (a pittance by Western standards), for the position of maid to a wealthy businessman. At first he'd treated her well and she'd been excited about accompanying him to London for a business trip; then, no sooner had they landed, than he transformed into an evil monster, dictating how she took her every breath. 'Do exactly as I say, or I will bring your sister here too,' he'd threatened. She loved her little sister and would do anything to protect her, so she'd resisted the natural instinct to run or rebel.

Forced into prostitution after less than a month, her beauty ensured that she was never short of customers, mainly at the higher end of the market: judges, policemen, even the odd politician. It was here that she'd encountered Professor Higgins, the only one who'd shown her any kindness. When an official investigation into trafficking in the UK had got too close, her captors had transferred their interests to Amsterdam, where she and her fellow slaves were sold to a ring of Loverboys, organised pimps; and here her misery had continued.

Terry felt intrusive and helpless. Now he'd heard her tragic tale he felt obliged to do something about it; but what could he do? Hers was the life of thousands like her, exploited, controlled and void of hope. Was it enough to simply write about it in the hope that the exposure afforded by a reputable national newspaper would somehow change things; force the authorities to act, or maybe to prick the conscience of one or two of the endless stream of 'tourists', happy to treat their fellow human beings as just another commodity, to be used and discarded? He looked into her eyes with pity. 'My name's Terry. What should I call you?'

'Terry; that is a nice name,' she replied, breathing deeply as the warmth of the whisky hit her throat. 'Do you want my professional name or my real name?'

'Well, I've told you my real name. Will you tell me yours?'

'Kim-Ly; it means Golden Lion.'

Golden Lion: it seemed fitting. The name of a beautiful, graceful, proud and formidable creature, the ruler of the jungle; when her parents had given her such a name they must have wished for fine things for their precious child, for happiness, love and prosperity. A golden lion should be free to roam as it pleases, thought Terry, not caged and mistreated, cowering fearfully in a dingy corner of sleazy captivity.

'And why did they hurt you?' asked Terry. 'What could you possibly have done to warrant such treatment?'

'I set up a meeting with the other girls, told them that if we got together we could fight for better conditions, better pay, health checks, that kind of thing. How could I have been so stupid as to think I would get away with it?' Kim-Ly felt her ribs and flinched. 'They told me this was just a warning and that next time they would really hurt me.'

Terry's typically professional approach was under threat as she sobbed into her whisky. 'I have to get you out of here,' he said on impulse; 'you can't stay here where they can do this again.'

'And go where?' she asked. 'There is nowhere to hide. They will find me and it will be worse for me and bad for you. They are dangerous men and their gang rules the District; they know all that happens here. Anyway, why should you help me? What is in it for you?'

'Does there have to be anything in it for me? Why can't it simply be a desire to do the right thing? They shouldn't be allowed to treat you like this.' Terry thought quickly. 'I know somewhere we can go, somewhere safe. It may be too close for comfort, but it will do for now until I can get you further away.'

What was he thinking? Maybe, for once, he wasn't thinking; an uncharacteristic impetuosity taking over his thoughts. He didn't even know if Pete and Sandra would still be here. They'd met at Glastonbury, three years ago, knee-deep in mud, and they'd each laughed at their mutual discomfort. Gemma and Sandra had got on like sisters and he and Pete had immediately found things in common; the same musical tastes, a love of old sitcoms and an annoying ability to recite them word for word.

'If you're ever in Amsterdam, make sure you look us up.' Pete's invitation had been genuine, but Terry knew that it was unlikely they'd ever see them again; the Christmas cards and e-mails had lasted a few years and then nothing. Terry had envied their lifestyle; a houseboat on an Amsterdam canal sounded romantic and free, a universe away from what had become an existence for Gemma and he. Sandra was a talented artist and made enough to finance their bohemian lifestyle and Pete seemed permanently chilled-out, drifting along with the flow, never fazed.

Terry held out his hands and, as Kim-Ly took them and he pulled her up, the sheet fell to the floor. The bruises now visible on her perfect legs, she stood before him in red silk underwear; her head bowed in shame, she whimpered from the agonising pain as her hand barely touched her ribs. Placing the sheet back around her shoulders, he watched as she threw some clothes and a few trinkets into a bag. He led her carefully to the door and peeked out to see an empty street; it was late, even by the twenty-four-hour clock of Amsterdam. A short walk to his door and they climbed the creaking stairs slowly. Breathing heavily, he felt the warmth of her body against his as he took her weight and helped her to his room.

'Here, change into these,' he said, passing her a pair of Barry's grimy, less than stylish jeans and a worn out Led Zeppelin t-shirt. 'No-one will look twice at you wearing these rags.'

'Whose are they?' she asked. 'They are obviously too small for you.'

'They belong to my flatmate; he's indisposed at the moment and won't be using them for a while. I must say they look better on you than they do on him.'

'Where are you taking me? You said you knew somewhere safe. There is nowhere safe from those bastards; we should stop this now.'

'Trust me, I have friends who will help us,' he said, in the slim hope that, not only would Pete and Sandra still be in residence at the somewhat vague address they'd given, but that they'd be willing to assist a man they barely knew with a desperate hooker in tow in the early hours. 'Only problem is, I'm not sure where exactly they are.' Terry scrabbled around in his bag for his address book. 'Ah, here it is. Do you know the way to Brouwersgracht? Not sure if that's the right pronunciation.'

'So, you are saying that you want to take me a stone throw from here in these horrible clothes, to a canal where you're not exactly sure where your friends are; and you call this safety?'

'They said you couldn't miss it, that their houseboat was the most distinctive on the canal,' said Terry, as he squashed the contents of his meagre wardrobe and his iPad into a small case. 'My friend Sandra, she's an artist and painted the boat herself, said it was some of her finest work; they sent me a picture, so I kind of know what I'm looking for. You'll like Sandra and Pete, lovely people, and I'm sure they won't mind if you stay with them for a few days.'

Terry was anything but sure; a long weekend among kindred musical spirits was one thing, battling the adversity of the elements, a joyful occasion despite the discomfort. Glastonbury was a special place; it brought out the best in everyone. There, strangers would actually talk to each other, pool their resources, build a bond of trust and generally have a ball; but here things were different; ostensibly a cool city, enlightened and free, but in its midst lay a desperate cesspool run by pimps and gangs with a vested interest in keeping it that way.

Kim-Ly sighed. 'Oh, OK then. You are crazy, but I will warn you. I am used to being mistreated and beaten, but they will not show you any mercy.'

'Don't worry, I have a black belt in Origami,' reassured Terry. 'They wouldn't dare mess with me.'

Her laughter was restrained, but with a distant hint of optimism, of freedom; the sound of someone who had almost forgotten how to laugh; and besides, laughing hurt her bruised ribs.

'Come on then,' she said, taking his hand. 'I know the way.'

And from that irrational moment, as he felt the softness of her hand in his, Terry was hooked.

3.

The sound inconsiderately punctured Sandra's dreams; a faint tapping, growing gradually louder as she stirred; tap, tap, she sat up, suddenly wide awake. Pete's snoring ceased temporarily, until he rolled over and began again.

'Pete, Pete, there's someone at the door,' she whispered, shaking him harder still.

His eyelids partially unstuck as he glanced at the bedside clock. 'What? It's four o'clock in the morning. Who the hell could it be?'

'Well, *I'm* not going to find out!' said Sandra.

'Suppose I'd better go then,' groaned Pete, as he rolled reluctantly out of bed and, still half asleep, made his way quietly to the door, where, by now, the tapping had become more urgent and insistent. 'OK, OK,' he shouted through the closed door. 'Who goes there?'

'It's Terry.'

'Terry! Terry who?'

'Terry. Terry from Glastonbury.'

'Who is it?' asked a curious Sandra, now standing behind him in her dressing gown.

'It's *Terry*. Terry from Glastonbury.'

'What the hell is *he* doing here and what does he want at this time of the morning?'

'A good question,' said Pete, turning his attention back to the still-closed door. 'What the hell are you doing here and what do you want at this time of the morning?'

'I need your help,' said Terry. 'Please, let me in and I'll explain.'

Pete turned to Sandra with raised eyebrows. Sandra nodded and Pete opened the door slightly and peeked out. He could see only Terry and was unaware of a desperate figure in the shadows behind him.

'You said to look you up if I was ever in Amsterdam,' smiled Terry, as Pete opened the door wider to allow him access. 'Hope you don't mind, but I have a friend with me. This is Kim-Ly.'

Sandra reacted quickly and caught Kim-Ly as she fell down the steps. At first, due to the scruffy attire, she thought it was a small man that had fallen into her arms; but, as she smelt the cheap perfume and looked at Kim-Ly's face, she saw that it was a strikingly beautiful woman. Kim-Ly could barely stand; the exhaustion of the walk to the boat had added to the extent of her injuries and the emotional turmoil of the evening; she had nothing left and had simply collapsed as she stooped through the door.

Helping her to the sofa, Sandra looked up inquisitively at Terry. 'So, what's the story?'

'She's hurt,' said Terry, 'and there will be people looking for her in the morning.'

'Shouldn't we get her to hospital?' asked Sandra. 'She's nearly passing out here. Pete, get some water.'

'Too dangerous,' replied Terry. 'I've got to keep her hidden, then get her as far away from here as possible.'

'Hmm, I've a feeling that it's best we don't know who's after her,' said Sandra. 'What *have* you got yourself mixed up in?'

'Not sure myself yet, but something tells me I may regret it.'

Sandra took another look at Kim-Ly and instinctively summed up the situation. 'And how's Gemma?' she enquired. 'I take it she doesn't know about this.'

'Nothing to do with her,' said Terry. 'Besides, she walked out on me months ago.'

'Sorry to hear that,' said Pete, as he handed Terry a beer. 'Here, you look like you need this.'

'Thanks, mate. Look, I'm sorry. I shouldn't be getting you guys involved in this, but this is the last place they'll look. Just a few days, till she's feeling better, I promise; then we'll be out of here.'

'And how long have you known this, er, young lady?' asked Sandra, gesturing at the now-sleeping Kim-Ly.

Terry looked at his watch and smiled sheepishly. 'About two hours. Look, we're not romantically attached; I'm just trying to help someone in trouble.'

'Very chivalrous I'm sure,' said Sandra. 'I'm not going to question your motives and of course we'll help, but she's not exactly the girl next door, is she?'

'No, she's the girl downstairs,' said Terry, staring at Kim-Ly's innocent-when-you-dream face.

Pete took in Terry's misty-eyed expression. 'Hey, snap out of it, old chap; bit old to be falling for a complete stranger, aren't you?'

Terry took a swig of his beer and answered with embarrassment. 'I haven't fallen for anyone. Like I say, I'm just trying to help a lady in trouble.'

Sandra shook her head. 'There are hundreds like her in this city, you know. What's so special about this one?'

'Look, she was being beaten up and I happened to be there, OK; nothing more to it than that.'

Sandra looked at Kim-Ly with sympathy, then turned to Terry. 'Hmm, if you say so. You can sleep on that chair over there for what's left of the night. We'll talk about this in the morning.'

Terry's attentive face was the first thing that Kim-Ly saw when she opened her eyes. She smiled weakly and tried to sit up. Unbeknown to her, Terry had been watching her sleeping for the last half-an-hour. She recalled little about her surroundings and, panicking at first, was unsure of where she was. Gradually, the events of the previous night came back to her and she relaxed a little; for the first time in years she felt safe, even if only temporarily.

She heard some clinking from the kitchen; then Sandra emerged with croissants and coffee on a tray. 'Ah, sleeping beauty awakes,' she said. 'How are you feeling?'

'A little tired and my chest hurts a lot,' said Kim-Ly, 'but I will survive. Thank you for your hospitality.'

'Wow,' exclaimed Sandra, 'you sure speak English well. Where are you from, Surrey?'

'It is a long story. I appreciate your kindness and my family would return it tenfold given the opportunity. Ah, what is that?' Kim-Ly jumped as Sandra and Pete's cat Tigger landed on the sofa beside her. 'Ah-choo. Ouch! – get that thing – Ah-choo. Ouch! – away from me – Ah-choo. Ouch! – cats make me – Ah-choo. Ouch! – sneeze, and sneezing – Ah-choo. Ouch! – hurts.'

As a hysterical Pete grabbed the bemused Tigger and put him outside, Kim-Ly looked up to see Sandra and Terry joining in the laughter. 'I am glad you think – Ah-choo. Ouch! – it is funny,' she laughed. 'Oh no, laughing hurts too; please, please stop.'

Slowly the hilarity subsided and, as Kim-Ly devoured her breakfast, she considered these strangers who had taken her in. Sandra she could tell was suspicious; she'd guessed her profession and her trust would be hard to gain. Pete appeared to be nice, friendly, easy-going and would do whatever Sandra said; and Terry, this tall, gangling hero, seemingly besotted with her after just one day. How could she repay him? She knew of only one way.

They were naïve, these good people, she decided. They did not have a clue as to the gravity of the situation, did not realise what risks they were taking by hiding her. Surely if they knew the truth of the bounty they had dredged up – that the sharks would not rest until they had recovered their valuable property – then they would throw her back into that carnal canal and plead ignorance. 'Kim-Ly; never heard of her,' they would say. Was she mixing her metaphors again? Professor

24

Higgins was forever chastising her for her conflicting sentences. Sharks did not live in canals, did they?

But what of her good friend Celina? She would be the first person the pimps would go to once they had discovered that their most profitable girl was missing. They would not believe Celina's denial. 'But I have not seen her since yesterday,' she would insist, but still they would threaten and torture her until she too would hurt like Kim-Ly. Would Terry, Sandra and Pete help Celina too? It was too much to ask, wasn't it?

Endless questions from Sandra were Terry's reward for offering to help with the washing-up; the inevitable interrogation. What was he doing in Amsterdam? What happened with Gemma? How did he meet Kim-Ly? Terry cautiously gave her the abridged version – he was in Amsterdam for work, he and Gemma had just drifted apart without him noticing, Kim-Ly lived downstairs from his apartment. He didn't want to elaborate; there were a lot of personal issues behind the circumstances in which he found himself, plenty of raw, uncompromising emotion to deal with; he hadn't even reconciled all this stuff in his own mind yet. He couldn't tell her about the undercover work he was supposed to be doing before he got sidetracked. He knew that he was here to do a job, that he had copy to submit to the paper by the end of the week, but the story was turning into a very different one; much bigger than he expected. He hadn't missed a deadline yet in his long and distinguished career, but the piece wasn't ready yet, not of the quality for which he'd become renowned; he'd rather it be right and late than substandard and early.

Respecting Terry's reticence, Sandra returned to the living quarters and attempted to get some answers from Kim-Ly, who matter-of-factly repeated the long and sorry tale she'd told Terry the night before. 'Oh, you poor girl,' said Sandra, the tears welling up in her eyes. She took Kim-Ly's hands and held them tight. 'You must stay here with us until we can get you away from here.

There's to be no argument; you will never go back there. From now on you have friends that you can rely on.'

She turned to an apprehensive-looking Pete and, without countenancing any argument, declared, 'We have an extra two mouths to feed; I'll write a list and you can go to the shops. Tonight we shall have a feast in celebration of Kim-Ly's freedom. What do you say?'

Pete knew better than to argue with a Sandra in this mood and, against his better judgement, replied, 'Whatever you say, dear. Would you like me to polish the best china?'

'Why not; it's been a while since we've had guests and I fancy cooking-up something special.' Sandra instinctively reverted to management-mode and considered only the cold practicalities. She was relishing her new sense of purpose and show of female solidarity; she'd never really thought about the human tragedies of their near-neighbours before and, a woman on a mission, she was determined that Kim-Ly at least would escape this misery.

She turned to the unshaven and tired-looking Terry, who smiled and said, 'Thanks, I knew you'd understand.'

'Oh, I think I understand alright. I'm not going to ask what you were doing in such a place and I'm truly sorry that you and Gemma have split up. My first impression is that you're heartbroken and you came here to forget, not primarily to work; although that must have been a convenient excuse. You can tell me if I'm wrong. ... No, I thought not. Right, you and Kim-Ly can spend a day or two hidden here while we consider what to do next.'

Kim-Ly looked on, listening intently to their conversation and reading their body language. Terry looked down at his shoes and shuffled his feet; Pete just seemed uncomfortable with the inconvenient interruption of his routine. Sandra spoke clearly, confidently; like someone who was used to being in charge. 'You must both get some rest; we'll eat and talk later.'

'But I cannot stay,' interjected Kim-Ly. 'I want to thank you all for what you have done for me, but I have a friend, Celina, who will be in trouble because I am gone. If I go back now I can make up a story to tell why I was not there. If not they will do to Celina what they did to me.'

'Then we must bring your friend here too,' concluded Sandra.

'Now hang on,' said Pete. 'What are you doing, setting up a home for fallen women?'

'And there is only one reason why they are fallen – men!!'

Pete and Terry exchanged glances and raised their eyebrows. 'But it wasn't me,' cried Pete, 'I didn't do it. I didn't cause the fall of womankind. Did you do it, Terry? Because if you did I think you should own up now.'

'Not me, mate,' replied Terry. 'I was somewhere else when it happened, honest.'

'Hmm, I guess some of you are OK,' conceded Sandra with a wry smile, 'but you can prove it by going to get Kim-Ly's friend.'

'No,' insisted Kim-Ly, 'it is too dangerous. Terry will be recognised; they will know that he was living upstairs and that he disappeared at the same time as me. I cannot let you risk your lives for me.'

'But nobody knows Pete,' insisted Sandra, 'he could easily blend in with all the sad, lonely punters; no offence, dear.'

'None taken,' Pete lied. 'Let's get this straight. You want me to go to the Red Light District – a place where you've previously forbidden me to venture, even out of curiosity – and bring home a prostitute without anyone noticing.'

'Well, when you put it like that, I suppose it does sound a bit dubious,' said Sandra, 'but it's all in a good cause and you'll be a hero, for a few hours at least.'

Pete shook his head and sighed in exasperation. 'And how will I know this, what's her name, Celina; and how will I get her out of there without attracting attention?'

Kim-Ly looked thoughtful. 'I can tell you which window to go to. The next one will be empty because it is mine. You could smuggle her out in disguise.'

And so it was that Pete (quiet, inoffensive, happy-go-lucky Pete) headed reluctantly to town, with rucksack on back containing a change of clothes for Celina; taking the first steps on the rather bizarre journey that would threaten the tranquillity of their happily humdrum lives.

4.

'Well, maybe you should go back to him then, if that's how you feel,' shouted Sam.

'Well, maybe I will,' replied Gemma, stomping out of the room and slamming the door behind her. She continued stomping as she climbed the stairs and threw herself on to the bed. Burying her head in the pillow, the truth hit hard; what a terrible mistake she'd made.

'I'm going to the pub,' shouted Sam, and the house shuddered with the full, angry force of the front door slamming shut.

When it came to relationships, Terry was Gemma's only reference point. Usually she kept the comparisons in her head, unspoken; but this time her thoughts had found voice, released by the half-bottle of wine she'd consumed with their evening meal and combusting spontaneously. Perhaps these feelings were unfair, but for once she'd allowed her inhibitions to be breached and had said what was on her mind; irretrievably. 'Terry would never have asked me to do *that*,' she'd blurted out before she could stop herself. Too late; the words had been spoken and could never be retracted.

But Sam wasn't such a bad bloke, she thought guiltily as she lay on the bed and studied the ceiling. Yes, he liked to partake in the odd drink and had a tendency to behave like a complete arse when doing so, but he cared about her and was usually kind and considerate. Perhaps she could make a life here and be relatively contented; happy in the routine domesticity she'd craved when Terry had been away. Yes, she should simply apologise for her *faux pas* when Sam returned and ask for forgiveness; explain that she and Terry had been together for a long time and that she needed time to adjust to this new life.

She didn't get the chance, as Sam returned drunk, clattering and raging, and threw all of her clothes and shoes from the bedroom window, scattering on the bushes and lawn below. His vitriol, delivered at a volume designed to wake the neighbours, sounded pretty conclusive. 'Now get out and don't come back.'

For a moment Gemma stood stunned, staring back at the house that had never felt like home. It was Sam's place, with all his history ingrained; in the masculine decoration, in every ornament, in every piece of furniture and on every bookshelf. With tears impairing her vision, she threw her meagre, strewn possessions into the back of her old Polo and drove precariously to her parents', her life in ruins. As Gemma fell sobbing into her father's arms, her mother looked on and sighed, then retreated to the kitchen to put the kettle on. Gemma had always been Daddy's girl.

'OK, what's happened now?' asked her mother as she handed Gemma a mug of strong black coffee. 'I assume this is to do with Sam.'

'Thanks,' said Gemma, the coffee spilling from her shaking hands. Mopping up the spillage with a tear-sodden tissue, she replied, 'Yes, it's to do with Sam. Are you happy now? I know you never liked him.'

'It's not a question of us not liking Sam,' interjected her father, 'we'd just got used to Terry, that's all. Nineteen years is a long time and Terry was part of the family. We've known him since you were both teenagers in love, with all that that entails; you can't simply erase all that history.'

'You don't have to tell *me*,' protested Gemma, 'that's the

problem; I can't forget either. I don't know which of them I want to be with and, now that I've burnt my bridges, *neither* of them will want to be with me. I'm on my own; a solitary old spinster.'

'Now hang on,' said her father, 'thirty-three is hardly old these days. You're still a very attractive young lady. The blokes will be knocking down the door once they know you're on the market again.'

"On the market again?" thought Gemma; it made her sound like a commodity to be sold to the highest bidder, but her father's rather dubious terminology did offer some comfort and reassurance. The truth be told, deep down she knew that he was right; she hadn't been short of offers during her faithful years with Terry, and Sam had simply been one temptation too far. For some reason a lot of men did seem to be drawn to her and she'd become adept at letting them down gently. Petite, blonde and with an aura of vulnerability; she'd inadvertently induced many a crush in fawning fellas, unknowingly reducing them to gibbering wrecks whilst innocently going about her daily business.

'Gemma probably doesn't want to think about being "on the market again" just yet,' said her mother; fully aware that, like most men, her husband could be a little insensitive at times. 'She only left Sam half-an-hour ago; at least give her a day or two before you put her on the internet.' She turned to her distraught daughter and took her hands. 'And what about Terry or Sam; do you still want a life with either of them and, if so, are you going to do anything about it?'

'Yes, maybe. Oh, I don't know,' replied Gemma. 'I just know that I miss Terry a lot and can't stop thinking about him and wondering what he's up to.'

'Well, there's your answer then. Why don't you swallow your pride and give him a call? You never know, he might be feeling the same way; I know he was devastated when you two split up; that's what he told us, anyway.'

'You've seen him?'

31

'Yes, he came round soon after you left him; he looked dreadful – unshaven, bags under his eyes and I'm sure he'd been crying. He wanted us to talk to you, persuade you to go back to him; we said it was none of our business and that you were old enough to make your own decisions.'

Gemma's younger brother Robbie entered the room with his usual bounce; a little taller than her, hair spiked up, immaculate white t-shirt and designer jeans. No matter how hard the times and how empty his wallet, he always seemed to find the cash for cool clothes. 'Hey, what's happening, Sis; why the long face?' Robbie worshipped his big sister and would never forget the support she'd given him during the hard times at school.

'Gemma's split up with Sam,' said her mother; 'she's a little upset.'

'Hey, he wasn't good enough for you anyway,' said Robbie, spraying crumbs from his biscuit. 'Come back and live here with us; it'll be like the old days when you came back from Uni and kept trying to set me up with your girlfriends. You were convinced that one of them would go for a toyboy.'

Gemma forced a smile. 'Yes, and at least one of them did, if I remember rightly.'

'Best days of my life,' grinned Robbie, 'it's not been the same since you left.'

'Robbie, that was over ten years ago. Isn't it about time you flew the nest too? It's not healthy still living with Mum and Dad at your age.'

'Can't afford to; it's been six months since my last job and that was minimum wage. Besides, Mum and Dad love having me here.'

'Hmm, it's an absolute pleasure,' said Dad. 'Look, if you two are going to live under the same roof again, temporarily I hasten to add, then I don't want you coming home drunk every night like you used to.'

'We've grown up a bit since then,' replied Gemma, 'we're more boring and responsible these days.'

'Speak for yourself,' said Robbie. 'Let's go out tomorrow; it's Saturday night and I'll cheer you up, teach you how to laugh again.'

Gemma thought for a moment. 'OK, why not; but I'm not going clubbing. I hate those places.'

'Absolutely,' said Robbie, 'just a quiet drink and a chat, that's all I'm suggesting.'

'Now where have I heard that before?' groaned Dad. 'Just remember that drink never solved anything; in fact, it usually makes things worse.'

Saturday morning and back in the reassuringly familiar family home, Gemma at least felt comfortable here among the magnolia walls, beige carpet and brown sofa, surrounded by glass cabinets filled with ornaments from her parents' many UK holidays. In their late-fifties and they'd still never ventured abroad; preferring instead to frequent homely B&Bs around the coast of this sceptred isle. 'We haven't seen all there is to see here yet,' her Dad would protest when it was suggested that they try something a little more adventurous, 'why would we want to go somewhere where we don't speak the lingo and can't stand the food?'

There in the corner stood the cause of the tiny scar above her left eye, the table that she'd crashed into after being tripped by Robbie when playing balloon football, against instruction to the contrary from Dad. The pictures on the wall were still the same, the collage of her and Robbie as kids, mostly taken at the seaside and featuring buckets and spades and ice cream; and there, above the mock coal fireplace, the landscape oil painting of the Suffolk coast, the yacht sails glinting gold and yellow in the sunset. Jess, the ancient family Labrador, stirred in the corner, a glint of recognition for Gemma through watery eyes and twitching tail. The old place even smelled the same, a sneeze-inducing mixture comprising essence of damp dog, pot-pourri and furniture polish, all vying for supremacy. Gemma glanced through the window at the swing between the two apple trees, over which she and Robbie had spent countless summer hours arguing about whose turn it was. Why was it still there? Maybe for the longed-for grandchildren that now seemed so unlikely.

Gemma sighed, sprawled with her legs beneath her, in stripy green slipper socks, pale blue jeans and white turtle-neck jumper; she held the phone close to her ear.

'I'm sorry, Gemma, but you know I'm not at liberty to divulge the whereabouts of our reporters,' said Chris.

'But it's me, Chris. Come on, we've been friends for years, surely you can make an exception; I need to contact him urgently, it's very important.'

'The only thing I can tell you is that he's out of the country and working undercover; and anyway, before he left he asked not to be disturbed, said he needed some time to himself.'

'Trust me, he'll want to hear what I've got to say,' insisted Gemma.

'Look, I'll tell you the truth; I'm a bit concerned myself. I haven't heard from him for nearly a week; his copy was due in yesterday and I've never known him miss a deadline before.'

'Is it dangerous, this place he's gone to?' asked Gemma. 'He's not in any trouble, is he?'

'It depends what he's unearthed; he's an investigative journalist and the people he's investigating are likely to object to being investigated. If they're on to him, then he could be in danger, but Terry's the best there is and he knows how to cover his back; he's been in many more precarious places than this.'

'Then at least pass on a message that I want to speak to him,' pleaded Gemma; 'ask him to give me a call.'

'OK, as soon as he reports in I'll let him know. He told me about what happened between you two and I'm really sorry. You were great for each other and I hope you can patch things up, if that's what you both want.'

'Thanks, Chris; I think it's what I want, not sure about Terry.'

'Well, if there's anything I can do …'

'Just get him home safely; the rest is down to me.'

Too noisy and too many people; the bar was heaving with skirts too short and tops too tight, complemented by alcohol and testosterone-fuelled would-be Lotharios out to make an impression. It'll end in tears, thought Gemma, as she cradled her gin and tonic and observed the weekend ritual mating-dance of the lesser-spotted suburb-dwelling prat; or maybe she was just jealous of these carefree revellers, many of whom appeared to be about half her age and oblivious to everything except their own immediate gratification. A flustered, overworked and underpaid student tripped and dropped a tower of empty glasses and the whole place cheered.

'Cheer up, Sis,' said Robbie, 'this was supposed to do you good. Do you want to move on somewhere else; the Capital maybe?'

'I said no nightclubs. I couldn't stand those places when I was younger and I'll feel well out of place now.'

'Are you kidding,' slurred Robbie, 'you'll be the best-looking girl there by far. Some of my mates will be there and I know just the guy for you.'

'No offence, Robbie, but I've met some of your mates before; barely a brain cell between them and that's occupied by one thought.'

'Hey, that's not fair; Stevie runs his own business *and* he's doing pretty well for himself.'

'Stevie? Not Stevie Reece? He owns a white van and he does odd-jobs; some of them very odd, as I recall.'

'Well, that's where you're wrong; he has two white vans now and his business is legit. Joey Sullivan works for him too and they make a great team.'

'Joey Sullivan!! It just gets better. Look, you go clubbing if you want; I'll get a cab and see you in the morning. I'm really not in the mood.'

'No, I'm not letting you get a cab home on your own,' said Robbie, trying to sound responsible. 'I promised Dad that I'd look after you and get you back in one piece.'

'Look, I'm the oldest, remember; and I'm more than capable of looking after myself. I know exactly what will happen; you'll just get even more pissed than you are already and it will be me bringing *you* home.'

'Just one drink, I promise; I need to see Jimmy One-Note, bit of business to sort out.'

'What kind of business; you're not wheeling and dealing in dodgy gear again, are you?'

'You know me, Sis,' smiled Robbie, with his best butter-wouldn't-melt expression, 'clean as a whistle.'

'Hmm, OK then,' Gemma sighed, 'but one drink and we're out of there. Why do they call him Jimmy One-Note anyway?'

'Well, you remember that band he used to roadie for; he started out as their bass player. I'll leave you to guess the rest.'

It had been many years since Gemma had frequented the Capital and now she remembered why: tacky colour scheme in red, white and black, music designed for torture played at deafening decibels, lights that made everyone appear to move in a staccato rhythm, drinks too expensive and any conversation necessitating high volume at close quarters. Robbie's entourage clocked him as they entered and waved them over.

'Hi, guys,' shouted Robbie, 'you remember my big sister Gemma.'

'Sure do,' leered Stevie, 'and looking better than ever, if I may say so.'

'No, you may not,' retorted Gemma, in a tone intended to let him know exactly where he stood.

'Hey, no need for that,' grinned Stevie; 'what's the world coming to if you can't pay a lady a compliment?'

Gemma shuffled uncomfortably as Robbie and Jimmy One-Note made their way to the bar and left her standing there with the others. Thankfully they paid her no attention as they scanned the dance floor in an attempt to determine their pulling strategy for the evening. 'How about that lot over there?' said Joey, pointing without subtlety at the very moment that one of the girls looked back at him, shook her head and mouthed, 'No chance!'

'Nice one,' said Stevie, 'you're like a bloody bull in a china shop. Got any other ideas?'

Gemma couldn't help but laugh and she cupped her hand and spoke into Joey's ear. 'Don't look, but there are four girls on the table to your left and, unless I'm mistaken, they've been watching you since we came in. I suggest you concentrate your efforts there.'

The voice from behind made her jump and a cold shiver ran down her spine as she felt his breath on her neck. 'Well, you certainly didn't waste any time,' sneered Sam. 'Having a good night are we?'

Gemma turned to face him and regained her composure. 'Not that it's any of your business, but I'm here with my brother and no, I'm not having a particularly good night. I notice that you're not exactly sitting at home crying into your beer either.'

Sam lurched in closer and the smell of alcohol forced her to step back. 'Who's this then?' he sneered, gesturing at a bemused Joey. 'Your next victim?'

Stevie stepped in between them and put a hand on Sam's shoulder. 'Hey, that's enough, fella. I don't think the lady wants to speak to you.'

'Lady, ha; she's a slag and you're welcome to her. Form an orderly queue, boys.'

Oh no, thought Gemma, here we go; she knew of Stevie's reputation, that he and Jimmy One-Note fancied themselves as the modern-day Kray twins. Rumour had it that they'd both been inside for GBH and he certainly looked pretty menacing, with gym-built bulging biceps and barrel chest; and Sam, his equal in height and build, seemed in no mood to stand aside.

'Now, that's not very nice, is it?' said Stevie. 'I think you should apologise now, then leave quietly and we'll say no more about it. I'll make allowances for the fact that you've obviously had too much to drink.'

In one flailing reflex, a defiant Sam pushed Stevie's arm away and took his best drunken swing. To the horrified on-looking Gemma, it all happened in slow motion as Stevie ducked and Sam landed on the floor with a dull thud that rivalled the techno-beat of the music. Undignified and sprawling, he had no time to stagger to his feet before two bouncers grabbed an arm each and dragged him protesting towards the exit, uttering a plaintive 'sorry' as he passed the relieved Gemma; a bloodbath averted.

Gemma turned to Stevie. 'Thank you, but there was no need for violence; I could have handled it.'

Stevie smiled. 'If you say so, love; you can repay me by taking me out to lunch if you want.'

'A tempting offer, but I don't think so,' said Gemma.

Oblivious to the recent drama, Robbie returned. 'OK, Sis? A gin and tonic wasn't it? I got you a double.'

Gemma downed it in one and grabbed Robbie's arm. 'Come on, we're going home; I don't know why I let you talk me into this.'

'But I'm just getting started,' protested Robbie. 'I was intending to get wide-eyed and legless and go a-searching for a girl that's wide-legged and eyeless. The night is still young.'

'Yes, but I'm not,' replied Gemma; 'please, get me out of this hell-hole.'

5.

Pete had been here before, though he hadn't shared this rather sensitive information with Sandra. It was a long time ago, in another life; before his escape from the rat-race, before barges and long before Sandra. Walking these seedy streets again, he felt like a different person to the young, fit, carefree youth he once was, as if it were someone else who'd been here all those years ago. As he crept past the Banana Bar, it all came flooding back to him.

You wouldn't know it to look at me now, he thought, as he caught his rotund reflection in a window, but I was once a half-decent centre-back in a reasonable local-league football team. Faint praise indeed, for a man who'd laid his body on the line for his team on numerous occasions, whether on the pitch or in the bar after the game. A long weekend in Amsterdam, their manager had suggested, receiving enthusiastic responses from all present. 'We'll have a couple of games with some Dutch opposition, take in the sights, if you know what I mean, and generally have a laugh. What do you think?' A unanimous yes and a determined posse of what could loosely be described as sportsmen had descended upon the Red Light District on the night prior to their first match; possibly not the best preparation for an important international encounter.

The Banana Bar was legendary, renowned and acclaimed for its beautiful girls and their impressive muscle control; and the lads were determined to take full advantage of the entertainment on offer. Goalkeeper training should be their first priority, they'd decided, and positioned the hapless Gordon to save the bananas, as these very talented ladies launched them across the room at incredible velocity. It didn't auger well for their forthcoming fixtures when he only managed to catch one, whilst protesting that they were too slippery. The alcohol was flowing freely and, although making a huge dent in their finances, the team soon got into the spirit of things. Much laughter ensued as one of the girls gyrated seductively upon the head of their shiny-headed full-back, claiming that she was in possession of the certain cure for baldness.

Back onto the street and they'd been enticed by a dodgy-looking character into a live show that proved to be somewhat bizarre and not at all what they were expecting. The back-street theatre was about two-thirds full and they'd sat in eager anticipation as a man in a bumble bee costume proceeded to deflower a lady dressed as a flower, the act graphically portrayed and undeniably real. The intended symbolism and artistic pretensions, however, were lost on the group of disbelieving, hysterical young men. And so the tone was set for the evening and, indeed, for the remainder of the weekend.

The following day saw a bedraggled bunch (seriously hung over from a lethal cocktail of lager and space-cake) take on the impressive total-football of what appeared to be the Ajax youth team. Goalkeeper Gordon (who by now had inevitably earned the rhyming-slang nickname Gordon Banks, due to his exploits in the Banana Bar and beyond), proved to be just as inept at catching footballs as bananas. The experience could only be described as a humiliating annihilation; a fifteen goal thriller without reply; after which the lads shook hands and predictably retreated to the bar to nurse the wounds to their national pride.

Through the hazy recollections, Pete indulged in a wry smile and wondered what had become of those hopeful, uninhibited, inebriated young dudes, the rest of their lives before them. Where were they all now? Probably family men, most of them; their youth and carelessness long behind them. If they could see him now they would never believe that he was here on a mission of mercy.

In surreptitious search of Celina, Pete attempted to carefully follow Kim-Ly's sketchy directions. The girls seemed to be closing in on him, each vying for his attention; a crooked, inviting finger here, a wink and a lick of the lips there; all of the windows looked the same, their inhabitants bored and disdainful, but mostly stunning nonetheless. He counted: seven windows along the right-hand side of the street, a vacant one, followed by one housing a pretty, long-legged lady sporting blonde curls and a top so tight as to threaten both his and her circulation; she stared down her nose and viewed him with undisguised distaste, but still he entered. Half-a-minute later and he was unceremoniously back outside on his arse, the lady insisting that her name wasn't Celina and that, no, she wouldn't accompany him back to his boat, where he had a friend for her. This, followed by a 'piss off and stop wasting my time'. Pete staggered to his feet and retraced his steps in an effort to regain his flawed sense of direction.

At a street corner café, an inebriated sailor was complaining vociferously that his particular preference was not on the menu. 'But I eat only fish heads and tails,' he shouted, then stood up and laughed, and zipped up his flies.

A short, shady figure in a pork-pie hat stood deep in thought beneath a lamp on the opposite corner, contemplating the tale of temptation and the tempted unfolding before him. With no visible reference points that coincided with his map, Pete approached him warily and, indicating his destination on the hand-drawn directions, said 'Excuse me; I appear to have lost my bearings. Do you know where this street is?'

The man shuffled nervously, pulled down his hat and turned the map upside down. 'You're in the right place, but at the wrong end of the street. It's that way, up there,' he pointed.

'Ah, yes, I see it now,' said Pete. 'Thank you. How stupid of me. Hey, hang on; don't I know you?' The man flinched and pulled down his hat still further. 'You're that author that was all over the papers and on the news a few years back,' continued Pete; 'big scandal with that MP and then that other business in America. Don't tell me, it'll come back to me.' Pete clicked his fingers. 'Joe Stamford, that's it. *That Bloody Book*, wasn't it? I have a copy at home, but hadn't got round to reading it yet. And what are you doing here? I would have thought you'd been through enough controversy without being seen in a place like this.'

'That was the idea of the hat,' the man whispered through gritted teeth, 'so that people wouldn't recognise me.' He glanced around nervously to ensure that no-one had overheard Pete's revelation. 'If you must know, I'm here to research my next book. It's based in Amsterdam and I can't write about somewhere unless I have a feel for the place. I'd rather you kept this to yourself; I could do without any more adverse publicity. I won't ask what *you're* doing here.'

'It's not what it looks like,' replied Pete. 'I too have an innocent reason for my presence. Here, autograph this, I'll say no more and you can forget that you ever set eyes on me.' He handed Joe a pen and the blank side of a leaflet for a live sex show.

'I already have,' said Joe, as he smiled and scrawled his name. 'Pleasure to meet you, whatever your name is.'

'Thanks. And I'll look forward to reading the new book; as long as I'm not in it.'

Pete glanced over his shoulder as he made his way along this boulevard of shame; the shady figure of Joe had disappeared into the shadows, as if he'd never been there at all. Had he imagined this curious meeting? Was he dreaming? Had he overdone the cheese and biscuits again? He shook his head at the odd turn of events that had brought him here, as if he were in the midst of a strange story; a figment of someone's warped imagination.

Wow, he thought, Celina sure is something to behold. Amazonian, barely clothed and bursting out of black lace; lithe and leggy, she looked down at him with deep blue eyes from atop a magnificent pair of heels, as she removed her meagre top. Pete gasped and shielded his eyes, thinking of Sandra. 'Whoa, stop! P-put that back on, p-please. I'm not here for that.'

Celina hesitated, gave him a sideways look and spoke slowly in a strangely sexy Eastern European accent. 'Then vhat are you here for? Don't be shy; I vill do vhatever you vant for the right price.'

'Jesus, now there's a thought,' said Pete, as he tried to look anywhere but at Celina.

He shakily removed a note from his pocket as well as a gold bracelet. 'Show her this bracelet,' Kim-Ly had instructed, 'she has always admired it and will know you have come from me.'

The next thing he knew he was pinned to the wall by a pair of enormous bare breasts and, surprised and shaken by Celina's strength, he couldn't move. 'This belongs to my friend,' she growled. 'Vhere did you get it? Vhat have you done vith her?'

'R-read the note.' Pete attempted to catch his breath. 'It will tell you that she is safe and that I have come to take you to her. Please, p-put me down and I'll explain. And for God's sake, put some bloody clothes on.'

Ignoring Pete's pleas to get dressed (after many years in the profession, Celina had few inhibitions), she sat down and began to read. 'Stay there and do not move,' she threatened.

'I wouldn't dare,' replied Pete, breathing heavily and worrying about his blood pressure. In an effort to avert his gaze, he took in his surroundings: a bare, soulless room, dimly lit by a single forty-watt light bulb and containing a perfunctory, solid-looking bed; so cold and uninviting for an act so intimate.

Eventually, Celina looked up with a slightly softer expression. 'And Kim-Ly, is she OK? Have they harmed her?'

'She is hurt, but my partner Sandra is looking after her,' replied Pete; 'she's in good hands.'

'And you say you vill take me there?' asked Celina, suddenly appearing more vulnerable.

'Yes, but we must be careful. Kim-Ly says that the pimps will be very angry and that they'll be watching you.' Pete emptied the contents of his bag. 'Here, put these on and we can walk out of here. No-one will suspect a thing.'

He wasn't so sure about this. Kim-Ly had neglected to mention Celina's striking stature and there was no way that Sandra's frumpiest rags, designed to discourage attention, would fit her. The Glastonbury XL t-shirt wasn't so bad and he had to admit that Celina filled it well, but the faded denim jeans barely reached below her knees; in some discomfort, she looked anything but inconspicuous.

Cautiously, Pete peeked out and scanned the street; it was peak-time and eagerly anticipant punters were everywhere, casually choosing their pleasure like selecting sweets from a shelf. Celina stood close behind him, with her breasts disconcertingly pressed against his shoulder blades. Sandra's sensibly packed sensible shoes had proved way too small, so Celina still towered above him in heels ill-designed for walking, let alone running should it become necessary. As they emerged hand-in-hand, she teetered on the brink of balance. An unlikely couple attempting to blend in with the throng, they made their way gingerly through the crowd; a crowd fortunately accustomed to the sight of unlikely couples.

'Just act natural and we'll be alright,' reassured Pete, his gaze straight ahead and purposeful, disguising his nervousness. He breathed a sigh of relief as they left the disreputable neighbourhood behind them and entered a more respectable district; but then he realised that it would be here that Celina would attract attention, out of place and out of the zone set aside for such women. Pete quickened his pace, peering into every nook and cranny, eager to escape this ludicrous situation.

'Please, slow down,' pleaded Celina, stumbling on stiletto stilts with all the grace of Miranda on Malibu; 'you try valking in these shoes and see how fast *you* can go.'

Pete looked around; all was quiet and still on a clear, starlit night and it seemed that, remarkably, he'd accomplished his mission without too much incident. Embarrassed to notice that he was still holding her hand, perhaps a little tighter than necessary, he withdrew it quickly. 'Sorry, never done anything like this before. Are you OK?'

He waited for an answer, but none came. Turning, he saw Celina: static, undignified and a far cry from the sexy lady he'd encountered just a short time ago, her heel caught fast in a drain cover.

A middle-aged couple, out for an evening stroll, stared as they passed; Pete on his knees and pulling hard at Celina's ankle, his head rubbing against a substantial thigh. 'Good evening,' said Pete, as if nothing were amiss, 'nice night for a walk.'

Eventually, the shoe jerked free and they continued on their erratic journey. 'Try to relax and look normal,' said Celina. 'Ve vill be found out if you keep jumping at every shadow.'

Pete considered his appearance, the most normal bloke on Normal Street; as normal as Norman Normal from Normanton. '*You're* telling me to look normal,' he said. 'Have you taken a look at yourself? Is it any wonder that I'm jumping at shadows with you beside me?'

'I did not ask you to come to my vindow tonight. I am only here for Kim-Ly. She is my friend and ve look after each other.'

'Then stop complaining and valk, I mean walk this way,' said Pete, 'this ain't exactly a picnic for me either, you know. Down here, it's not much further.'

Pete shuddered as a twig cracked behind them, a sound akin to a crack of thunder in the still of night. He stopped and peered around, but could see nothing. Taking Celina's hand again, they walked on in silence, oblivious to the stealthy shadow in pursuit that darted in and out between trees, walls, cars.

* * *

Barry clutched his boarding pass in sweaty hands, his eyes darting this way and that, sensing danger in every passing face. Leaning on his stick and limping painfully to the departure lounge, he couldn't wait to board that plane home and put as much distance as possible between himself and this awful place. He felt naked without his camera; it was part of getting dressed in the morning and he would no more have thought about leaving home without it as he would his jacket, shirt and trousers; which, incidentally, was about all he had left. No luggage, no coat, no strength, but worst of all, no camera. 'Two more days,' the doctor had advised, 'then we can let you go home to recuperate.'

That was before the visit from an agitated Terry, suggesting that he may want to discharge himself a little earlier and that it wouldn't be safe to return to their apartment to collect his things. Barry had listened in disbelief as Terry had recounted the sorry tale of the last twenty-four hours. He'd worked and socialised with Terry before on numerous occasions and had always admired his dedication to the job in hand; Barry was surprised at this uncharacteristic lack of professionalism.

'You've done what?' he exclaimed. 'The girl downstairs; I know who you mean, she's absolutely gorgeous, but for God's sake, Terry, is she worth putting your life at risk for, not to mention hers, your friends on the boat and, more importantly, mine. We've been in plenty of places where people need help and you've always kept your distance, remained professional. What was it you once told me, when I wanted to buy food for those street kids in Bombay? "We're here to report what's happening, not to get involved. Simply by showing the world the injustice and poverty we are contributing to its eradication". What's so different about a girl screaming in the flat downstairs? Don't tell me, I think I can guess.'

'Look, I know I've been a complete dickhead and I'm now fully aware of the potential impact of my actions, but I wasn't thinking straight. I'm sorry, I let my heart rule my head and now it's too late to turn back. That's why I'm here; to warn you that things could get a little risky around here.'

'Hmm, are you sure it was your heart ruling your head and not another part of your anatomy?' Barry snatched his passport and attempted to stand. 'You're a stupid bastard, but we've been through a lot together and I suppose in some ways I understand, bearing in mind what happened between you and Gemma. Now, the least you can do is to help me to the bus station.'

'Thanks, mate, that means a lot. Gemma tore my world apart and I'm not sure I can live in the same place any more; there are too many memories, maybe it's time to move on. Saw her the other week on the High Street with her new fella and had to duck into the nearest shop; turned out to be a lingerie specialists. How do you think that made me feel?'

'Look, I've been through the odd break-up myself, you know, but this is all a bit drastic and dramatic, isn't it? All a bit spur of the moment and not thought through.'

'Perhaps, but look where safe and secure got me. It's time for a little spontaneity, time for some adventure.'

'And what do you want me to tell the guys back at the paper?' asked Barry. 'This would make an interesting story, you know; probably better than the one you were supposed to be writing.'

'Tell Chris that I just couldn't take any more; that I got stressed-out and needed a break. Tell him to take it off my holiday; he knows all about Gemma and I – he'll understand and cut me some slack.'

'And after this "holiday", what happens then; are you coming back?'

'I don't know. Have to see how things pan out, I suppose. We'll have to get away from Amsterdam; but from there, who knows?'

'Well, you've obviously made up your mind, but please think about the fall-out; there are a lot of people could get hurt here.'

'Hey, you know me, Barry,' Terry smiled, 'I'm just a big pussycat; wouldn't hurt a fly.'

47

Purloining a walking stick on the way, Terry had assisted Barry to escape the hospital without detection; then to the bus, where they'd shaken hands and wished each other luck. 'You're going to need it, mate,' said Barry.

Striding purposefully ahead, Terry was oblivious to Barry's shake of the head and weak wave from the window. Barry sat back, closed his eyes and tried to blot out the pain in his leg; relishing the thought of home, he was relieved to be out of hospital, albeit against medical advice.

The Customs officer had appraised him with a contemptuous look, but allowed him through. Pale and drawn, attempting not to look conspicuous, he felt guilty and self-conscious, even though he'd done nothing wrong. So what's new, he thought; I always feel like this when I go through Customs.

As a relieved and knackered Barry boarded the plane, events on the other side of town were taking a dramatic, macabre turn.

'Celina, this is my partner, Sandra,' said Pete; 'welcome to our humble abode.' He flopped down on the sofa, exhausted. 'Where the hell is Terry?' he asked. 'I'll kill him for getting us into this crazy situation.'

Kim-Ly and Celina hugged and giggled like long-lost friends and withdrew to talk about recent, unexpected events.

'Terry had to pop out for a while,' replied Sandra, 'said he had some business to attend to. Wouldn't say where he was going; only that it wouldn't take long. How did it go? You're both back safely, so must have been successful.'

'Don't ask. I'd rather not go through anything like that again if it's all the same to you; and the next time you want to adopt the missionary position and save lost souls, you can go yourself.'

Sandra sat down beside him, put her arm around his shoulders and gave him a peck on the cheek. 'My hero,' she beamed. 'Doesn't it make you feel good to save a damsel in distress?'

'Trust me, that young lady is more than capable of looking

after herself; it was me that was in distress. I need a drink.'

He was just about to stand to fetch himself a beer when an almighty thud hit the cabin door. 'Jesus, what was that?' exclaimed Pete. 'Who is it? Who's there?' No answer.

Kim-Ly and Celina cowered in the background, hiding behind Sandra, scared and shaking.

'Who are you? What do you want?' asked Pete again. Still there was no answer.

Finally, a voice spoke faintly from the other side; the voice of Terry in shock and fear. 'Oh my God, no; Pete, open the door please.'

Pete gasped as he did as instructed, closely followed by two frightened screams that could be heard miles away. Wedged in the doorway lay a limp and motionless man, eyes wide and bulging, blood trickling from the corner of his mouth, a gun hanging from his trigger finger; and there behind him stood a paralysed Terry with a vacant expression and a hammer in hand.

Then all was quiet, apart from a whimpering Kim-Ly; until Pete uncharacteristically took charge, suddenly assertive after his recent adventure and recognition as a hero. 'Sandra, take the girls into the bedroom, please. Terry, for God's sake don't just stand there; can you get this guy out of the doorway?'

Terry said nothing as, still in shock, he held the prone figure beneath the arms and dragged the dead weight to one side. Pete emerged and joined him, taking the man's wrist and feeling in vain for a pulse. 'My God, man, what have you done? I think you've killed him.'

'H-he had a gun,' stammered Terry, 'he was about to kick the door in. W-what was I supposed to do?'

'And where did you get the hammer? Did you just happen to have it on you at the time?' enquired Pete.

'F-found it lying on deck; must be yours I suppose.'

'Great,' said Pete, 'I was using it to fix the generator; it'll have my prints all over it. So, who is he?'

'No idea. I saw him following you and Celina back to the boat, must have been on your tail since you picked her up.'

Pete considered the turmoil that Terry had inflicted upon their peaceful life and finally lost patience. 'Look, we were perfectly happy before you turned up with hookers and dead bodies. Do you really think that a brief encounter at Glastonbury a few years ago gives you the right to impose upon our friendship and hospitality this much?'

'Do you think I planned it?' replied Terry. 'How could I have known it would end up like this?'

'So, you're saying that this is the first time you've killed someone,' said Pete.

'Absolutely. I'm not in the habit of hitting people with hammers, honest. I've seen death, it's part of my job; but I've never been responsible for it before.'

'So what shall we do with the body?' enquired Sandra.

Pete and Terry jumped. 'Bloody hell, will you stop creeping around?' said Pete. 'Where are Kim-Ly and Celina?'

'Inside and very scared,' replied Sandra; 'apparently you've just killed one of the big cheese pimps and these guys don't fool around. There will be people looking for him and it won't take long before they put two and two together and link this with the disappearance of Kim-Ly and Celina.'

'Phew, I hope she's worth it, man,' said Pete, shaking his head and looking the bemused Terry in the eye. 'This is some serious shit you've got us all into. Come on, help me with that tarpaulin. If no-one else has seen us, then there's no reason why they should trace him here.'

'You guys are taking this very well,' said Terry. 'If I were you I would have kicked us out on day one. I'm really, really sorry.'

'So you should be,' said Sandra, 'but we are where we are.' She thought for a moment, then concluded, 'We'll use that old anchor to weigh down the body and toss it over the side. I was going to paint it for decorative purposes, but I can get another.'

'Shouldn't we call the police?' suggested Pete, shocked at Sandra's apparent nonchalance and seeing a previously unknown side of her. 'We may need some protection if this chap is, sorry was, a dangerous criminal.'

'No, we don't know how much influence these people have,' said Sandra. 'It has been known for perpetrators of organised crime to exert power over authority. It only takes one copper to be caught with his pants down and that's it: blackmail and control.'

Pete and Terry carried the heavy anchor and placed it carefully on top of the prone body.

'Hey, have you done this before?' Terry asked Sandra, as he threw in the murder weapon and clumsily tied the end of the tarpaulin. 'You seem to be very conversant with the disposal of bodies.'

'No, she just reads too many crime novels,' said Pete. 'Now, can we stop chatting and get this over and done with. Are those knots going to hold?'

'Yeah, I used to be in the Scouts,' admitted Terry. 'Long time ago, but I'm pretty sure they're right.'

Pete surveyed the surrounding area to ensure no-one was watching and motioned for Terry to grab the other end, but the combined weight of anchor and body proved too heavy to lift.

'Need some help vith that?' asked a voice from behind; and there stood a statuesque and unfeeling Celina. 'I hated that bastard; he treated us like shit and it vould be an honour for me to throw him to the fishes.'

Pete nodded and within seconds a splash; the deed was done.

At first impervious, Terry felt as if he'd just played a part in a movie; pure fantasy. Wearing a glazed expression, he sat down next to Kim-Ly. People like him didn't kill, did they? He was a decent chap, salt of the Earth, a diamond geezer and generally an all-round nice bloke; this couldn't really be happening to him. The shivers began, the cold sweats; and through the haze of shock he saw Pete standing over him with a large brandy. He was just about to take it, gratefully, when Sandra cruelly snatched it away. 'Brandy for shock is a fallacy,' she stated. 'Hot, sweet tea, that's the answer; here, drink this.'

'But I don't take sugar,' protested Terry.

'It's purely for medicinal purposes,' said Sandra. 'Drink it quickly and you won't even notice the taste.'

Terry grimaced as he did as ordered. 'Ugh! Can I have that brandy now, please?'

'Not until the shock has subsided,' said Sandra. 'You'll need a clear head to discuss the implications of what you've just done and to work out what to do next.'

They sat in silence for ten minutes while Terry regained his composure, Kim-Ly holding his hand in her lap and Celina expressionless, staring straight ahead. Attempting to clear his head, Terry turned to Pete. 'Can anyone trace him to here? Did you leave any trail?'

'Not unless you count the stiletto prints and the overpowering aroma of cheap perfume that a dog without a nose could follow.' He went on, despite Celina's glare, 'No, I don't think so. I'm assuming the guy was on his own, otherwise we'd have been inundated with his mates by now.'

'Well, I know one thing,' said Terry, 'I have to get Kim-Ly and Celina out of Amsterdam sooner rather than later. We'll be on our way first thing tomorrow and out of your hair. This is my responsibility; I'm the one who created this mess, it's up to me to clear it up.'

'And where will you go and how will you get there?' asked Sandra.

'By train; down through Belgium and France and then the ferry back to England.'

'Well, firstly, they're likely to be watching the train station and, secondly, how do you intend to get these young ladies across borders and through Customs? I doubt very much that they have their passports with them.'

'Our passports are fake,' confirmed Kim-Ly. 'And the pimps hold them for safe-keeping, in case we try to escape.'

'Then do you have any better ideas?' Terry asked Sandra. 'We can't stay here.'

'Yes, I think I do. Been turning things over in my mind since you got here,' said Sandra, tapping her head. 'I believe I may have the solution. We're all going on a cycling holiday. I'll arrange the hire, get some new clothes for the girls and cycling gear for all of us. Why should anyone look at us twice? Holland is full of cyclists on account of it being so flat.'

They all considered this strange proposition. 'But I haven't ridden a bike in years,' protested Terry. 'I'll fall off before we get to the end of the street.'

'You'll soon pick it up again,' said Sandra, 'it's like riding a bike.'

'And I have never ridden a bike,' admitted Kim-Ly; 'we could not afford one where I come from.'

'Then perhaps a tandem will be required for you and Terry.'

'A tandem; it almost sounds like a good idea,' conceded Terry, 'but there's no reason why you should put your lives at risk too.'

'We're in this up to our necks,' said Sandra, 'whether we like it or not; harbouring a murderer, disposal of the body, etc. Besides, it will seem more convincing if there are more of us. They'll be looking for just you and the girls.'

'Me, a murderer? Think I may have grounds for claiming self-defence. What do you think, Pete?' asked Terry. 'Fancy a cycling trip?'

'First, I've heard of it, but yeah, why not; in for a penny, as they say. I could do with losing some weight and Sandra's right, we're implicated too, thanks to you.'

'That's settled then,' decided Sandra. 'We lie low here tomorrow, until I've sorted out the bike hire, the route and the disguises, and then we hit the road. Now I suggest we all get some sleep; that's if we can.'

6.

'Good night?' asked Gemma's Dad, as he watched her half-heartedly push some cornflakes around her bowl. Gemma raised her eyebrows as if that were all the answer required and said nothing.

'Yeah, just like the old days,' replied an annoyingly bright Robbie. 'Gemma started a fight and I had to bring her home.'

'What? We wouldn't have been in that Godforsaken shithole in the first place if it wasn't for you,' protested Gemma. 'I wanted to come home, remember?'

She'd finally cried herself to sleep at three o'clock in the morning and was not in the mood for Robbie's incessant jovial banter. Ideally, she would have preferred to stay curled up in bed all day, hidden away from the world and unsolicited advice, but her father had insisted that she surface by ten. 'Your Gran's coming over,' he'd said, 'and you hardly ever make the effort to see her; the least you can do is to show your face.'

Gemma's Gran was a forthright, outspoken lady, with little time for self-pity. She'd been hardened to the world by the loss of half of her family in the Blitz and believed in people dealing with their problems and moving on; just as she'd had to in the most tragic of circumstances when she was still but a child. The story had had a profound effect on a teenage Gemma when she'd asked Gran for help with her history project on World War Two;

54

Gran had lost her mother and older sister that day, along with her childhood and innocence. Now there was nothing that the world could throw at her that she couldn't overcome. If Gemma was searching for a sympathetic ear, then she knew she wouldn't find it on the side of Gran's head. Still she remained tearful, the lack of sleep adding to her miserable mood.

Gran entered the house with her familiar irrepressible flourish, her booming voice announcing her arrival to the whole street as she hugged hello. It wasn't long before Gemma's Mum brought Gran up to speed with the situation and she needed little encouragement to set about putting Gemma's world to rights.

'You must find Terry and tell him how you feel,' she'd said, countenancing no argument. 'If he still loves you, then he'll come back; if not, then you must either get used to living alone or find someone else. There's no point in wasting time moping around and trying to change things you can do nothing about. Everyone makes mistakes in life; the important thing is to deal with them quickly and move on.'

'You make it sound so cold, clinical and easy,' said Gemma.

'Not cold and clinical; it's simply a question of survival. Of course it hurts, but you have to look after number one and take control, because no-one else can determine your destiny. Your grandfather was not my first love, you know, neither would he have been my first choice, but we rubbed along OK together and, in time, I grew to love him, I suppose; got used to having him around the place and I sure as hell miss him now he's gone.'

'I miss him too,' sobbed Gemma, the tears welling up again as she lay in her Gran's arms, just like she had when she was a child. She didn't notice as Gran, too, brushed away a tear.

The next day, and with Gran's words still ringing in her ears, Gemma approached the newspaper office with apprehension. She'd only been here once before, when Terry had been taken ill and was in no fit state to travel home alone. 'It's a well-known medical fact that man-flu is worse than childbirth,' Terry had proclaimed, after she'd got him home and put him to bed.

Fluorescent-lit, buzzing with all the excitement of breaking news, telephones ringing incessantly; a modern, open-plan office full of intensity and people going about their business as if all was fine. Didn't they know that Terry wasn't there and that the paper couldn't function without him? A bored-looking young receptionist showed her to Chris's office and knocked on the door.

'Come in, Gemma, sit down,' said Chris, smiling. 'Good to see you again. Mandy, could you bring us some coffee, please?' He turned to Gemma with a more serious expression. 'There has been a development, but I can't tell you much more than I did the other day, I'm afraid. I had a call from Barry, the photographer who was working with Terry. He says that Terry's OK, but that he's decided to take some holiday and he doesn't know when he's coming back. I'm willing to cut him some slack, given the circumstances and the good work he's done for us in the past, but this is a cut-throat business and we can't have our reporters missing deadlines and disappearing without warning. Barry has called in sick too and said he won't be fit for work for several weeks. God knows what they've both been up to.'

'Then please tell me where he is,' pleaded Gemma, 'I can talk some sense into him if I could find him.'

'Why don't you just call him?'

'I've tried, but he either has his phone switched off or he's not answering. Besides, what I have to say, I want to say in person, not over the phone.'

'Then I'm sorry, but I can't help you,' said Chris. 'It's not my place to divulge his whereabouts; and anyway, I can't even be sure that he's still in the same place that we sent him. It's been weeks since we last spoke.'

Gemma emerged onto the busy street, the sanguine sunshine a stark contrast to her miserable mood. She was down-hearted, but at least now she had a new lead: she knew where Barry lived from the time that Terry had insisted that they give him a lift home after the office Christmas party. It was miles out of their way, but public transport had long since retired and, given his somewhat inebriated state, no taxi would take him. Gemma had insisted that Terry clean up the car the next day.

The suburban, tree-lined streets all looked the same as she weaved between the parked cars, but Gemma had been blessed with a photographic memory: she only had to visit a place once to be able to find it again if required. Approaching Barry's drive, she considered her tactics: simple – pretend that Chris had already told her about their assignment and ask Barry to fill in the details. She remembered Barry as a trusting soul and, although she felt bad about tricking him, the means justified the end. Gemma rang the doorbell and waited ... and waited. She was about to give up when a shadow appeared in the hallway, making slow progress to the door.

'Gemma, what a nice surprise; how are you?' A gaunt, unshaven Barry smiled through his pain, the stick taking his weight.

'Oh my God, Barry, whatever's happened to you?' replied Gemma, shocked at his withered frame and drawn features.

'A little accident, that's all; it's nothing that a little rest won't cure.'

The cogs of her mind turned quickly: Barry is hurt, *ergo* Terry may be too. She took Barry's arm and helped him to the untidy living room; a newspaper lay strewn on the floor, open at the sports pages, a foil container hosted the pungent remnants of yesterday's takeaway and half-a-dozen empty beer bottles stood, like monuments to Barry's decline, on the coffee table.

'Can I get you a drink?' he asked.

'No, you sit down and let me get them. Tea or coffee?'

'Strong coffee, please. Hey, it's great to see another human being; haven't seen a soul since I got back.'

Gemma made her way to the haphazard kitchen and located the coffee and mugs, deciding to take hers black as she opened the rancid milk and took a step back. The fridge was bare, apart from a few bottles of lager and a piece of mouldy cheese.

'Jesus, Barry, how are you surviving? Isn't there anyone to look after you?'

'No. I get along OK by myself. Haven't spoken to my parents for years, my brother's in Australia and girls don't tend to stick around too long.'

'I wonder why?' said Gemma, removing a grubby sock from the chair between finger and thumb and sitting down. 'When's the last time you had a decent meal? No, don't answer; I can see it's been a while. No arguments, I'm getting the groceries and I'll cook you something before I go. Now, what's the story? Who did this to you?'

Barry hesitated, unsure how much to give away. 'All part of the job; we all know the risks before we go to these places.'

'You don't have to tell me; I always went through hell when Terry was away. Didn't know from one week to the next where they were going to send him. This one didn't seem so dangerous though, from what Chris told me.'

'You've spoken to Chris?'

'Yes, he brought me up to speed. I know where you've been and what you've been working on.'

'You wouldn't think it would be such a bad place,' said Barry, 'but believe me, it has its fair share of evil bastards.'

'And Terry, is he OK?' Gemma probed further.

'He was when I left him; well, physically anyway. His scars are not visible to the naked eye.'

'Look, I know I've hurt him, but I want to put it right. I have to see him, Barry.'

'You may be too late. Amsterdam's probably not the best location to send someone on the rebound; there's a lot of temptation and comfort on offer for a man in such a condition.'

'Amsterdam! So that's where he's decided to take his "holiday".'

'You didn't know, did you?' exclaimed Barry. 'You've just fooled me into revealing his location. Well thanks, Gemma; and there was me thinking this was a social call.'

'I'm sorry, Barry, but I had to find out. How can I find him when I get there?'

Barry thought for a moment. 'Right, I'm going to tell you the truth because I don't want you having a wasted journey. He's kind of met someone else, but there are likely to be people who are not very happy with their budding relationship. Let's just say that the lady in question is of dubious merit, but obvious desire, and that Terry thought her chosen career was beneath her, even though there have been many people beneath her and, indeed, on top of her, if you get my drift.'

'Oh my God, you can't be serious; he's fallen for a hooker?'

'He'll probably deny it and say that he was merely helping a girl in trouble, but from where I'm standing that's about the size of it; and I must say that I can see the attraction. Sorry to be the bearer of bad news, but it's probably for the best that you know how things stand.'

Gemma put her head in her hands and sobbed. 'It's all my fault, I've driven him to this; how could I have been so stupid.'

'Look, I know he was devastated when you split up; I doubt that he's thinking straight at the moment.'

'And your injuries; are they to do with the people he's upset?'

'Probably caused by the same people, but not the result of anything Terry did. No, I just took some pictures that I shouldn't. I was already in hospital when it all happened, otherwise I might have been able to persuade him that his obsession might not be good for his health.'

'Obsession? Is that what it is?'

'Maybe, maybe not; who knows the inner-workings of a broken heart?'

'Please, Barry, I have to speak to him before this goes any further. Where is he?

'No idea, I'm afraid. When I left he was planning on leaving

Amsterdam pdq; they'd been lying low on a barge with some friends of yours – now what were their names?'

'That'll be Sandra and Pete.'

'Sandra and Pete, that's it. I suggest you call them to check the lie of the land.'

Robbie listened to Gemma's tale in disbelief. 'Are we talking about Terry here?' he leered. 'Didn't know he had it in him; always had him down as a one-woman man.'

'He was before I messed things up,' said Gemma, 'and this isn't funny. I'm glad Terry's gone up in your estimation, but this is my life we're talking about. I'm going to Amsterdam, regardless of what anyone thinks.'

'Not on your own you're not; I'm coming with you.'

'What for? To see if Terry can get one for you too?'

'You think I'm really shallow, don't you?' protested Robbie. 'I want to come to look out for my big sister; could be some dodgy territory you're getting into and you're gonna need someone on your side. I've got nothing better to do; it's a no-brainer.'

'A no-brainer; I hate that expression. If it's a no-brainer, then it's a decision you're well equipped to make.'

'Hey, come on, Sis; you know it makes sense,' replied Robbie, choosing to ignore her bad pun. 'When are you going?'

'As soon as I can book the flight.'

'Can you get the time off?'

'Yes, I'm due some holiday, or I could just take the time off with stress; God knows I've earned it.' Gemma had been thinking of airing her grievances at work for some time. With qualifications and experience to match the best of her colleagues, she'd been overlooked for promotion once again at Bardsley & Cavendish. It was jobs for the boys as usual at this most traditional of traditional law firms.

'OK, but aren't you going to talk to your friend Sandra first?'

'No, she might warn Terry that I'm on my way and that would

spoil the surprise, wouldn't it?'

'Then I'm definitely offering my services as chaperone; I want to see his face when you turn up unannounced. I wouldn't miss this for the world.'

7.

A balmy evening in Amsterdam on the *Christina*, a floating, peaceful hideout, the sun setting slowly, the aroma of simmering curry wafting through the still air; a relaxing aura and laid-back mood, despite the threat so close and menacing. In the galley, a contented Sandra and Pete prepare dinner, in their element in their natural habitat, Celina lounging lazily on the sofa, watching some dubious European 'talent' show, Terry and Kim-Ly standing on deck, getting to know each other.

'What are you thinking about?' asked Terry, as Kim-Ly gazed into the distance.

'About home, my mother, father, brother, sister, my village. I want to go back there to explain what happened, why I disappeared. They must think I am dead. I promised to write, to tell them all about my adventures in London, but I was too ashamed of what I had become. What will they think of me now? I will be disowned, cast out for bringing shame on my family.'

'None of this is your fault. If they love you, as I'm sure they do, they'll understand and welcome you back. How could you have known what you were going to? You were only fifteen, still a child and as trusting as a child will be.'

'Tell me how you come to be this understanding.' Kim-Ly looked into Terry's eyes. 'You do not know me; you do not know the bitterness inside, the fear of men. How can I ever trust anyone again?'

'You can trust me,' said Terry, taking her hands. 'Please, let me help you.'

Kim-Ly pulled her hands away. 'And who is Gemma? I heard you and Sandra talking about her.'

'Gemma is my ex; we split up and it's over. I am free to see anyone I please.'

'And why me; why not any other shop-window dummy from De Wallen? What makes me so special?'

'Have you never taken a look in the mirror?' asked Terry, as if the answer were obvious. 'You are so beautiful; you can rise above this and learn to love and trust again. You're a golden lion; you can do anything you wish.'

Kim-Ly smiled and Terry melted again; then the smile turned to disdain. 'You make it all sound possible,' she said, 'like it is so easy to forget all that has been done to me, the years of abuse and shame. I am a prostitute, Terry; that is what they have made me and that is what I will always be, until I am so old that no-one wants me any more. That is the only way I can be free.'

'You told me that you tried to arrange a meeting with the other girls to obtain better conditions. If you were prepared to do that then you must have some fight in you, a desire to stand up for your rights. You have a right to freedom and to make your own decisions.'

'Yes, and look where fighting for my rights got me,' argued Kim-Ly, raising her top to show Terry the bruising on her ribs. 'Some girls actually choose this profession, you know. They want to please men for a living; they are the ones who are in charge of their lives and do this on their own terms. The likes of Celina and I who are forced into it, we are just slaves.'

'It doesn't have to be that way,' insisted Terry. 'My job has taken me to some awful places and I've seen some dreadful things, but the one thing that shines through all the dirt, despair and misery in the world is the human spirit. I've seen people in the worst poverty imaginable, but those people have bigger smiles and show greater generosity than the richest men in the world. It's that kind of spirit that can change things, make things happen.'

'And this job you have, that takes you to such awful places that you have to share a gutter with the likes of me, you never told me why you were here and what you do.'

Terry hesitated; his profession had been somewhat tainted of late and, in the eyes of the public, was little better than Kim-Ly's, but he decided honesty was the best policy. 'I'm a journalist. I was sent here to do a story on the sex-trade and the men behind it.'

Kim-Ly nodded knowingly. 'Ah, now I understand,' she said, 'and I am part of your story, your way behind the scenes. It all makes perfect sense now.'

'Is that what you think of me?' said Terry, deeply offended. 'I have risked my life to get you out of there; not to mention imposing on my friends and the small matter of killing our unwanted guest and disposing of the body.'

'I did not ask you to come to my room and to interfere in my life. These are choices you have made. I warned you about these men and no-one would be dead if you'd left when I told you to.'

'True,' conceded Terry. 'OK, tomorrow you can go back where you came from if that's what you want. Here am I talking about freedom; who am I to try to persuade you to stay against your will? And you have my word that I won't write a syllable of what happened here.'

Kim-Ly considered Terry's words and looked into his eyes. There was an honesty about this man, a dependability, a glint in those blue eyes, a rugged charm in that unshaven face; and she couldn't deny that she was attracted to the quiff of oily black hair that she thought made him look a little like Elvis. She stood on tiptoe, pulled his head towards hers and brushed her lips against his. Terry needed little encouragement to respond and soon they were enveloped in each other's arms, neither wanting to let go. Kim-Ly sobbed as she realised that this was the first time that she had actually kissed a man because she wanted to, then rested her head on his shoulder as Terry sat down upon an antique treasure chest that Sandra had thoughtfully placed there for this very purpose.

Perhaps I could be happy, thought Kim-Ly. Perhaps this man could be my saviour and take me away from here. She was just about to lift her head to speak when she saw a shadowy figure on the towpath, his eyes darting this way and that, looking into every boat that he passed. Then she recognised him; the dead man's brother. 'Terry, quick, we must hide, they are here; they are looking for us.' She pulled Terry down behind the side of the boat and they sat as silent as their heavy breathing would allow.

Terrified, they heard the footsteps coming closer and closer. Terry held her tight and prayed to a God that he didn't believe in. As the footsteps ceased, they could hear the rasp in the hunter's smoky breath as he stood above them and observed the boat and surrounding area. A clamorous cough rattled his ribcage and they saw the phlegm land on the deck but a few feet away. Kym-Ly shuddered and let out a sigh as their enemy cursed and moved on.

'Phew, that was close,' said Terry. 'It's not safe to be standing around talking; we must warn the others.'

A scratching sound nearby picked at the edges of Terry's already frayed nerves. 'What the hell's that?' he whispered.

Kim-Ly tensed and squeezed his arm. 'I do not know, but I am scared. Can we go inside now, please?'

'Agghh! What in the name of God. …' Terry jumped as he felt something wet on his arm, then jumped again as Tigger leapt on to his lap, eager to cultivate the friendship that had blossomed when Terry had fed him his leftover salmon sandwich at lunchtime.

'Bloody cat!' exclaimed Terry. 'You scared the life out of me.'

'Ah-choo. Ouch! – Oh, no – Ah-choo. Ouch! – not again – Ah-choo. Ouch! – get that thing – Ah-choo. Ouch! – away from me – Ah-choo. Ouch!' Kim-Ly pushed Terry and the cat away and stood to run inside, just as Celina opened the door and shouted, 'Kim-Ly, Terry, dinner is ready.'

From the shadows, the retreating man turned at the commotion and, in one movement, drew his gun and shouted, 'You! Where is my brother? I will teach you bitches to run away.' Reactions surprisingly quick for one of such bulk, he launched himself onto the boat above the still-seated Terry's head. Terry reacted in a flash and grabbed his trailing foot and the man crashed to the deck, his stocky frame landing with a dull thud as his head hit the corner of the chest. He lay motionless, undeniably unconscious, but Celina wasn't about to wait for him to wake up. Grabbing a nearby wrench, she rained blows upon his head until a pool of deep red blood formed around him.

Terry held back her arms. 'Jesus Christ, stop. What are you doing?'

'The same as you did. Let me go; let me finish it. That bastard deserves to die, just like his stinking brother.'

Pete poked his head through the door. 'Hey, what's with all the noise? You haven't killed anyone else, have you? Ah!'

A feeling of *déjà vu* prevailed as Pete felt in vain for a pulse, then fetched a tarpaulin, threw in the murder weapon and, for ballast, an anvil he'd been using for making brackets for hanging baskets, before Terry had commandeered his hammer. Once more, assisted by Terry and Celina, he secured the body and dropped it over the side: a splash and the deed was done – again.

'Do you have to leave your bloody tools lying all over the deck,' complained Sandra. 'I'm forever tripping over them and they make far too convenient murder weapons.'

'So, I suppose all this is my fault?' answered Pete in indignation. 'I won't have any bloody tools left if this lot carry on like this.'

'What can I say, mate?' said Terry. 'I know I keep apologising, but I *am* truly sorry.'

'Was he alone?' asked Sandra. 'We're not expecting any more visitors, are we? How did he find us?'

'I think he was just wandering,' said Kim-Ly, 'looking for his brother. He has probably been all over the city. I did not see anyone else.'

'I have some brown paint,' said the ever pragmatic Sandra. 'You can paint this part of the deck to hide the blood stains. This makes our little cycling trip tomorrow all the more urgent. Now, I don't know about you, but I'm starving; once you've finished your painting, then dinner is served.' She turned and retired to the galley, leaving Pete and Terry again in awe of her apparent cold-blooded composure.

The curry was eaten in stunned silence, appetites blunted and mood subdued. They all felt obliged to do justice to this culinary masterpiece, but their hearts weren't in it. Terry nudged a piece of chicken around his plate, Pete chewed absentmindedly, Kim-Ly ate in small, dainty mouthfuls and Celina stared into the distance and said nothing, her food untouched. Only Sandra ate heartily; she'd put a lot of effort into this and would be damned if she'd let the small matter of another dead body put her off her Chicken Makhani (or Chicken Mankini, as Pete insisted on calling it).

Conversation was stilted and, as the evening wore on, they sipped at their beer, wine, brandy, whichever was their tipple of choice. Sandra was growing increasingly concerned about one of their guests; understandably withdrawn, Celina retired to a chair in the corner and folded her arms across her stomach, her head down as the spasms hit, followed by cold sweats, anxiety and cramps. This time the hot, sweet tea wouldn't work and Celina was slipping into delirium.

Kim-Ly worriedly held Celina's hand. 'I know what is wrong,' she said; 'this is more than shock.' Carefully she rolled back Celina's sleeve to reveal the pin cushion that was her abused arm. 'This is how they control her,' she said, the bitter, angry tears welling up. 'She is dependent on them for this evil drug and now she needs her fix. They tried to do this to me too, but I refused. I told them that I would do what they wanted without the heroin. I have seen what it does, the lives it has destroyed and I said no, that I would kill myself before I would allow that stuff into my body. Celina used to fight them, you know, before they turned her into an addict; she was braver than me and would tell them where to go when they tried to make her do things she did not want to do. But now her bravery is gone and she is reduced to this habit that she cannot control.'

'Cold turkey,' said Terry. 'I have seen it before and it's not nice to watch.'

'So what do we do?' asked Sandra.

'Nothing,' answered Terry. 'In the case of heroin, cold turkey is extremely unpleasant but, providing she has no other medical condition, it is not dangerous. We must wait for it to take its course and then help her to stay away from it. Her first and only thought will be to go back to get more, but we must watch her like a hawk and keep her with us at all times. Kim-Ly, will you be her guardian?'

'Yes, it is my duty. I will stay with her tonight and tomorrow. I will be her conscience.'

Terry was a trifle disappointed. He was hoping that Kim-Ly might need a little comforting after the trauma of the last few days, but her obvious concern and loyalty to her friend served only to further stoke the fires of his affection, to raise still more his opinion of this enigmatic lady.

Sandra shook her head and looked at Pete. 'Look, I know you're not entirely convinced about our involvement in this adventure, but don't you see that we can't just turn our backs and pretend that this isn't occurring on our doorstep? We can't prevent it happening to someone else, but at least we have the opportunity to help two girls to escape, to save two people from slavery.'

Pete observed Celina's suffering. He knew that she was a loose cannon and a disaster waiting to befall their humble existence, but, against his better judgement, he'd grown to like her, to acknowledge the flickering candle of her spirit: burning dimly, but alight still.

'You're right, as usual,' he nodded.

'OK, the bikes are being delivered first thing tomorrow. I suggest we start packing so we can make an early start.'

8.

Gemma always insisted on the window seat; she liked to watch the ground become detached from the wheels, to gaze down as the airport, people, houses, roads, cars, grew small and distant, like a random Google satellite map. It evoked a feeling of liberty, of leaving behind all the day-to-day nonsense and drudgery; a feeling of transient freedom, of going on holiday.

Terry had been by her side the last time she'd flown, his hand on hers as they'd taken off, anticipating a sun-soaked, chilled-out fortnight in Italy. Neither of them were ones for lying on beaches; they preferred harbours, boats, cafes, castles, history, culture, wandering among the locals, soaking up the atmosphere and sampling the cuisine. She closed her eyes in distant reminisces; she could still feel the sea breeze in her face as they strolled along the stunning Sorrento coast, still taste the cheese, wine, bread, salami, olives. She licked her lips as she recalled those succulent sardines, fresh from the fishing boat, simply grilled and straight onto their plates, no need for garnish or dressing.

'You OK, Sis?' asked Robbie, jolting her from her dreams and sending her plummeting back down to earth, thankfully only metaphorically.

Gemma sighed. 'No, not really. What the hell am I doing, Robbie? What am I expecting to find when I get there? Terry's not going to be very pleased to see me, is he? I'm the one who broke his heart, the one who destroyed all those memories, who shattered the unspoken trust between us. Now he's found someone else; I should just wish him luck and we can both get on with the rest of our lives.'

'Well, I assume we're going all this way because you still love him and you want him back,' replied Robbie. 'You'll stand at the junction of lust and love, next to this new lady that he's picked up on a street corner and say, "sorry, I cocked up, can we go home now, please?"; and he'll take one look at you and see that the only place he belongs is by your side. He'll say to himself, "That's Gemma, the only girl I ever loved; that's Robbie's big sister that is, and there ain't no-one on this Earth better than that." He'll turn to this floozy and say, "Look love, it's been a bit of a laugh, but there must have been a misunderstanding. This is the lady for me; always has been, always will be".'

Gemma forced a smile. 'That's almost profound. What movie did you get that from?'

'Just telling it like it is,' said Robbie. 'No fella in his right mind would turn you away.'

Gemma considered Robbie's words. It hadn't always been thus between them and, during her early teenage years, when the hormones and acne had seriously taken hold, they used to fight like cat and dog. Back then everyone was her enemy, the whole world was against her and Robbie instinctively knew just which buttons to press to wind her up. It had taken university to put things in perspective, for her to mellow in her own space and to realise that her family weren't so bad after all. Robbie, too, had grown up while she was away, no longer the baby of the house and, although he would never admit it, he'd missed his infuriating sibling. Now things were fine, they looked out for each other; a mutual respect and unconditional support had grown, there forever, wherever they may roam.

Gemma didn't feel like the girl he thought she was, though, like the heroine in Robbie's fairy-tale ending; but nevertheless, his

71

confidence in her and his misguided adulation did rekindle her resolve: she determined to at least locate Terry and present him with a decision to make.

The stewardess stopped beside them. 'Any drinks, Sir, Madam?'

'A gin and tonic, please,' smiled Gemma, 'and whatever my little brother wants.'

'So, where are we going?' asked Pete.

'Well, the first stop is Gouda,' replied Sandra, 'about 52km away. I've rented us a self-catering place on the outskirts. Should be fairly quiet and out of the way; we can lie low until we decide on our next steps.'

'52km!!' exclaimed Pete, 'that's over thirty miles, isn't it? I'm not as fit as I used to be, you know.'

'None of us are, dear' replied Sandra, 'but we must put some distance between ourselves and Amsterdam; and you can't deny that we could both do with some exercise. Terry's right to want to get the girls out of the country and back to England; maybe Kim-Ly can claim asylum and Celina is an EU citizen. We will find a way and once they're gone we can come back home and live on our boat with the two dead bodies beneath it. That's if you haven't got the taste for adventure and want to help more girls to escape.'

'No, thank you,' said Pete, shuddering at the thought. 'I'm all for a change of scenery, but I'll be happy to return to our boring old existence when this is all over, if you don't mind; you're the one who seems to be relishing all this.'

Sandra hugged him. 'I wouldn't say that relishing is the right word exactly; I just can't see any alternative. All I'm doing is applying practical, logical solutions. This set of circumstances has been thrust upon us and we have to deal with it. I'm simply trying to think of the best way out, that's all.'

Nerves frayed and eager to leave, Pete watched in disbelief as Terry and Kim-Ly wobbled precariously, scattering a strolling family as they practised the art of not only riding a bike, but of steering a tandem. The whole thing would have been comical were he not so worried about them drawing unwanted attention to themselves; after all, they were hardly inconspicuous. Terry winced as his nether regions came into painful contact with the crossbar after using his feet for brakes, their progress halted just inches from the water's edge. They'd decided that Kim-Ly should initially concentrate on balance, while Terry did all the pedalling; but the weight of the loaded panniers and a lack of confidence and speed meant a hazardous ride.

Eventually, they decided that they had mastered sufficient forward motion for the journey to commence and the unlikely convoy set out on their bizarre escapade. Pete took a look at his fellow cyclists and had to admit that they almost looked the part: with full cycling regalia, rucksacks and a shared sense of purpose. 'Just let me know how much this all costs,' Terry had said, 'you will be fully reimbursed, I promise.' Thank God for that, thought Pete; all this equipment and accommodation must have cost a fortune.

Sandra led the way, in charge and in possession of the itinerary and map, closely followed by Terry and Kim-Ly, growing in poise with each revolution of their wheels. Then came Celina, quiet, withdrawn, but with spasmodic shivers and pain after the come-down; and finally Pete, bringing up the rear, mesmerised as he involuntarily contemplated the hypnotic sway of Celina's voluptuous, shapely buttocks that threatened to swallow the saddle whole, shrouded in luminous yellow Lycra.

They cycled in nervous silence, along canals and back-streets, glancing surreptitiously at everyone they passed. Their bags were weighed down with bottles of water, as if on a training exercise for some kind of triathlon.

'Why do we need all this water?' Terry had asked. 'We'll be stopping for a piss every five minutes if we drink all this.'

'It's not for us,' replied Sandra, 'it's for Celina. I've been reading on the internet about the effects of going cold turkey. She'll lose her appetite, she'll suffer depression, anxiety and panic-attacks, she won't be able to sleep and she'll be in a lot of pain. The website recommended plenty of water for detox and hydration, painkillers and flu-relief remedies to lessen the effects, and support from friends and family. As we're the only friends she has, that bit is down to us; we'll have to take it in turns to watch her, day and night, to ensure that she doesn't slip away back to her old life and habit.'

Terry had nodded in agreement. 'Then load my bag up with as much water as possible. I take it you've done a rota for the watch.'

'Of course.'

Pete looked thankfully over his shoulder and breathed a sigh of relief as they finally left the city and emerged into the countryside; taking a lungful of air, he realised that they may just have got away with it. He could tell that Terry too was feeling more relaxed, as his dulcet tones caught the breeze – "*When it's spring again, I'll bring again, tulips from Amsterdam. ...*" Sandra and Kim-Ly couldn't help but laugh when Pete joined in for stereo effect – "*With a heart that's true, I'll bring to you, tulips from Amsterdam.*" Celina, though, didn't seem to be amused and simply continued pedalling, head down and moribund. Maybe she'd never heard of Max Bygraves.

Savouring a different world with sunshine-lit country lanes, the light wind behind them aiding their progress, the only sounds were the leaves rustling in the trees, the birds singing, the occasional passing car, with drivers considerate to cyclists, a refreshing change and welcome respite from their previous lives. The few people they passed smiled and nodded, unaware and disinterested in this strange cycle-chain-gang as they rode on, through beautiful verdant countryside and sleepy villages.

The lunch of stamppot with rookworst and beer in a welcoming roadside bar would have been idyllic, were it not for their concern for Celina, her eyes staring blankly into the distance, the confused expression and frequent shudders. Kim-Ly sat beside her and spoke softly, reassuringly: 'It will be OK, you can beat this; we will not let anyone hurt you any more.'

Celina's obvious distress attracted unwanted attention from the concerned landlord (sporting an impressive mullet and moustache combo), who feared a potential medical emergency on his busy premises and an exodus of customers. 'Is she OK? Would you like me to call a doctor?'

'Thank you, but she's just feeling a little under the weather,' replied Sandra, 'we can take care of her and we have the right medicine from a doctor in Amsterdam.' The landlord walked away, looking unconvinced.

'Time to move on, I think,' said Sandra. 'We've a long way to go and we don't want to arouse suspicion.'

Pete and Terry stared wistfully at their half-finished beers. 'I was enjoying that,' complained Pete. 'Do we have to go yet?'

'Yes, let's go,' decided Terry. 'We can chill-out when we get there. We're still too close to the scene of the crime for my liking.'

'I cannot do this any more,' said Celina. 'Please, let me go back. I vill only be trouble and you vill be quicker vithout me.'

'No chance!' exclaimed Pete. 'Do you think I risked my life getting you out of there for nothing? You're one of us now, whether you like it or not. We will go as fast as you can and stop for breaks whenever you need one.'

'Pete is right,' said Kim-Ly. 'We are a team, partners in crime I think you call it.'

'Ve have done nothing wrong,' said Celina. 'They deserved to die. Vhy should we run?'

'Because the police may not see it that way and because the mob won't stand for two of their brothers disappearing off the face of the Earth,' replied Sandra. 'Come on, let's get going.'

They rode off again in convoy, in the same order, though not singing this time; somehow the novelty of their little adventure had already worn off. Behind them, the landlord watched and twisted his moustache between thumb and forefinger, as they disappeared around the bend.

'So what happens now?' asked Robbie. 'There's obviously no-one in. Are you sure this is the right boat?'

'Definitely, yes. I've seen pictures and it's called the *Christina*.' Gemma took her Blackberry from her bag. 'I didn't want to call Sandra, but there's no alternative. All the shutters are down and everything is locked up; looks as if they've gone away. Perhaps they're on holiday.' The phone rang and rang. 'No answer.'

Gemma jumped at a voice from behind. 'Ze lieten vanochtend op de fiets.'

They both turned to see a man in his sixties with greying hair and slight stubble, casually dressed in blue jeans and check shirt. 'I'm sorry, we don't speak Dutch,' said Gemma.

'I can speak Double-Dutch,' said Robbie. 'Fluent in it, in fact.'

The man held out his hand and shook first Gemma's, then Robbie's. 'My name is Johan and I am the neighbour of Pete and Sandra; they left this morning, on bicycles. They have always been good neighbours and very quiet, but some strange things have been happening for the last few days. They have had visitors who come and go at different times and there are screams and noises at night and things thrown into the water. Pete has always been good to me, helping to fix things on my boat, so I ask no questions.'

'My name is Gemma and we are friends of Pete and Sandra. We were in Amsterdam, so we thought we would drop in and surprise them. Do you know where they were going?'

'No, but they were carrying much on their backs, as if they were going for vacation.'

'And who was with them?' asked Gemma.

'One man, very tall, and two girls, I have never seen them before; very good looking girls, both of them. They did not look like cyclists; saw them this morning, the tall man and one of the girls were on a cycle made for two. What do you call it?'

'A tandem.'

'Yes. They did not look like they have been on one before.'

'That sounds like Terry,' said Gemma; 'he's not been on a bike since he was a teenager.'

'You could go to the cycle hire company,' suggested Johan, '*Cycle Netherlands*; their signs were on the bicycles and they might tell you where they were going.'

'And do you know where we can find *Cycle Netherlands*?'

'In the city you can ask. They are well known.'

Locating *Cycle Netherlands* wasn't hard, but extracting information from the proprietor was. 'I'm sorry, Madam, but we cannot tell you about our clients; we have a policy of privacy and the information that our customers give us is secret.'

'But I have a very important message for one of the party,' implored Gemma. 'It is essential that I contact him.'

'Then the only thing I can suggest is that you give the message to me and I will try to get it to them.'

'No, it is too private,' said Gemma. 'I will try to phone again.'

'Can we hire two bikes, please?' asked Robbie. 'May as well do a bit of sightseeing while we're here.'

Gemma stared at him. 'What? We're not here for sightseeing. Where the hell do you want to go?'

'Trust me, it's a good idea,' said Robbie. 'I'll explain later.' He turned to the man behind the counter. 'Now, my good man, do you have two bikes available?'

'Yes, we do, sir. How long would you like them for?'

'We'll start with a week. Can we extend that if we need to?'

'There is a number on the hire agreement; just call that and we can add further days to your credit card.'

As they wheeled the bikes outside, Gemma glared at Robbie. 'What's going on? Why do we need these bloody things for a week? They're not cheap and we're not here for a holiday, you know.'

'Look, while you were talking to that guy I managed to pick

up some useful information. So much for their privacy policy; the book was wide open on the counter. I assume your friend is named Sandra Moore, party of five, two lady's bikes, one man's and one tandem, and they're heading for a place called Gouda. What do you say to a little bit of exercise? Some country air, a few windmills and the prospect of a happy reunion at the end.'

Gemma smiled. 'Hey, well done. So, how far is Gouda?'

'No idea. Let's check it out on this map they've given us. What scale is it?'

Gemma pored over the map and exclaimed. 'Jesus, that's over 50km, about thirty-odd miles. Hope you're feeling fit.'

'Well, we're not going to be able to cover that today,' said Robbie, looking at his watch, 'but we could make a start and stop somewhere along the way. Good job we're travelling light.'

'You're enjoying every minute of this, aren't you? The mystery, the chase, the adventure.'

'Well, it sure makes a change from bumming around back home. Nothing ever changes; the same old faces in the same old haunts, and there are no work prospects. I'm applying for jobs every day and getting nowhere; then there's the trip to the job-centre every two weeks to sign on and have your soul sucked out. I don't want to still be living at home with Mum and Dad, it's embarrassing at my age; but what choice do I have?'

'I'm sorry. I've been so obsessed with my own problems that I never thought about yours. When this is all over and we get home, we'll sit down and plan out your future. Work out what you really want to do with your life and decide on a strategy to make it happen.'

'You make it sound so easy. The Old Man's OK, you know, helped me out with money on numerous occasions. I guess he remembers the time when I was flush, working on the building-sites during the boom and bringing in good money. The fridge packed up and he commented that it was overworked because it was always full of my lager; I had a new fridge delivered the next day. Paid for them to go on holiday once too; admittedly it was when I was seeing Susan Whitchurch and wanted the place to myself, but that's beside the point. I had money and was happy to share it. I want to work, to make my contribution, but just because I've got no skills to speak of, everyone thinks they can pay peanuts and treat you like shit. The minimum wage is an insult, whether you're cleaning toilets or stacking shelves; and it makes me sick, the sodding politicians saying, "we're all in this together". The Big Society, my arse! It's just a way of getting people to work for nothing. And you know who really winds me up?'

'Who's that?' asked Gemma.

'The bloody weatherman.'

'The weatherman.'

'Yes,' Robbie continued his rant. 'Haven't you heard them every night? "And take care on your commute to work in the morning, the roads could be treacherous" or "Looks like it's going to be a sunny start to the working-week"; do they not know that half the bloody country's unemployed. Maybe I'll just take off and see the world, work my way from one place to another. There's got to be more to life and this little escapade is already giving me the taste for travel.'

'Let's see if you still feel the same after cycling for thirty miles,' said Gemma, putting a comforting arm around his shoulder. 'Come on, let's hit the road.'

9.

Tranquil, that was the word; a secluded old farmhouse about five miles out of town at the end of a deserted lane; a little run-down, but full of character and definitely discreet. Sandra returned with the keys from the farmer.

'This is perfect,' said Terry. 'How did you find this place?'

'There wasn't much choice, to be honest,' replied Sandra. 'It was the only decent accommodation available at short notice. I just took what I could get.'

'Well, no-one will find us here,' said Pete. 'And we have it for a week. Is that right?'

'Yes, should give us time to work things out and for Terry to make the necessary arrangements to get the girls out of the country.'

Sandra turned the key in the lock and they all followed her inside. The furniture and design were more modern than the exterior had suggested and comfortable sofas and chairs in pale green and cream surrounded a polished pine coffee table. The living room was light and airy, with a door leading onto a well-equipped kitchen.

Kim-Ly and Celina had been exploring and returned with questions. 'There are only two bedrooms; where will we all sleep?' asked Kim-Ly.

Sandra smiled. 'Pete and I will have the double room and

you and Celina can go in the twin room. As Terry is the one responsible for all this, he can have the sofa-bed.'

'Thanks,' said Terry. 'I don't mind; could sleep anywhere at the moment, I'm absolutely knackered.'

Pete felt his aching thighs. 'I think we all are, mate. Let's see if we can cobble together something to eat while the ladies get settled.'

The welcome hamper in the spotless kitchen was a sight for sore eyes, well stocked with ham, cheese, bread, tomatoes and salad, along with five bottles of beer. 'Great,' said Terry, searching for the bottle opener, 'Sandra sure knows how to organise a holiday. Look, there's a table and chairs in the garden; we can watch the sun go down from there.'

A group of 2-Tone cows from the neighbouring field watched curiously as Pete and Terry made themselves comfortable. 'Looks like it's going to rain,' observed Pete; 'some of the cows are lying down.'

'But not all of them,' replied Terry. 'How do we know which are the Michael Fish and Wincey Willis of the bovine world? The ones that are standing obviously think it's going to be fine.'

'Scattered showers, maybe?' suggested Pete. He placed the hamper on the table, sat down and clinked bottles with Terry.

'Cheers,' said Terry, 'and thanks again. Bet you wish you'd never set eyes on me at Glastonbury.'

'Prost!' smiled Pete. 'Hey, we didn't have any plans for the next few weeks and it's good to get away, to be honest. I sometimes miss the mobility from when I was my own boss on my own boat; a different place every day if I wanted, or I'd stay for a while if I found somewhere I liked.'

'But you're happy here, aren't you, with Sandra? She's a great girl and you won't find anyone better.'

'Yeah, I'm well aware of how lucky I am and I love Sandra and living in Amsterdam; at least I did until you exposed us to its less-appealing side. So what happened, between you and Gemma?'

'Guess she got bored with me; we used to just go walking and talking, you know. We were genuinely happy with the simple life; and then my job started to take me away too much. It's ironic really; there's you, wishing you could be on the move again, and here's me, regretting that I was never home. Can a man ever be totally contented?'

'Perhaps not,' said Pete; 'we're forever wondering what might have been if we'd made this decision or that. Talking of which, there's the lovely Kim-Ly. You've some decisions to make there if I'm not mistaken about the way she looks at you.'

'Do you really think so? Do you think she likes me?'

'Well, given her ex-profession I shouldn't think that she has a very high opinion of the male gender, but you've certainly made her think twice, put doubt in her mind. Of course she likes you; you'd have to be blind not to see it. Doesn't it bother you, though, to know that she's been with so many men?'

'I can't see it; all I can see are those eyes and that smile, the fighting spirit. Even after all she's been through, there's still a kind of innocence about her, Pete. Do you not see it too?'

'Yeah, I guess so. You've got it bad, haven't you?'

Terry sighed. 'I think I have, yeah; but it'll probably end in tears.'

Kim-Ly smiled, sat down next to Terry and took his beer. 'This is a nice place,' she said, brushing back her hair and taking a swig. 'I think we will enjoy our time here. What have you two been talking about?'

Terry blushed. 'Oh, just about the strangeness of life and love. How's Celina?'

'She is not well. She has lost all the food she had at lunchtime. Sandra is with her and they will come out soon.'

'We won't eat until they are both ready,' said Terry.

Pete made an excuse about checking out the sleeping arrangements and wandered back inside, leaving Kim-Ly and Terry alone. Gently, he led her to the bottom of the garden, where they silently viewed the tall trees separating fields populated by more 2-Tone cows, silhouetted against an orange sky. A small concrete bunker nestled in the corner of the meadow, a sombre reminder of the German occupation and devastation of World War Two.

'So, what do you want to do with your freedom?' asked Terry. 'If you could have your wishes come true, what would they be?'

Kim-Ly thought for a long time, still staring into the distance. 'And are you the genie that is going to grant my three wishes?'

'I will if I can,' replied Terry, only just stopping himself from an inappropriate *Carry On* comment about rubbing his lamp first. 'What is your first wish, oh mistress?'

'I want to go back to London, finish my studies with Professor Higgins and take my exam. Then I would like to return to Vietnam to see my family and become what I wanted to be when I was a child – a teacher. I know that I can do it, as I have taught Celina to speak English and now she is almost as good as me. I would rather not go back without my qualification; I must accomplish something to make them proud and to explain why I have been away so long.'

'All achievable,' said Terry, 'except that we will have to find the professor first and his name is not likely to be Higgins.'

'How do you know that is not his name?'

'It's from an old play, *Pygmalion*, by George Bernard Shaw, later made into a musical called *My Fair Lady*. The story tells of a common Cockney flower girl, Eliza Doolittle. A Professor Higgins makes a bet that he can pass her off as a duchess at some upper-class garden party and he sets about teaching her to speak posh and act like a lady. I suspect that you may have been the unwitting subject of a similar wager by *your* professor, except that he was unable to complete the experiment due to his exposure in the newspapers.'

'But he was always kind to me,' protested Kim-Ly. 'I cannot believe that he would do all he did just to win a bet.'

'Never met the guy, so I can't question his motives,' replied

Terry. 'All I'm saying is that the story is remarkably similar; and the name Higgins all but confirms my theory.'

'But what does it matter if he wins his bet, if I too can benefit by learning and passing my exam?'

'A good point; in the play Eliza is emancipated by her newfound confidence, but she still returns to her roots. Professor "Higgins" has done a very good job; your English is already better than most native speakers.'

'And what about you?' asked Kim-Ly. 'Will you be in trouble for not writing the article you were sent here for?'

'Perhaps. I have a good relationship with my boss and a reputation in the business, so I think I can be away for a while. They won't put up with it for too long, though; missing a deadline is the final curtain in journalism. If the worst comes to the worst, I'll go freelance.'

'Then you must write my story,' insisted Kim-Ly. 'We will write it together and I will also translate it to Vietnamese; if it stops one girl from following my footsteps, then it will be worthwhile.'

'It's a good story,' admitted Terry, 'the papers would pay good money for it, but I will not exploit your misfortune for financial gain.'

'Wow, a journalist with a conscience; that is a rare thing these days.'

'We are not all bad,' said Terry. 'I entered this profession to expose injustice and corruption, and that is my mission to this day. I can't be bought.'

'Then you can tell of the injustice and corruption in my life and change it for the better.'

Terry considered the logic behind her words, the good intentions. 'It will have to be written sensitively, to avoid glamorising the profession and the people who control it.'

'Sensitively, yes; then you are the man who can write it.'

'OK, we'll do it,' concluded Terry, 'but first we must get back to London.'

Kim-Ly gazed into his eyes. 'Thank you, Terry. Thank you for rescuing me and for not thinking of me as just another sex-object.'

But you are one of the sexiest women I have ever seen, thought Terry, as they kissed long and tenderly.

Sandra waved to get their attention. Celina had recovered somewhat and they were both sat at the garden table with Pete, waiting to eat. Terry reluctantly released Kim-Ly from his arms and they made their way back up the garden, hand in hand.

'Sorry to shatter the moment,' said Sandra, 'but I'm starving.'

'Yeah, me too,' conceded Terry. He looked at Celina. 'How are you?'

'I am OK for now,' she answered. 'Sandra has been good and, vith everyone's help, I vill beat this.'

'We will make sure that you beat it,' said Terry; 'we will not think about the alternative.'

'Terry, come and help me to get some things from the kitchen,' said Sandra. 'I can't carry everything and Pete looks like he's there for the night.'

As they entered the kitchen, Sandra removed her phone from her pocket. 'I have a missed call; it's Gemma. I will have to call back. What do you want me to tell her?'

Terry held out his own phone. 'I have a few of those too. I don't know what to tell her; that's why I've not returned her calls. Besides, she was the one who ended it; I don't see why I should have to tell her anything.'

'You were together a long time,' said Sandra; 'surely you owe her some kind of explanation.'

'An explanation for what, exactly? For moving on, for trying to rebuild the derelict, condemned building of my life, for daring to consider an existence without her?'

'Yeah, but there are ways of moving on; couldn't you have tried internet dating? I hear it's all the rage back home.'

'I didn't plan all this, you know; and it's nothing to do with Gemma.'

'And you no longer have any feelings for her?'

'Of course I have feelings for her. Where do you want me to start? Anger, dismay, sadness, loss, pity, love. ... Oh God, what am I supposed to do?'

'How the hell should I know? I'm no expert in relationships,' said Sandra.

'Can you call her back, find out what she wants?'

'Why not? I may as well add agony-aunt to my list of duties: harbouring criminals, accessory to murder, nursemaid to an addict, tour organiser and general dogsbody. OK, I'll speak to her, but not tonight; I've had enough for one day. I'm tired and hungry, and I have a sore arse from spending all day on that bloody bike.'

'It was your idea,' pointed out Terry.

'And it's worked so far, hasn't it? I didn't see anyone on our tails, did you? Come on, you ungrateful bastard, carry that tray.'

Stamppot with rookworst were all they could offer; the speciality of the house. Gemma and Robbie had cycled as far as they could before the stunning sunset warned of imminent nightfall. The welcoming roadside bar, though, wasn't as welcoming as it first appeared. 'We are no longer serving food,' said the landlord, as he met them at the door, 'but I can let you have what is left over and we have one small twin room vacant. There is no other accommodation for ten kilometres.'

'Thank you,' said Gemma, 'that will be fine. I guess we have no choice; we need to eat and sleep.'

For once, Robbie was silent and simply nodded his agreement as he removed his cycle-clips, purchased at the hire shop because he didn't want to risk getting oil on his Chinos. He wiped the sweat from his brow and looked forward to whatever was left over, not caring what it was as long as it staved off his hunger. As they tucked in appreciatively, he had to admit that the stamppot and rookworst wasn't bad: mashed potatoes, mixed with unidentified mashed vegetables, accompanied by a very tasty smoked sausage; and the extra burnt bits from the bottom of the pan were a bonus.

A group of athletic-looking fellow cyclists adorned the bar area, swigging lager from bottles and laughing uproariously at some in-joke. Robbie felt out of place and puny as he squeezed apologetically between them to order drinks for himself and Gemma; at least he'd removed his cycle-clips, but still they looked at him as if, somehow, he wasn't cool.

'I guess those are the guys who belong to them flash bikes outside,' observed Robbie, as he returned and handed Gemma her drink.

'Yeah, better let them leave first in the morning. Don't want them to see you with your cycle-clips on. They may think you're not cool.'

Robbie seemed offended. 'Hey, this isn't my natural habitat, you know. A chap always looks uncool if you take him out of his comfort-zone. Not really bothered about how I look, to be honest; doesn't matter to me what other people think.'

'Yeah, right,' smiled Gemma, 'you've always been a *poseur*, a bit of a peacock.'

'Well you've got to keep up appearances, even though you may feel like giving up sometimes. Look at the Modfather, Paul Weller; have you ever seen *him* looking anything less than immaculate?'

'No, I haven't, but then I haven't seen him wearing cycle-clips either.'

'Will you stop going on about those bloody cycle-clips. I'm not ruining a perfectly good pair of strides just for the sake of vanity. I'm prepared to look like a prat in a place where nobody knows me.'

They hadn't noticed the landlord hovering behind, waiting for them to finish. 'Was everything OK, sir, madam?' he asked, as he stepped in to clear away their empty plates.

'Very nice, thank you,' replied Robbie. 'Please give my compliments to the chef.'

'And are you in Holland on holiday?'

'Not exactly; we're on a mission to locate a friend of my sister's here,' said Robbie, gesturing at Gemma. 'We have reason to believe that he and his companions are heading for Gouda on bikes and left Amsterdam this morning.'

'How many companions did he have with him?' asked the landlord.

'We think four; one man and three women.'

'I think they were here at lunchtime; two Englishmen, one English lady, an oriental lady and another who did not say anything, but looked very ill. They insisted that she would be fine, but I think she should see a doctor. You could not miss her: very tall, with bright yellow cycle shorts.'

'That sounds like them,' said Gemma. 'Thank you, we will leave early in the morning.'

'Breakfast is served from seven o'clock,' said the landlord, looking at Robbie with a smile, 'and do not forget your cycle-clips.'

'How can he take the piss out of my cycle-clips with a mullet like that?' said Robbie, turning to a hysterical Gemma, as the landlord walked away, his shoulders shaking with mirth. 'That's it, I'm going to bed.'

'Yeah, me too,' laughed Gemma. 'Could be a long day tomorrow.'

Floating, searching, diving, up for air, searching again, the little girl no longer there; where could she be? Another dive, deeper this time, but still no sign. Splashing in panic, Natalia could not simply disappear; down once more, the pressure building, fighting for breath; how could she stop searching, how could she live with her best friend gone? Thrashing and revolving, sinking; the water, blood red now, two figures descending, on their way to the depths.

The evil grins, the staring, vacant eyes. Blood drips from every orifice: nose, mouth, ears and eye sockets. A head turns, caved in and smashed, brain exposed, blood, blood and more blood. She tries to scream, but no sound emerges, thrashing and drowning, the silent scream, the silent scream.

'Celina, Celina, what is wrong? Do not worry, I am here; wake up, wake up.'

Open eyes, seeing nothing; still the scream won't come, a hand in hers, a frightened call. 'Celina, Celina.'

She sat up straight in bed, shivering, shaking, sobbing, sweating. 'She's gone, she's gone. Oh, Natalia, please forgive me. I tried to save you but ...'

Celina awoke suddenly. 'Kim-Ly, vhat happened, vhere am I? Who vere those men in the vater?'

'It is OK, they are gone. You have had a bad dream. Here, drink some water. You are safe now. Who is Natalia?'

Celina took a sip, stared manically around the unfamiliar room and tears filled her eyes. 'She vas my best friend, back home in Poland; ve vere only eleven years old and ve vent to svim in the lake. Natalia could not svim very vell and she drowned. It vas my idea to go to the lake; I knew she vas not a strong svimmer, ve should never have been there.'

Kim-Ly looked at her friend, transported back in time by her dream – she was that eleven-year-old girl again, devastated, helpless and inconsolable. She did not know what to say, so just encouraged her to drink more water.

'More vater?' protested Celina. 'Vhy do you think that vater is the answer to everything? Sandra, she makes me drink vater all the time too. Do you not see that vater is the problem, not the solution?'

'It is to help make you better,' argued Kim-Ly. 'It will do more good than those other poisons you have put into your body.'

'Can it bring back Natalia? No; vater took her from us. Can it help me to forget her? No; only the drugs can do that for a little vhile. Can it change that I ran avay from home in shame at vhat I had done to her? Can it change vhat I have become, a cheap prostitute, selling my body to survive and to feed my filthy habit? Can it change the fact that I have battered a man to death and threw him into the vater? Can it make the nightmares go avay?'

'No, only you can do that. You made a mistake, but it was not your fault. You were only a child and you must not punish yourself for the rest of your life. There is a saying in my country – "*Cái khó bó cái khôn*". It means adversity brings wisdom. We must all learn from mistakes and move on to better things. We have a chance now, a chance to escape from that terrible life, to go where they cannot hurt us any more. We must repay Terry and Sandra and Pete by showing them that we are better than what we had become.'

'But I am not as strong as you.'

'You used to be stronger than me,' replied Kim-Ly; 'it was you who protected me when I first came to Amsterdam, showed me the way to survive, to keep as safe as possible. I will never forget your kindness and now it is my turn to look after you.'

Celina smiled weakly. 'Thank you, Kim-Ly. I vould probably be already dead vithout you. OK, ve are a team, but it vill not be easy.'

'Nothing worth fighting for is ever easy,' said Kim-Ly. 'Now, we must sleep. Sleep is the best cure for a bad day.'

10.

Terry yawned, scratched his balls through his boxer shorts and opened another cupboard – empty. He took another look in the fridge, hoping that a breakfast of eggs, bacon, sausage, mushrooms and tomatoes had miraculously appeared there overnight – empty. 'It's no good, we're gonna have to go grocery shopping,' he concluded.

'You're right,' Pete concurred, 'but there are five of us. It's a little way into town and how are we going to carry back enough for all of us on pushbikes?'

'Been thinking about that,' said the ever-pragmatic Sandra. 'You two can take the tandem and do the shopping; one of you returns with the tandem and the other brings back the groceries in a taxi.'

Terry looked at Pete. 'Why didn't we think of that?'

'Because you're men, perhaps? Here, I've written a list. Reckon it's about eight kilometres to town. If you leave now you'll be back by late morning.'

'And will you three ladies be OK here by yourselves?' asked Terry.

'I'm sure we'll survive,' answered Sandra, 'and it will give me a chance to make that phone call.'

Terry glanced nervously at Kim-Ly to check if she was listening, but no, she was staring serenely through the open window, taking in the landscape and the fresh country air: a vision of beauty in a simple, yellow cotton dress that hugged her body like he wanted to. He turned back to Sandra and sighed. 'Thanks. When this is all over I'll get us all weekend tickets for Glastonbury and I'll pay for your flights and expenses.'

Sandra smiled. 'Hmm, tempting offer, but you can meet some dodgy characters there, you know.'

'Too right,' agreed Pete. 'Let's go then, and I'm sitting at the front; all I saw yesterday were four backsides. No offence, but it quite spoiled the vista.'

Terry looked over his shoulder and waved as he and Pete weaved their way down the lane, avoiding most of the potholes. He felt temporarily relieved to be away from Kim-Ly, away from temptation, away from decisions other than what kind of cheese to buy. He didn't even have to decide which way to steer, as Pete was taking care of direction; all he had to do was relax and pedal and, for now, that was enough. He could get used to this, the breeze in his hair, the near-solitude, the open road, troubles behind him; but he knew that he had a responsibility to finish what he'd carelessly started, to Kim-Ly and Celina, to Pete and Sandra, who'd so selflessly come to their rescue.

'You OK, mate?' asked Pete, without looking round. 'Sandra told me about Gemma's calls. What are you going to do?'

'Join a bloody monastery!' replied Terry. 'It's the only answer, isn't it?'

'You don't even know what she wants yet. Could be to tell you that she's found that old Morrissey album and would you be so kind as to collect it as it brings back too many memories.'

Terry laughed. 'Yeah, she never quite understood my infatuation with Mozzer; thought he was a miserable git, couldn't see the sardonic humour. You know, I'd just started to feel free; for the first time really, as I couldn't recall an existence without Gemma. Why does life have to be so complicated?'

'I suggest that you find out what it's all about first, before you start jumping to conclusions. Let Sandra talk to her.'

'But what if she wants me back?'

'No good asking me, pal. Having to choose between two beautiful women is way beyond my realm of experience. You just do what feels right, I guess.'

'That's easier said than done; whatever happens, someone gets hurt.'

'Just make sure it's not you this time.'

Well-stocked and spacious, the supermarket had everything on their list and much more besides. Pete was excited to discover some rookworst nestling among a succulent and varied array of sausages. 'Hey, reckon we could rustle up some stamppot to go with this?'

'Don't see why not; seemed pretty simple to me.'

Pete added some particularly tempting Belgian chocolates to the pile, along with a newspaper; and, mercifully, the shopping was complete. 'Sure we've forgotten something,' he said, studying the list, 'but I've had enough. Who's taking the taxi?'

'You can if you want. I'm enjoying the cycling and it will give me time to think, and to delay whatever's waiting.'

The lady at the checkout eyed them curiously as Terry paid by credit card. Given the fact that this was another fine mess he'd gotten them into, he felt obliged to pay for everything associated with their little trip. With taxi ordered, they sauntered out into the car-park, pleased with their hour's shopping.

'Hey, where's the bike?' exclaimed Terry. 'Sure we parked it over there.'

'Yeah, that's the place, I remember that sign. Didn't you lock it up?'

'No, I thought you had. Let's talk to that security chap.'

'Are you mad?' said Pete. 'Next thing you know he'll call the cops and they'll start asking awkward questions.'

'Good point,' conceded Terry. 'Great, that's all we need; now we're stuck in the farmhouse without transport. Still, at least we're insured, I suppose; good job they wouldn't let us take the bikes without cover.'

'Well, there's nothing we can do about it now,' said Pete. 'Come on, here's our cab. I can just imagine Sandra's reaction when we turn up without it.'

Little was said as the taxi wound its way out of town, Terry deep in contemplation and Pete engrossed in the paper. The taxi driver tried in vain to make conversation, but could get nothing from these reticent Englishmen.

'Can you actually read that thing, or are you just looking at the pictures?' Terry asked Pete.

'I get by. Thought that, as I'm living here now, I should make an effort to learn the language. Sandra is better than me, though, as she is at most things. Some interesting stuff in here, good news that I'll tell you when we get back.' He nodded towards the driver to indicate that said news was for Terry's ears only.

They stood among the bags of groceries as they watched the taxi disappear round the corner. 'So, what's in the paper that's so secret that it can't be spoken in public?' asked Terry.

'Best go inside first,' said Pete; 'the girls will want to hear it too.'

Sandra glanced up from her book as they entered, laden with shopping and looking sheepish. 'OK, what's happened?' It seemed her instincts had immediately picked up that something was wrong.

'Do you want the good news or the bad news?' asked Pete.

'Bad news first and then you can try to cheer me up with the good news.'

'Where are Kim-Ly and Celina?' asked Terry.

'In the garden, getting bored and irritable; not a lot to do round here. Come on, spill the beans.'

'Well,' said a cringing Terry, 'we've kind of lost the tandem.'

'Lost it! What do you mean, lost it?'

'It was stolen, while we were in the supermarket. Think we collectively forgot to lock it up.'

'Jesus, is everything you two touch a disaster? You're like a modern-day Laurel and Hardy, except they were funny.'

'Hey, no need for that,' said Pete. 'We brought home some rookworst, *and* the ingredients to make stamppot.'

Sandra shook her head in exasperation. 'And is that the good news?'

Pete handed her the newspaper. 'No, that's the good news,' he said, pointing at a headline on page two.

Sandra read intently and smiled. 'Hey, that *is* good news. We could be in the clear.'

Terry was growing ever more frustrated. 'Is anyone going to share it with me?' he asked.

Sandra translated the article aloud. '"*Gang Warfare Hits Amsterdam*" is the headline. "*Rival drugs and prostitution gangs are at war in Amsterdam after the disappearance of two pimps and two girls has sparked bad feeling and accusations between combatant Turkish families. Police are attempting to keep the peace and to ascertain the facts but, despite denials, there is suspicion that the two men in question have either been kidnapped or murdered and that the girls are working elsewhere.*" It goes on to talk about the history of the rivalry between these two factions and that there is little love lost between them. "*The police have made no comment, except to say that their investigation continues*".'

'I wouldn't start celebrating just yet,' said Terry; 'if investigations are continuing, there's no telling what they'll unearth.'

'Yes, but if they think it's down to gang rivalry, it will at least buy us some time,' reasoned Pete.

'I guess so,' answered Terry, unconvinced and distracted. He turned to Sandra. 'Did you talk to Gemma?'

'I did. Do you want the good news or the bad news?'

'There's good news?'

'Depends which way you look at it.'

'Just tell me what she said.'

'Well, she says she's sorry. She made a big mistake and that, although she doesn't deserve another chance, she wants you back.'

'I was afraid of that,' said Terry.

'She's here,' said Sandra.

'What? Where?' exclaimed Terry. 'In the house?'

'No, no, here in Holland with her brother; she's serious, Terry. They're in Gouda and I've arranged for you to meet her tomorrow at noon, at a bar/restaurant called De Zalm.'

'Well, thanks for that.' Terry flopped down in the armchair and put his head in his hands. 'So she's here with her crazy brother. Oh God, what am I supposed to tell her about Kim-Ly, about everything that's happened?'

'She already knows about Kim-Ly, been speaking to that photographer friend of yours; and she's still come all the way here to find you. Says a lot about how serious she is, I think.'

Kim-Ly entered, smiling and stunning. 'Ah, my hero returns,' she said, as she sat on Terry's lap, draped her arms around his neck and kissed his forehead.

Pete looked on in sympathy, raised his eyebrows and shrugged as he caught Terry's desperate plea-for-help expression. 'Better get this shopping put away then,' he said, in a clumsy attempt to change the subject. 'Anyone for stamppot and rookworst for lunch?'

Sandra was right; there wasn't a lot to do round here. Quiet and out of the way was the only criteria she'd stipulated when arranging their accommodation; and that, it certainly was. She'd found an old pack of cards in a drawer and she, Kim-Ly and Celina were simultaneously wondering how long they could amuse themselves playing Rummy. Perhaps Patience would be more appropriate, she thought, as Celina won yet another hand. The sound of inebriated laughter emanated from the kitchen and Terry and Pete sounded as if they'd already consumed the six bottles of wine they'd brought back from the supermarket. 'I'll face the music tomorrow,' Terry had said; 'for tonight, I will attempt to forget. Would you do me the honour of assisting me, Pete?'

Pete liked a glass of vino as well as the next man and had taken little persuading. Kim-Ly looked concerned as she listened to their drunken guffaws and Sandra tried to reassure her. 'Let them have a good time; it's their way of letting off steam, of dealing with things. They will both suffer for it in the morning.'

'But we have seen what drink does to men,' said Kim-Ly. 'Celina and I, we see it every night in our job.'

'Not Pete and Terry,' said Sandra. 'I have seen them both drunk before and they just get even more stupid than they are already. They're harmless, honest; but if it makes you feel better I will go and have a word, ask them to take it easy. And don't keep referring to your job; it's not your job any more. It's finished and you don't have to go back.'

Sandra stood and made her way to the kitchen door, where she watched, unnoticed for a few minutes the men at the table, two bottles empty, and a third half-full. Both had a pen in hand and were scrawling on scraps of paper whilst giggling hysterically.

'If you could have any actor, past or present, to play the lead role, who would it be?' asked Pete.

'Orson Welles, definitely,' replied Terry.

'Orson Welles; wasn't he in *Steptoe and Son*?'

'Nah, that was 'orse'n'cart.'

They both collapsed in heaps of hilarity, Terry banging the table, with tears in his eyes. Then Pete looked up to see the unimpressed figure of Sandra, framed in the doorway. 'Hello, love,' he grinned, 'would you like to be in our sitcom?'

'Is that what all the noise is about? You're writing a sitcom.'

'Yes,' slurred Terry, recovering from his fits of laughter. 'Thought it was about time somebody wrote another classic, like *Porridge*, *The Likely Lads*, *Blackadder*; you can't beat those halcyon days.'

'And you think you two could be the modern-day Dick Clement and Ian La Frenais, do you?' said a sceptical Sandra. 'Come on then, make me laugh, let's hear some of it.'

'Well, it's still in its infancy at the moment,' admitted Terry; 'we don't really have a plot or a theme yet, just a few set pieces.'

Pete continued with the story so far. 'There's this Scotsman who has a week off because he has a wee cough. Under doctor's orders he heads down to the New Forest to recuperate in the fresh air. He was last seen stroking one of the ponies and saying, "I'm feeling a little hoarse".' Once again, they both got the giggles, pleased with their evening's work.

'You forgot to mention that he also had flat feet,' added Terry, between chuckles, 'and that the doctor prescribed a foot-pump.'

Sandra shook her head in dismay. 'Hmm, I've a feeling that when you read all this back in the morning, it won't seem quite as funny; sounds like a Hampshire-based *Last of the Summer Wine* to me. Why don't you just admit that you're writing this sitcom on the thinly veiled premise that the creator of this book has a few bad jokes that he can't weave into the narrative.'

'True, but it could be a hit,' said Terry.

'I very much doubt it; it's no worse than some of the competition, but I think it may need a little more substance and a more contemporary stance,' argued Sandra. 'What demographic are you aiming at, exactly? It's like that joke of dubious taste about Acker Bilk that you told us last night; you need to be of a certain age to get it. *I* know that Acker Bilk is a jazz clarinettist of some repute and that his trademark is his bowler hat, but the yoof are unlikely to have heard of him, are they? And secondly, bowler hats belong to the days of Captain Mainwaring. It's well past its sell-by date and, if a joke has to be explained, then it's simply not funny; the spontaneity is gone.'

'I disagree,' said Terry. 'That may be an old joke, but great comedy is timeless, just like great literature, art, music. What's your favourite song? *Strange Fruit* by Billie Holiday, isn't it? That's pretty old and you argue, with some justification, that there's been nothing to match it since for social commentary and emotional gravity. We read and listen to stuff that was created long before we were born; comedy is no different: it simply requires some historical context, that's all.'

'I just think it will have to be more cutting-edge if you want it to sell,' concluded Sandra.

'We will take on board your critique, but we may return to our sitcom at a later date.'

'I can't wait,' said Sandra.

'What about our band, then?' asked Pete.

'Your band?'

'Yeah, why not? I play the guitar, Terry reckons he can sing and thinks he looks a bit like Elvis.'

'Is that Presley or Costello?'

'We could have Kim-Ly and Celina on backing vocals,' continued Pete, 'and you can play the tambourine or something if you want.'

'Now, there's an offer I can't refuse. And do you have a name for this band?'

'The Black something or other,' declared Terry. 'Haven't decided yet; every band with Black in their name is cool.'

'Like Black Lace.'

'OK, maybe that's the exception that proves the rule.'

'Look, I only came in to say ease up on the drinking; you're frightening the girls. It won't make it go away, you know, Terry; all it will do is numb the senses and make it harder to make the right decisions.'

Terry appeared to sober up before Sandra's eyes, his expression changing from dopey to grumpy in one moment. 'Why do you have to be right all the time?' he asked. 'It must be quite a responsibility, being everyone's conscience.'

'Hey, steady on, old chap,' said Pete, 'I think Sandra's done pretty well in making the decisions so far, and I for one am happy to follow her lead.'

'Yeah, I'm sorry,' conceded Terry. 'We'd probably have been locked up by now, if not for you.' He fumbled with the lid and eventually managed to screw it back on the bottle. 'We'll save this for tomorrow, I think. Goodnight.' Stumbling clumsily, he didn't seem to notice as he smashed his shoulder on the door frame and continued his erratic progress to the bedroom. He emerged seconds later. 'That's Kim-Ly and Celina's room; I shall retire to the sofa-bed like a good boy and complain no more. I bid you goodnight once again.'

Kim-Ly looked unimpressed as he slumped down on the sofa between her and Celina and proceeded to untie his shoelaces and remove his shirt. 'Ladies, I wish to sleep, so, unless you fancy a threesome, I suggest you vacate my bed.'

'Time we all went to bed, I think,' said Sandra, and ushered a sad Kim-Ly from the room as her eyes told that the sheen had faded somewhat from her knight's shining armour.

Back in Amsterdam, events were taking a macabre turn as the police investigated the mysterious appearance of a body – floating, bobbing and staring, with a frozen expression of anger and shock.

11.

Gemma sipped at her spritz and surveyed the square, wondering if Terry would turn up. The waiter had asked if she would like to see a menu, but she had declined, insisting that she was waiting for a friend and that they may eat when he arrived. Despite all they'd been through together and the knowledge that nobody knew Terry as well as her, she felt nervous; her palms were sweaty and her heart was beating fast, as if in anticipation of a blind date. Who was this strange man she'd agreed to meet; a man who could so callously disregard their history and casually hook up with a prostitute, so soon after their parting? Did she really know him? The jealousy was insidiously eating away at her insides, threatening to leave her bitter and twisted. Sadly, she gazed into the distance, searching for her first love, and questioned once again why she was here. Was that a chill in the air, or were her involuntary shivers from within?

She recalled the happy hours they'd spent in places such as this, their favoured haunt of al-fresco dining, relaxed and contented, people watching as the world drifted by and they ate in silence; no need for words, they each knew what the other was thinking. The waiter hovered annoyingly, with a disapproving expression. Gemma could see that this was their busiest time of day and that a lone woman making her spritz last as long as possible was not the kind of customer they coveted.

Observing the other clientele, mainly couples exhibiting various degrees of affection, she wondered how much turmoil was concealed beneath their ostensibly happy façades. A young couple on the next table held hands across the condiments and gazed lovingly into each other's eyes. Two older gentlemen adopted a similar stance, immaculate in slick slacks and shiny shoes, shirts unbuttoned too far, cravats and hats.

'Hi, Gemma.' She jumped at the reassuringly familiar sound of his voice from her blind side and, caught off guard, her reply emerged as a squeak. 'Terry.'

Terry smiled, sat opposite and ordered a beer. 'You're looking good,' he said, 'but then, you always did.'

In her head she'd rehearsed the words a hundred times, the words that would bring him back, make him see sense; but somehow they wouldn't come out. 'Do you want to eat?'

'Be rude not to,' he replied, glancing towards the still-hovering waiter. 'I guess, by the name of the place, that fish is the speciality of the house.'

'Yes, the salmon salad looks good.'

'Two salmon salads it is then.' He waved at the suddenly attentive waiter and ordered their lunch, along with two more drinks. 'So, what's a nice girl like you doing in a joint like this?'

'Just happened by and thought I'd sit and wait for a guy like you.'

'So, how are you?' asked Terry.

How could she answer a question like that? She was distraught, her life in tatters, empty; a Terry-shaped void in her soul. Gemma tried to stay calm, to keep her composure, but she could feel the tears welling up. 'Oh, Terry, what happened to us? Where did it all go wrong?'

'Look, I don't see the point of raking up the past, of revisiting the accusations. We had that conversation when you walked out, remember?'

'But I've come all this way to say sorry, to say that I made the biggest mistake of my life and to ask your forgiveness. Is it too late for us, Terry?'

Terry stared back at her, a confused expression on those once-assured features. 'What do you want me to say? That everything's OK, let's go home and live happily ever after. You put me through hell, Gemma. I was just starting to come to terms with things and now you turn up and turn everything upside-down again.'

'Yes, I've heard about your way of coming to terms with things.'

'What's that supposed to mean?'

'Well, come on, Terry; you're not that desperate, are you?'

'You know nothing about it. You know nothing about Kim-Ly.'

'Kim-Ly, so that's her name. And was she worth what you paid?'

Terry looked as if he couldn't be bothered to be offended. 'I don't have to defend myself to you, but for your information I haven't paid her anything and we haven't slept together. Chris sent me here to do a piece on the sex trade. Kim-Ly was in the flat downstairs; I heard her screaming; she was being beaten by two men and I went to help, as I hope you would expect me to do. I must admit that things have got a little out of hand since then, but she is an innocent victim, Gemma; she didn't ask to be taken from her family and to be treated as a slave.'

'You always were a sucker for a sob story.'

'True, but there's much more to it than that. You'd like her, Gemma, you should meet her.' Terry hesitated, as if he'd just heard his own voice; his expression said it all: why didn't he think before opening his mouth? 'Hang on, maybe that's not such a good idea.'

'OK, why not?' said Gemma, in desperation. Their salmon salads arrived, giving her the time to observe Terry cringe at what he had impetuously suggested.

Terry thanked the waiter and turned to Gemma with a shocked expression. 'Are you serious? What could possibly be gained from the two of you meeting?'

Gemma rolled a tomato around her plate. 'Look, you're right; it was me that screwed up and destroyed what we had, but we're both grown-up now, Terry. We're no longer those spotty adolescents that exchanged glances across the classroom. If you want to move on, then you will have my blessing, but I'm not giving up without a fight.'

'A fight? Not sure who'd win that one,' said Terry with an uncomfortable smile, 'but I think Kim-Ly might be a little more street-wise.'

'I was speaking metaphorically.'

'This is fucking weird,' said Terry. 'I can't believe I'm even considering it.'

'We can deal with this like adults, can't we?'

'You've got to give me time to think about it, to talk to Kim-Ly.'

'OK, no pressure. Now, let's just enjoy the food and the ambiance; we used to love dining in places like this, remember?'

They ate in silence, no need for words; but this time neither knew what the other was thinking. As Terry attracted the waiter to ask for the bill, a familiar figure cycled across the square.

'Hello, stranger,' said the ever-effervescent Robbie. 'Gemma said to come to her rescue at two o'clock. Doesn't look like she needs rescuing, though; are you two getting along OK?'

'Nice cycle-clips,' smiled Terry, as he stood and shook Robbie's hand. 'Good to see you; come and join us.'

Robbie got down from his bike, propped it against a plant pot and, with a frown, removed those bloody cycle-clips. Terry called the waiter back over and ordered two more beers and another spritz, as Robbie sat down beside Gemma. 'Keep an eye on that bike,' said Terry; 'apparently there's a fair bit of cycle theft around here.' He continued to regale them with the tale so far (leaving out the bit about the two murders): of Sandra and Pete's support, of the enemies they'd made, of their escape from Amsterdam. 'I have to get Kim-Ly and Celina out of the country and to London.

Thinking of sailing from Rotterdam, but they have no passports.'

'I can get you passports,' said Robbie, avoiding Gemma's glare, 'or at least I know a man who can.'

'Robbie, how do you know a man who can get passports?' asked Gemma. 'You told me you'd cleaned up and didn't mix in those circles any more.'

'I have, Sis, honest; but I still have a few phone numbers and a couple of people who owe me one – that's if they're not inside by now.'

'What do you need?' asked Terry.

'Not much; names, dates of birth, countries of origin and photos, that's all. Oh, and it'll cost you a monkey each. I can post the details and pictures back home and have them back within the week.'

Gemma looked from one to the other with concern. 'I can't believe I'm sitting here listening to you two planning to smuggle two girls out of the country using fake passports. Do you know what the consequences would be if you got caught? Why can't you just go to the police or the British Embassy and ask for protection and asylum?'

'It's a little more complicated than that,' said Terry. 'We could do without the police asking questions.'

'Why is it so complicated? What have you got to hide? What haven't you told us?'

'It's best you don't know,' warned Terry. 'I don't want you being compromised.'

'OK, no questions asked,' agreed Robbie, without his sister's consent, but definitely with her disapproving, withering look.

Terry looked Robbie in the eye. 'Are you sure about this? Why should you help us?'

'For old time's sake, and to ensure that you treat my sister with respect. I don't want her getting hurt.'

Terry turned to Gemma. 'I would never intentionally hurt anyone, but I can't see a way out of this without somebody losing

105

out. I will bring Kim-Ly and Celina to town and find one of those passport-photo machines. If I can, I will get them to come and meet you. It's only fair that you should know who you will be rescuing, but the only thing I ask is that you treat *them* with respect too; they are human beings with feelings, just like you and I.'

'Respect, absolutely,' said Robbie. 'So, this Celina, what's she like then?' he enquired with an unsubtle wink at Terry.

'Nice girl, but with lots of issues; and she'd have you for breakfast.'

'No problem; do you think she'd like a full English?'

Gemma and Terry grimaced in unison.

Emotions all over the place, a bemused Terry swayed along the now familiar country lanes back towards the farm-house. Crapulent from last night's wine, complemented by lunchtime beer, he knew that he shouldn't be on the road; that two wheels could be as dangerous as four. He stopped in a copse to clear his head and relieve his bladder and, as the trees closed in around him, he observed a colourful butterfly flitting from one bluebell to another. It would live for just a few weeks and then its journey would be done; a simple, but brief and beautiful life. He tried to put things in perspective: that his life, and that of those he affected, would one day be insignificant in the infinite scheme of the Universe. He thought of those who had come before him, of their effect on the world; the vast majority of the human race, from the beginning to now, were flesh turned to dust and without significant influence. The best that could be hoped for was to create another human being to continue your journey, something he'd thus far failed to do. It was a longing that he seldom shared, that the one thing he craved above all else was to become a father, to be responsible for another life. Who would be the one to share life's ultimate experience, to add real meaning and to justify his existence: Gemma or Kim-Ly? Who was he to assume that either of them would want to contribute to his dreams?

Best face the music, he thought, as he remounted the bike and continued his journey. How would Kim-Ly react to the news that Gemma was here and wanted to meet her? He'd told Kim-Ly, honestly, that it was over; that he was a free agent and could date whoever he wished. Now things weren't so clear-cut and he knew not which way to turn. He vowed to tell her the truth; she'd had more than enough deceit in her life and he would not be the one to add to it. The note he'd left her, apologising for his ungentlemanly behaviour the previous night, would hopefully pave the way for civilised discussion.

Terry skidded to a halt as he rounded the wall and turned into the drive. The orange and blue diagonal stripes on the white police van reflected bright in the sunlight and his heart sank; they'd been rumbled already. Wheeling his bike cautiously, he found a hedge to hide behind with a good view of the house. He wondered if he should simply walk in as if he had nothing to hide and say, 'Good afternoon, officer, how can we assist you?', but he decided to remain hidden and await developments. He waited and waited, ready to jump out and come to Kim-Ly's rescue if undue restraint was used. Who was he kidding? He'd probably just climb from his hiding place with his hands in the air and give himself up.

Then, at last, through the window, he could see a burly policeman talking to Sandra and, seconds later, they both emerged, blinking in the sunshine; closely followed by Pete, Kim-Ly, Celina and, bringing up the rear, another, smaller police officer. Oh God, they're all under arrest, he thought, as the policeman escorted Sandra to the back of the van and opened the door. He offered his arm to help Sandra up the step and turned to Pete. 'I suggest that you lock-up your tandem in future, sir. Bicycle theft is very common in Holland; you are very lucky that we found this one and that the hire company told us where to find you.'

Terry jumped as a flurry of feathers rattled the branches above him and a pigeon landed with little thought for the nerves of the man below. Terry had worked in war-zones, yet somehow he found his current situation more scary. He tried to make himself smaller as the policeman looked his way, wondering about the cause of the commotion. The pigeon shat disdainfully on Terry's head, spread its wings and flew away as the policeman returned to the task in hand, apparently satisfied as to the source of the noise.

From the van a wheel appeared and Pete and Celina looked relieved as Sandra handed the tandem down to them. Pete shook the policeman's hand. 'Thank you, we will be more careful next time.'

'We hope you enjoy your stay in Holland, sir,' said the policeman; 'you are truly blessed to be sharing your vakantie with such beautiful ladies.'

The back of the departing police van was a welcome sight and Terry coughed as the dust rising from the drive enveloped him, covering his pigeon-shit-encrusted hair. They all turned to see Terry emerging sheepishly from the bushes. 'Hi, what's happening?' he asked, as if he spent most of his time hiding in the undergrowth. 'I've only been gone a few hours and you have already attracted the local constabulary.'

'Terry!' Kim-Ly ran towards him and flung her arms around his midriff. 'Where have you been? We were very scared when the policemen came, but they were very nice and have brought back the bike.'

The guilt turned his face an embarrassed shade of red, as he returned Kim-Ly's hug. 'Just some business to attend to in town,' he said, and looked to Sandra for help.

'Phew, that was a close one,' she said, changing the subject. 'Frightened the crap out of us when they knocked on the door, but they didn't suspect anything. They found the tandem in a dyke on the edge of town and traced us through the hire company's details on the crossbar. Best go inside. I need a drink.'

Making his excuses, Terry retreated to the shower to wash the pigeon poo from his quiff and consider his predicament. He took a deep breath and let the steam clear his airways, as the hot water bounced off his body and regenerated his senses. He tried to convince himself how fortunate he was to have two gorgeous women vying for his affections; but somehow he didn't feel lucky. Logical, detached thought, that was the answer. Consider the pros and cons of each scenario.

Suddenly his thought processes were rudely interrupted and he gasped as the naked Kim-Ly joined him beneath the shower. He'd dreamed of this moment since he first set eyes on her in that Amsterdam back alley and, despite the doubt so recently put into his mind, he was powerless to resist as her firm body pressed invitingly against his. Expertly, she knew all the right strings to play and the order in which to play them, the music of love building slowly and rhythmically. It was everything he'd imagined and more as her warm mouth found his and she wrapped her legs tightly around his waist. For those perfect moments they were as one, their bodies and souls moving to a sensorial metronomic beat; they shuddered in harmony as the symphony reached its crescendo, then collapsed helplessly in each other's arms. How could something that felt so right, so natural, be wrong, thought Terry, as he gazed into Kim-Ly's eyes and marvelled once again at her radiant smile. The golden lion had irrevocably caught her prey.

'Wow,' said Terry, as they tenderly dried each other's bodies with soft white bath towels. He could think of no words to describe the experience they'd just had.

'Yes, wow,' agreed Kim-Ly, as she ran her fingers through the hairs on his chest.

Terry looked thoughtful; was this the right time to talk to her about his surreptitious liaison with Gemma? He wanted this feeling to last forever and couldn't bear to shatter the moment.

Kim-Ly kissed the end of his nose and took his hands. 'What is wrong; why do you look so serious?'

'I need to talk to you, but not here. Let's get dressed and take a walk in the garden.'

Her tiny, soft hand was enveloped in his as they reached the fence that separated them from the open fields. They stood in the shade of a magnificent old ash tree and a gentle breeze cooled them down after their hot shower. Well, here goes, thought Terry, as he bit the bullet. 'It's Gemma, she has come to Gouda to find me; she wants me to go back to her.'

Kim-Ly let go of his hand and hung her head. 'And that is where you have been today, to meet her.'

'Yes, we were together for a long time, since school; I thought at least I owed her a face-to-face meeting.'

'And what have you decided? Who will you choose?' Her voice sounded small and lost.

Terry hesitated then gently lifted her chin. 'I think I have chosen you, if you'll have me.'

'And had you made that decision before or after we made love? Is it me you want, or just my body, like all the others?'

'Well, one wouldn't be much good without the other; you can't have a person without a body in which to contain them.'

'You know what I mean, Terry. I am free, thanks to you, and I will never go back to being used for sex.'

'I cannot deny that the initial attraction was physical,' said Terry, trying to pick his words carefully, 'but I have since come to know that the person within is as beautiful as the body without. Yes, I still have feelings for Gemma, you can't simply erase the past, but I was not lying when I told you it was over between us.'

Despite his eloquent words, Kim-Ly still looked unconvinced. 'Then prove it to me; take me to meet her and let me hear you tell her about us.'

A vision of the *Gunfight at the OK Corral* entered his mind and he shook his head. 'What is it about you two; are you that much alike? Gemma already knows about us and she wants to meet you too. Her brother is also here and has volunteered to help us by getting passports.'

'Does he work for the British Embassy?' asked Kim-Ly with a confused expression.

'Not exactly,' replied Terry, smiling at the thought. 'Robbie is a good man, but his lifestyle is somewhat unorthodox, not to say pushing the boundaries of legality.'

'And what is in it for him?'

Terry could understand her distrust of people, her reason to search for an ulterior motive behind every act of kindness. 'There is nothing in it for him. I will have to pay him one thousand pounds, but the people who supply the passports will probably get all of that. Oh, and he would like to buy Celina breakfast.'

'But he does not know Celina. I think Gemma's brother sounds very strange.'

'Strange; yes, that's Robbie.'

'And if I meet Gemma, will she hate me?'

'No, Gemma's not the type to hate anyone, but I don't know how either of you will react. Maybe I should just introduce you and let the two of you talk, while I go for a beer with Pete and Robbie. I feel very uncomfortable about all of this, you know, and I don't want to hurt anyone.'

'And if you go for a beer with Pete and Robbie, will you behave as you did last night?'

'I'm sorry about that, but I was very worried about today. What can I do to make amends?'

Kim-Ly smiled. 'You already have; in the shower.'

Terry blushed and they kissed again, wet and wonderful, long and lingering, tongues too; a splendid sensation that, at least for now, erased all doubt from his mixed-up mind.

12.

The Loverboy Brothers: that's how they were known on De Wallen, feared, hated and revered in equal measure, always smartly dressed and sporting expensive watches and jewellery, the immaculate Mercedes that they shared; all of these material possessions were ill-gotten recompense for their carefully cultivated reputation as the meanest, toughest drug dealers and pimps in town. If you knew the Loverboy Brothers, then you either stayed out of their way, or you were beholden to them. The girls they controlled were hand-picked for their vulnerability, tempted by the attention, the flash car and the flashed cash; then, once hooked, they were exploited and used without mercy. A lucrative trade, but the girls saw little reward for their labours: food and basic lodgings were the best they could hope for, betrayed by those they had fallen for and trusted.

Now there was only one Loverboy Brother left: the brains of the operation and the one who'd dragged them to the top of the tree, albeit a tree bearing fruits rotten to the core. Emre stood sadly with the police officer, his head bowed as the diving team raised the tarpaulin shroud to the surface. He'd already identified the body of his older brother Arhan and it didn't take a sixth sense to assume that the second body now bobbing on the surface would be that of his beloved younger brother Doruk. Drops of rain hit the water, creating gentle undulating ripples that slowly reached the water's edge, as if his brother was reaching out to him. The raindrops and ripples demonstrated that every event had a cause, and Emre vowed that the effect would be severe and bloody for those responsible for his brothers' eventuality.

Eventually, the body was winched out of the canal, the tarpaulin cut open and his worst fears were realised. Doruk seemed at peace, with his short life behind him; only twenty-two years old and they could hurt him no more. Emre said a silent prayer, tears of sorrow and wrath in his eyes. He nodded acknowledgement to the policeman to confirm that it was his brother and he walked resolutely away.

When they'd flown the nest and set out on their adventure, Emre had promised his parents that he would look out for Doruk, protect him from the evils of the world. His father would turn in his grave. How could he tell his poor widowed mother that both of his brothers were dead? How could he tell her how they earned their living? How could he bring such shame on his family? She would be heartbroken; not only for her loss, but for the loss of the values that she and her husband had bestowed upon their offspring. 'We did not bring you up to behave in such a fashion,' she would wail through her grief. 'You see how it ends, when you treat others this way. I disown you for the disgrace that you have brought upon us; never again will you darken my door.'

Emre vowed to uncover the truth, to wreak revenge for this outrage and make someone pay for this blatant affront to his authority. Already there had been blood, the head of the rival gang challenged and his pleas of innocence ignored. Emre had to admit, though, that his denial had sounded pretty convincing, his alibi intact and watertight. So, if not his adversaries, then who would be so brave or so stupid as to murder his brothers? Celina and Kim-Ly? Perhaps, but not alone; they would have needed assistance to perform such an act and to dispose of the bodies.

He'd never trusted that Kim-Ly. 'She is too clever; you will have to watch her because you will never fully control her,' he'd warned Arhan; but his warnings had fallen on deaf ears. Arhan had grown greedy, as he'd realised the depth of her allure, the top rate money she could command for repeat custom from wealthy clients.

'Then come with me to let her know what will happen if she disobeys,' Arhan had replied. 'She is rebelling against me by asking the other girls to join with her. A Hookers Union,' he'd laughed; 'have you ever heard anything so ridiculous?'

Emre had held his furious brother back as he'd threatened to kill Kim-Ly. 'Stop; are you crazy? Her screams will be heard across the city. Enough, Arhan. How will she earn you any money if you beat her so badly?' Now he wished that he'd let Arhan continue, turned a blind eye while he finished the job.

Could this be Kim-Ly's revenge, her break for freedom? Where was she now? He would like to ask her some questions. Emre hadn't reached the height of his profession without gleaning inside information from the police; tip-offs before drug raids, prior warning about new laws limiting cannabis use in coffee bars and reducing the number of prostitution windows. The police were some of his best clients and he had no hesitation in using this relationship to his benefit. Now he would await developments on the official enquiry into his brothers' deaths and determine his strategy from there. In the meantime, he had two funerals to arrange and little solace to offer his family.

Gemma's heart sank when she saw Kim-Ly; how could she compete with such beauty? Seemingly about ten years her junior and with features unblemished by the tragic life that Terry had described, Gemma looked down to see them holding hands, a cruel and obvious statement of his intent. She felt the tears coming again; not tears of jealousy and ire, but of resignation and defeat. In a belated act of sensitivity, Terry released Kim-Ly's hand and, with an embarrassed shuffle from one foot to the other, he introduced the two most important people in his life.

'Gemma, this is Kim-Ly, Kim-Ly this is Gemma.' He stood back, looking lost as Gemma shook her rival's hand.

Trying desperately to regain her composure and to remain dignified, Gemma welcomed Kim-Ly. 'It's a pleasure to meet you,' she lied. 'What would you like to drink?'

'A cappuccino, please; that would be a civilised drink to have on an occasion like this.'

'A cappuccino it is.' Gemma smiled through gritted teeth as she turned to Terry. 'OK, you can bugger-off now. Kim-Ly and I have a lot to talk about.'

'And do I get any say in the matter?' asked Terry.

'None whatsoever,' said Kim-Ly; 'we will see you later.'

Terry sighed. 'What can I say that I haven't said already? This is fucking weird. Well, I'll leave you to it then. I hope you enjoy your little chat. Call me when you've finished.'

'We will,' said Gemma. 'Bye-bye.'

They both watched as Terry turned away and, with another shake of the head, strode across the busy but spacious piazza. It was cheese market day and the pungent aroma wafted among the bustling throng of tourists, here for that very purpose. Statues of Burgundian counts and countesses stared down at them from the walls of the imposingly Gothic Stadhuis, its spiky towers reaching for the overcast sky. Gemma had chosen this cafe the previous day for its quiet, homely nature, an ideal place for such a momentous meeting; but today it was buzzing with people of all shapes, sizes, hues and cultures, each hauling carrier bags full of cheeses, of all shapes, sizes, hues and cultures.

The awkward silences, interspersed with stilted small-talk, lasted until their cappuccinos were served, each suspiciously weighing up the other, until Gemma broached the subject that was on both their minds. 'Terry has told me a lot about you, how you've had such a tough time, how he rescued you and how he feels about you.'

'Yes, Terry is a wonderful man.'

'And do you love him?' asked Gemma. 'Have you ever loved before?'

'That is a cruel question. I have not had the opportunity to love. It is used as a dirty word where I have worked. There *was* a boy from my village, but we were both young, barely teenagers. Quan begged me not to go when I left, but I promised I would return. I should have listened to him. Terry is the only man I have trusted since I was taken from my home. He is special, Gemma, as you should know.'

'Yes, he is … and that's why I am here.'

'Then why did you let him go? He has not told me much about you, except that you were together since school, that you broke his heart and that he thinks it is over between you.'

The words cut like a knife. If Terry thinks that it's over, then what the hell am I doing here? Gemma thought for the hundredth time. She recalled her Gran's wise words: *"If he still loves you then he'll come back; if not, then you must either get used to living alone or find someone else. There's no point in wasting time moping around and trying to change things you can do nothing about. Everyone makes mistakes in life; the important thing is to deal with them quickly and move on."* What could she do? If this is an infatuation, a crush, a temporary aberration, then let it take its course, she said to herself. If not, and it is true love, then I may as well give up.

'I guess I'm chasing a lost cause,' she sighed. 'I wanted to give him a choice to make, the chance to come back to me, but it seems he has already made his decision.'

'I am not sure if his decision is final,' replied Kim-Ly. 'He says that he still has feelings for you, that there is a lot of history.'

'Perhaps, but what is history but the past? It seems that you are his future and I can only wish you both the best of luck. I want him to be happy after what I put him through.'

'And you are prepared to give him up that easily?' said Kim-Ly. 'Most women would not be that understanding and I was expecting to have to fight for him.'

'Ha,' Gemma smiled weakly. 'Terry said that you are streetwise and would win the fight easily.'

'Then if we are not going to fight, can we be friends?' asked Kim-Ly.

'I don't know. My heart will break anew every time I see you together, but maybe I'll get used to the idea, given time. Terry was right: he said I would like you and I do. I had no right to judge you because of your profession. I can see why he has fallen for you, and now I have to make a fresh start and get on with my life.'

'You are very beautiful,' observed Kim-Ly; 'you will not be on your own for long.'

'Thank you,' smiled Gemma. 'A few more comments like that and perhaps we can be friends. I cannot compete with you on the beauty front, though.'

'But I do not feel beautiful within; I have lived a bad life.'

'Not bad, just unlucky,' replied Gemma, 'until now, that is.'

'Terry says that your brother will help us to get to London.'

'Yes, and I'm not too happy about it,' said Gemma. 'Robbie will be in a lot of trouble if he gets caught, but there's no talking to him once he's made up his mind.'

'I would like to meet Robbie,' said Kim-Ly, 'he sounds like he is a character.'

'A character, yes, that's Robbie. You will meet him this afternoon. Now, shall we order some lunch? We may as well keep this as cordial as possible.'

'This steak is as pink as a baboon's bottom,' complained Robbie. 'I knew I should have gone for the chicken. Why do they always insist on undercooking their cows on the continent? I didn't want it cremated, but the least they could have done is threaten it with a flame.'

Robbie's observations barely registered with the preoccupied Terry, but Pete wholeheartedly agreed with him. 'Yes, I'm forever sending back steaks after I've asked for them well-done and they turn up dripping with blood; and the waiter always looks offended, as if it's a personal affront to the reputation of the house.'

Robbie and Pete had only just met, but they were already getting along like long-lost friends, their senses of humour cynically similar. Their other companion however, had temporarily mislaid his mojo.

Pete turned to Terry. 'You OK, mate?' he asked. 'Nothing you can do about it, you know. Let them sort it out between themselves. I'm sure they'll reach an amicable agreement.'

'What, like Gemma during the week and Kim-Ly at weekends?' replied Terry.

'You should be so lucky,' said Pete.

'Hey, that's my sister you're talking about,' said Robbie. 'I've yet to meet the lovely Kim-Ly, but she must be something else if you're thinking about dumping Gemma for her.'

'She is; and Gemma dumped me, remember.'

'Yes, I know, and I told her that Sam was a tosser; but now she knows that she cocked up. Can't you give her another chance?'

Terry didn't reply, but stared into his beer as if the answer might be there.

'Jesus, what's that?' sniffed Robbie, as an old man sat at the next table and placed his carrier bag on the floor beside him. 'What you got in there, pal; the dirty socks of the Gouda football team?'

The old man stared back at him through a grey beard, reminiscent of Uncle Albert's from *Only Fools and Horses*, and shrugged his shoulders. 'Ik snap het niet.'

'He says *non-comprende*,' said Pete. 'It is cheese market day and you'd better get used to it; the whole town will smell like that today. Sandra and I went to the one in Alkmaar last year and there's no escaping the stench. We purchased some fantastic cheese, though – best I've ever tasted – and no-one came near us on the train home.'

Finally, Terry joined the conversation, the lure of cheese seemingly awakening his senses. 'We must buy some to take back with us tonight; cheese is a vice that I could never give up. I know it's bad for the cholesterol, but you can't beat a good piece of cheese.'

Robbie stared at him. 'I'll do a deal with you. I'll buy you as much cheese as you want if you give up your other vice.'

'I'm sorry, Robbie, but no can do. I know you love your sister and so did I, but I think my mind's made up; that's unless Gemma's persuaded Kim-Ly to change it for me, if you know what I mean, because *I* sure as hell don't.'

A defeated Robbie poked at the inedible pink remnants of his steak with his fork; no point in attempting to resuscitate it, best let it lie. 'What more can I say?' he conceded. 'At least I tried.' He'd always respected his prospective brother-in-law and, much as he wanted to, he couldn't bring himself to harbour any bad feeling.

Terry's phone rang and it nearly dropped between fumbling fingers; the resultant conversation brief and to the point. Terry raised his eyes toward his expectant audience. 'We've been summoned to meet them in the square in one hour. It seems that they haven't killed each other yet; in fact, on the contrary, I'm sure I heard laughter as Gemma hung up.'

Pete waved across the bar as Sandra entered, closely followed by the striking figure of Celina, resplendent in a simple body-hugging white t-shirt, complemented by a tight red mini-skirt. Their shopping trip had obviously done little to tone down Celina's appearance and she was unknowingly turning heads as usual. 'Wow!' exclaimed Robbie. 'I see what you mean; can't wait for breakfast.' He doffed an imaginary cap and nodded, as Pete made the necessary introductions.

'So, how did it go?' asked Pete.

'First, I vanted to see a priest,' replied Celina, 'to make a confession for the first time in many years. He said that God could save my soul. I told him that I had no soul left to save. Then ve vent to the doctor, he tried to give me methadone, but I spoke

119

vith Sandra and ve decided that I should not svap vone drug for another. He said it is very hard to give up vithout help and that he could recommend a place for rehab, but I have no insurance and no money. Looks like I vill have to do this by myself.'

'Not by yourself,' said Sandra, as she placed a supportive arm around Celina's waist; 'you have us, remember. So, this is the notorious Robbie, is it? Terry has told us a lot about you.'

'None of it is true,' grinned Robbie, his gaze diverted towards Celina. 'Mistaken identity, and I have a rock-solid alibi.'

Sandra turned to Pete with a serious expression. 'How much have you told him?'

'Pretty well everything, but without the gory details.'

Sandra laid the day's newspaper in front of Pete. 'Well, maybe it's time he knew the gory bits too. It's only fair that Robbie should know what he's getting into.'

'Oh, shit!' said Pete, as he took in the news. 'Now what do we do?'

'What's up?' asked Terry.

'The game's up,' replied Pete, and he went on to translate the headlines. '"*Police Search for Missing English Couple in Murder Hunt*". Apparently, the suspects were seen leaving on bicycles, accompanied by one man and two women. It goes on to give some pretty detailed descriptions, although I'm not sure about mine – *"an overweight, middle-aged, balding man"*, for God's sake; that's hardly fair, is it?' He looked to Sandra for reassurance, but none was forthcoming.

'Murder hunt?' exclaimed Robbie. 'Look, I'll be the first to admit that I've been involved in some dodgy stuff in my time, but murder?!! What the hell have you been up to?'

Terry brought him up to speed with recent events, then concluded – 'This has gone too far. We should give ourselves up, explain what happened and rely upon the mercy of the courts. What's the Dutch justice system like?'

'How the hell should I know?' said Pete. 'I've not had any

experience of it and had no bloody reason to think that I ever would; until you turned up.'

'I vill not give myself up,' said Celina. 'You go back if you vish, but I know that Emre, the only brother left, has friends in the police. You can ask Kim-Ly and she vill say the same.'

'Then we have no choice,' concluded Sandra. 'I suggest we meet with Gemma and Kim-Ly and decide what to do from there. We need to split up, into pairs perhaps or at least into threes; they will be looking for five people and it won't take long for them to trace us through *Cycle Netherlands*. The police here know where we are staying, so we can't go back there.' She turned to the smitten Robbie with his mouth still agape. 'Are you still prepared to help us?'

He winked at Celina, who responded with a brief and barely visible smile. 'Yeah, why not, in for a penny, as they say; and I've got nothing better to do. Did you get the passport photos and the money?'

'Yes, all sorted this morning,' replied Terry, as he handed over a brown envelope containing the agreed fee, photos and information.

'OK, but we no longer have time to do this by post,' reasoned Robbie. 'I'll get a flight home this evening and bring them back in the next few days. You can add my travel costs to the two monkeys. Can't see any other way that you'll get out of the country and it's gonna have to be soon, preferably before they've alerted every airport and port. I'd better get going before Gemma finds out; she'll only try to talk me out of it. I'll call you when I get back and arrange where to meet you.'

'Wait,' said Terry, 'I can order your tickets on my iPad; it'll be quicker and we can see what flight you can get on. It's not like queuing for a bus, you know.'

'OK, may as well get another beer then,' agreed Robbie. 'What's everyone having?'

Fifteen minutes later and it was all organised. 'You are flying from Amsterdam at 8 p.m. and there are regular trains from

Gouda, so you'll have plenty of time.' Terry shook Robbie's hand and gave him a hug. 'Thanks, mate. I don't know why you're doing this, given the circumstances.'

'No, nor do I. Look after Gemma till I return.' A firm handshake and a good-to-meet-you for Sandra and Pete; another wink at Celina, and he was gone.

A house on fire couldn't have got on any better than Gemma and Kim-Ly. The cappuccino had evolved to spritz and the effect had temporarily eased any bitterness and rivalry. They laughed about many things, but mostly about Terry. Both agreed that he was a decent chap, despite the faults that Kim-Ly had yet to discover, but that Gemma took delight in sharing. 'He farts a lot after a curry and he has an annoying habit of scratching his balls in the morning; apart from that, he's had one careful owner and is in reasonable condition for his age.' Suddenly, it dawned on her what was happening, the meaning of her words, so casually thrown away; and the joke wasn't funny any more. An uncontrollable sob caught her throat and she made her excuses and retired distraught to the bathroom.

Kim-Ly saw them coming across the square and counted – one, two, three, four; who was missing? She was disappointed that all were present and correct except Robbie, as she'd been looking forward to meeting him. The serious expressions became more pronounced the closer they came and her smile was met with nervous glances into each corner of the Markt.

'Where is Gemma?' were Terry's first words: no smile, no greeting.

'She will be back soon; she seemed very upset.'

Sandra sat beside Kim-Ly, placed a reassuring hand on her arm and laid out the newspaper in front of her. 'We have some serious decisions to make. It looks like they're on to us.'

'Oh dear.' Kim-Ly shivered, as Gemma returned with her composure partly regained.

'Why the long faces?' she asked. 'You can't be feeling any worse than me. Where's that brother of mine?'

Sandra pointed towards a vacant table in the only quiet part of the café. 'Come over here and I'll explain everything.'

The others sat in silence and watched as they awaited Gemma's reaction. 'What? You can't be serious?' A few more illegible words from Sandra, and Gemma continued vociferously. 'Well, how did you expect me to react? How dare you get us mixed up in this; we've just got Robbie back on the straight and narrow and now you've sent him back to all those dodgy characters that he used to hang around with. This is far worse than *anything* he's ever done before; it was all petty stuff, mostly harmless. This is in another league altogether. No, I won't keep my sodding voice down.' Her chair crashed to the ground as she stood, wiped away a tear and stormed out with a parting shot at Terry. 'You're a bloody fool and I hope you'll be very happy together.'

'Gemma, please come back,' pleaded Terry; 'let's talk about this.'

'Gemma, I am sorry,' shouted Kim-Ly. 'You said we could be friends.'

'Go to hell!!'

'Hmm, she took that well,' observed Pete, as he watched Gemma stride purposefully away.

'An understandable reaction, I'd say,' said Terry. 'How did you think she'd take it? I'll give her a call in an hour or so, give her a chance to cool down.'

'I think it may take longer than an hour,' said Sandra. 'Well, I propose that we remove ourselves from the throng; don't know about you, but I feel pretty conspicuous in the midst of all these people. Any suggestions as to how we split up; who goes with who and where to?'

A passing policeman smiled at Celina and she seemed to shrink as she cowered in her chair. 'Can I stay vith you?' she asked. 'I feel safe vith you and Pete.'

'What, you want to stay with the missing English couple that the police are searching for in a murder hunt?' asked Pete. 'I can't think of anywhere safer.'

'Of course you can,' said Sandra, ignoring Pete's flippancy. 'That leaves Terry and Kim-Ly; and Gemma, if you can get her to come round.'

'OK,' sighed Terry. 'I don't suppose that I have any choice; but I've said it before and I'll say it again, this is fucking weird.'

13.

It was Hoofdinspecteur Bomkamp's birthday, but he didn't feel much like celebrating. Fifteen years he'd been in the police force and, through sheer hard work and endeavour, had deserved every single one of his rapid promotions; yet, sadly, his achievements had become irreversibly tainted by that one impulsive indiscretion. He was convinced that nobody knew, but was aware that many suspected that his involvement with the Loverboy Brothers was less than professional. Now two of them were dead and their hold on him was no longer as strong. He knew that Emre was a formidable opponent, but alone and without the support of Arhan and Doruk, perhaps he could be beaten.

Every morning when he awoke, Bomkamp felt the guilt and the shame; and today was no exception. He knew full well that he wasn't the only one, and that some of his superiors and colleagues had also succumbed to temptation; that the only reason Emre and his sleazy siblings had been allowed to thrive was due to the fact that they literally had the police by the short and curlies.

His children bounced on the bed in excitement as he opened his presents and he gave them a hug and kiss for each of his years. His wife Aline observed the annual ritual with a look of adoration: a successful man and two wonderful children reflected in her wide blue eyes. How could he ever again be worthy of such devotion? Following his daily routine, he dressed once more in the immaculate uniform that filled him with both pride and dishonour, his rank confirmed by the gold crown above a gold bar on his sleeve. He took a familiar look in the mirror as he combed his distinguished greying hair and a steely resolve overcame him; it was time to do justice to his position, to repay some debts and to throw off the sordid shackles of blackmail.

He knew not the reason for the sudden disappearance of the English couple from the boat, nor the identity of their companions; but it could not be coincidence that the bodies of his adversaries had appeared so soon after. Forensics had determined beyond reasonable doubt that blunt instruments, in the shape of the recovered hammer and wrench, had been the respective causes of death. From the evidence presented thus far, Bomkamp deduced that anyone who could overcome the brutal and ruthless Arhan and Doruk would be serious criminals; probably involved in the international drugs trade. The seemingly innocent bohemian appearance of the boat and the reportedly laid-back demeanour of its inhabitants were obviously a front for prostitution and trafficking, a convincing cover for their covert activities.

He had already been granted charge of the case and he would run a lean, efficient ship in his endeavour to trace the absconders. With the enlisted assistance of the neophyte Hoofdagent Van Otterloo, no questions would be asked and his every order would be followed in order to impress. Van Otterloo was a bright kid and his wiry frame and baby face concealed a logical and investigative mind; he would be the Watson to his Holmes. Legend had it that Van Otterloo's grandfather had been a detective of some repute, but he always changed the subject when asked. 'I want to make my own way in the force on merit,' he would insist, 'not live off the reputation of my ancestors.' Their first mission would be to determine the whereabouts of their prey; after which, he would demand back-up if required.

His wife straightened his collar and admired the gold cufflinks that she had taken great pleasure in selecting for his present. They kissed goodbye, as they did every day, but this time there was an electricity in the contact; a fleeting reminiscence of their long-ago courtship.

'I have to work away for a while,' he declared. 'There is an important case that requires my leadership and I cannot say how soon I will return.'

'Is it to do with the two murders on Brouwersgracht?'

'You know that I cannot talk about my work. I will call you and the children every day and I will return once the case is resolved.'

He knew that Aline would accept his explanation without question, as she had a hundred times before. 'OK,' she sighed, 'but do you have to go on your birthday?'

'I am afraid so. There are fugitives that must be caught and I suspect that they may try to leave the country. It is imperative that I pick up their trail before it goes cold.'

Aline kissed him again. 'Please be careful, there are treacherous people out there. Remember, you are a father as well as a policeman.'

'Do not worry, there is no-one can outwit your favourite Hoofdinspecteur. I will be back before you have even missed me.'

Two hours later and Van Otterloo and he were on the road to Gouda. These people had done little to cover their tracks and it was almost as if they wanted to be caught; they may as well have put signposts on every corner. He had an address from *Cycle Netherlands*, detailed descriptions of his quarry, numerous sightings along the way and confirmation from his colleagues in Gouda that they were indeed staying at the specified location. He had declined their offer of assistance, declaring that he would prefer to work stealthily and avoid spooking his prey into flight before he'd got the chance to work out what they were up to.

Following a nourishing luncheon of stamppot and rookworst, they had gleaned further information; another couple, purporting to be brother and sister, were also in pursuit of the assumed murderers. The man's petty criminal demeanour had been somewhat dissipated by his cycle-clips and the lady was petite, blonde and very attractive. They were about half a day behind the other motley quintet and the landlord thought there was something suspect about all of them.

Bomkamp was also aware that the chain of chase would not stop there; that Emre, with enough contacts in high places to ascertain the *modus operandi* of every police operation, would be on their tails too. And so be it; Bomkamp would happily lead him directly into the lion's den, where the dangerous gang would hopefully do to him what they did to his brothers. Then he could start again, perform his job with integrity and justify his family's pride. That was his nebulous plan in a nutshell; what could possibly go wrong?

They approached the farmhouse furtively, any attempts at subterfuge hindered by the silence. Every step on the gravel produced a crunch like a giant eating cornflakes. Peering through windows, peaking round corners, trying door handles; stillness prevailed and the place looked deserted.

'Can I help you, officer?'

Bomkamp hopped out of his hide and Van Otterloo rushed from the rear of the house to see a grizzled old man standing in the drive, his weathered features obscured in the shadow of a large hat. Strands of unkempt hair strayed at acute angles and his clothes were ill-fitting and grubby; Bomkamp wondered if he were a scarecrow that had wandered in from the field. The old man's wrinkled eyes darted from one to the other.

'Who are you?' asked Bomkamp.

'My name is Thomas; I am the farmer that owns this place. They left yesterday and did not return; looked like they were heading for Gouda. All of their things are still in the house and they have brought plenty of food and drink. They were a strange group. The police were here before, two days ago. Is there anything wrong?'

'We just want to ask some questions. Did you speak to any of them?'

'Only the English lady who collected the keys; she seemed very nice. It was the others who were a bit weird. Not that I have any experience, but the other two girls looked like ladies of the night.'

'How could you tell?' asked Bomkamp.

'Just by the way they carried themselves, the way they looked, the way they walked; kind of provocative.'

'So, if you have "no experience", on what do you base this theory?'

The old man shuffled uneasily. 'Just a hunch, that is all. I cannot tell you anything else.'

'Hmm, if you say so. Can you let us in, please? We would like to take a look around.'

The farmer leant on the doorframe as the detective duo scrutinised every object and upturned every cushion, searching for any trace of the identities and plans of this assorted crew. 'Looks like they were intending to come back,' concluded Van Otterloo; 'their things are scattered everywhere, things that you would not leave behind.'

'My guess is that they have discovered that we are onto them,' said Bomkamp; 'maybe read it in the newspaper and decided that it is not safe to return. They have left a few clues behind, though; can you tell me what they are?' He enjoyed testing his officers, giving them the opportunity to come up with the answers. It was his way of assessing their ability and deciding which of them had the best prospects for advancement in the police force.

'There is this leaflet on heroin addiction, sir,' observed Van Otterloo, 'evidence of our suspicion that they are involved in the drugs trade. This notebook is interesting – contains a few pages of scribbles and connected words like prostitutes, pimps and drugs gang, all written in English; as if somebody were making notes for a story. There is a pack of chicken breasts in the kitchen, presumably left there to defrost; which indicates that they were intending to return yesterday to eat. I have laid out some of their clothes and conclude that we are looking for one tall man, another

129

man of shorter, but somewhat bulkier frame and three ladies, one size forty-six, who dresses in more casual attire, and the others, one tall and one short, who definitely dress to impress; you should see some of their undergarments, sir.'

'Control yourself, Van Otterloo,' said Bomkamp. 'Some very good detective work, well done. What about this copy of best-selling novel *That Bloody Book* by Joe Stamford on the coffee table? It suggests that we are dealing with some cultured criminals, as well as ruthless ones. We already know that at least two of them are English and that, based on the observations of our farmer friend here and your rummage through their drawers, two of the females could indeed earn their living improperly. I deduce that we have stumbled upon a plot to oust the Loverboy Brothers as the undisputed top dogs of the Amsterdam underworld and that, as well as disposing of Arhan and Doruk, they have also taken two of their best girls as a further challenge to Emre's powers. A dangerous game, but one in which they are currently a few steps ahead of both us and Emre. It also appears, from the testament of our landlord with the mullet, that they are being pursued by another couple. God knows where they fit into the jigsaw, but I intend to find out.'

'I would also argue, sir,' said Van Otterloo, 'that the discovery of *That Bloody Book* on the coffee table is merely another blatant and crass attempt by the author to sell his other book, and is not in any way a measure of the cultural credentials of our five fugitives. Furthermore, the term "rummage through their drawers", in this context, is more befitting of a 1970s English sitcom – *Are You Being Served*, maybe – rather than a conversation between two modern-day Dutch policemen. I think the author is taking liberties with both era and genre. How else would I know of such things?'

'All of this is true,' conceded Bomkamp, impressed with the discernment of his young detective, 'but we have, among the detritus of their brief occupation of this establishment, some decent clues as to their origin and character.'

'So, what happens now, sir?'

'I propose that we head for Gouda and ask some questions there. Their journey thus far has been less than circumspect and I suspect they will have left a trail that you would not need a sniffer dog to follow.'

Pete had seen more than enough and was quickly losing his patience. 'How do you expect to blend into the background when you're wearing *that?*' he asked Celina. 'You're not touting for business any more, you know.'

Celina, still wearing the eye-catching white t-shirt and red mini-skirt ensemble, glared at him. 'I know no other life except to tout for business. If you vant to take me shopping I vill happily get something more boring but, as I have no money, this vill have to do for now.'

The oleaginous hotel manager had eyed them suspiciously upon booking in, but now, as they stood at the bar, he was staring directly and not too subtly at Celina's never-ending legs beneath her taut and tantalising derrière. The tightness of her attire left little to the imagination and Pete looked decidedly out of place at her side. Thankfully, Sandra joined them and placed herself adjacent to her partner; 'he's with me' was the unspoken statement.

'Can't you get Celina kitted out in something more normal?' Pete asked. 'Wherever we go there are eyes following us and I'm damn sure it's not me they're looking at.'

Sandra let out a tired sigh. 'OK, I'll try, tomorrow. Can't we just relax this evening? Our little adventure is starting to catch up with me. We're far too old for all of this, you know.'

Pete kissed her cheek. 'Yeah, I know what you mean. You've been fantastic and I'm really proud of you. It'll all turn out OK in the end, you know.'

'You think so?' replied Sandra, looking less than convinced. 'I wonder how Terry's getting on with his *menage à trois*. I can't imagine what Gemma's going through; it must be awful for her to be rejected like that.'

'This isn't easy for Terry either, you know,' answered Pete, on behalf of mankind; 'he doesn't know which way to turn at the moment.'

'Seems to me he's made his mind up,' said Sandra.

Celina listened attentively to their conversation as she tried to ignore the indelicate leer of the hotel manager. 'Kim-Ly is a good person, you know. She is beautiful, loyal and trustvorthy and any man vould be lucky to catch her. If Terry has any doubt, then he should be honest and let her go.'

'Oh, I don't think he has any doubt,' said Sandra. 'I'm just saying I feel sorry for Gemma, that's all.'

Gemma had never felt so alone; in a strange room in a strange country, even her brother had deserted her. She pulled the tear-soaked pillow around her ears once more and attempted to blot-out the world outside. What had she been thinking of when she came here? Yes, she'd made some mistakes, but it seemed harsh punishment to be treated so callously by those she loved and who, she thought, would at least have a modicum of feeling for her too.

The decor had the tourist trade specifically in mind and a series of cheap Dutch clichés adorned the white walls and twee Dutch dresser: Delft tiles depicting windmills and quaint houses with lace curtains, clogs, cows, dolls and more bloody windmills. Oh, how she longed for her mundane job and her home. Home? Where was that now? Was it back with Mum and Dad and Robbie? Had she really regressed so far?

Her phone rang once more and she could ignore it no longer. 'What?' she shouted and awaited Terry's response.

'How are you?'

'How the bloody hell do you think I am?'

'I'm sorry.'

Gemma said nothing.

'Where are you?'

'Why should you care?'

'You know I care. Can we talk?'

'I think everything's been said, hasn't it?'

'Maybe, but we don't have to be enemies, do we, after all we've been through?'

Gemma hesitated, then sighed. 'I'm in a guest-house on a street called Lage Gouwe, by a canal. Meet me there in half an hour.'

'We found a dingy place last night,' said Terry, 'but it stank and was full of bugs. Now we can't find anywhere to stay. Is there any room there?'

'Are you serious?'

'Please, Gemma, we could be in big trouble here and I doubt that it's just the police that are looking for us.'

'OK, I'll find out if they have another two rooms. You're not sleeping with *her* under the same roof as me; surely you have at least that much sensitivity.'

Gemma used the half an hour wisely, making herself look more than presentable, restoring her dignity and composure. Her head held high, she saw them through the window, Kim-Ly hiding behind Terry as they approached, looking shamefaced and guilty. Gemma met them at the door, the awkward silence lasting forever before she spoke. 'They have one more twin room; Kim-Ly and I will sleep in there and you can wallow in your own shit and consider what you've done.'

Terry looked to Kim-Ly, who nodded her approval. 'Thank You, Gemma' she said. 'I am truly sorry for what has happened.'

'Oh. I don't blame you,' said Gemma, glaring at Terry. 'Come on, they're still serving food and I need a drink.'

More silence as they ate and drank bottles of Grolsch, punctured by vacuous small talk and nervous laughter. 'So, what's the plan?' asked Gemma eventually.

'We lie low and stay away from Sandra, Pete and Celina until Robbie gets back, hopefully with all the paperwork in order,' replied Terry. 'Then we head for Rotterdam and book a ferry back to the UK; looks like Hull is the only place where they go direct and, as it's not a major tourist route, we can hope to slip under the radar.'

'At least I'll be able to say that I've been to Hull and back,' said Gemma; 'seems pretty apt.'

'Robbie rang earlier; says he's called in a few favours and that he hopes to be back tomorrow.'

'I'll never forgive you if he goes down for this,' said Gemma. 'You know how easily led he is and you're just taking the advantage.'

'He offered to help us; I didn't coerce him in any way. Besides, I think he likes Celina.'

'She's got big tits and a short skirt; of course he likes her.'

Looking thoughtful and sad, Kim-Ly had said little. 'Celina and I, we have caused too much trouble. Let us leave and make our own way; we will all have a better chance of escape if we go our separate ways. Terry, you should go back to Gemma, where you belong.'

Gemma shook her head. 'And do you know how miserable Terry would be? You have inadvertently started a chain of events that no-one could have predicted. Now we must let those events take their course and see where they lead us. I don't want him back against his will and he would spend the rest of his life wondering about you. No, destiny has brought us to this point and now we have to deal with things as they are.'

'Ever the pragmatist,' said Terry. 'Thank you, Gemma, thank you for not hating Kim-Ly, for not hating me.'

'Bollocks!' pronounced Gemma. 'Now, let's sleep on it. I've had more than enough for one day.'

Meanwhile, the determined Bomkamp and Van Otterloo were methodically scouring the city's hotels and guest-houses for English visitants.

14.

Robbie was absolutely knackered; the early morning flight had necessitated a 4 a.m. alarm and he was half-asleep as he approached the guest-house. Terry had promised him as much breakfast as he could eat and he licked his lips in anticipation of croissants, jam and fruit juice; they may even have some bacon if he were lucky. He glanced up at the window to see Terry looking down and was just about to wave when, out of the corner of his eye, he saw two policemen approaching. Terry saw them too and shrank back behind the curtain.

'Goedemorgen, meneer,' greeted the older, more important-looking one. 'Wat brengt u deze delen?'

'Sorry, Officer, or is it Superintendent?' said Robbie, thinking that a bit of flattery wouldn't do any harm. 'Don't speak the lingo, I'm afraid.'

'Ah, an Englishman, interesting; and what business do you have here, sir?'

A barge meandered leisurely along the canal by their side. Three boisterous children shouted 'hello' and waved frantically from the deck. Robbie considered making a run for it while his inquisitors' attention was diverted, but thought better of it; the younger of the two officers looked pretty athletic. Instead, Robbie used the distraction to attempt to concoct a plausible story. They all waved back at the children and smiled.

'I am a travelling salesman,' answered Robbie, thinking on his feet. 'I am here for a conference that starts tomorrow.'

'And what is it exactly that you are selling?'

'Sex-toys,' said Robbie, coming out with the first thing that came into his head and immediately regretting it.

'Sex-toys,' repeated the Superintendent; 'big business these days and I suspect that sir makes a very good living.'

'I get by,' said Robbie, feeling the nervous beads of sweat breaking out on his forehead.

'We are on the lookout for some natives of your country, sir, in connection with a high-profile case. Would you mind if we take a look in your bag?'

'Not at all, Superintendent, I've nothing to hide,' said Robbie, his nonchalance belying an inner turmoil. He anxiously considered the contents of his case and surrendered himself to the inevitable.

'Hoofdagent Van Otterloo, would you be so kind as to do the honours?'

'Yes, sir,' obeyed the younger man, as he hunched down on the pavement and began delving into Robbie's personal effects. Discarding t-shirts and underwear, he pulled out a phallic object and assessed its girth and length. 'This backs up his story, sir,' said Van Otterloo, handing over item one. 'I am not sure where you insert the batteries, though.'

The superior officer took it between thumb and finger and deliberated upon its use, whilst Van Otterloo continued his search.

'What about these, sir?' he said, passing him two round pieces of plastic, the circle broken by two protruding nodules. 'Very clever in that they are flexible and can fill two orifices at once; they have these angular bits for enhanced stimulation and they are modular to cater for the capacity of the user.'

Robbie looked on helpless as the superintendent removed the lid from the phallic object and sprayed it beneath his nose. 'May I apologise, sir, for the deviant mind of my officer here and compliment you on your choice of deodorant.' He held up the two circular pieces of plastic and continued. 'And if I am not mistaken, these are a pair of cycle-clips. Van Otterloo, you really must get out more and spend less time on the internet.' He turned his attention back to Robbie. 'If you truly are a supplier of goods to the sex-toy industry, sir, may I ask where your real samples are?'

Robbie looked at this comedic double-act in disbelief and replied, 'Gone are the days of the travelling salesman with a suitcase full of samples. My entire catalogue is contained on a memory-stick and I will be presenting my array of products via PowerPoint at tomorrow's conference. If you are looking to spice-up your sex lives you are welcome to join us and see what's on offer.'

'A kind offer, sir, but I think I will pass. You are free to go and I hope you have a pleasant stay in our country.'

Robbie breathed a sigh of relief as he tried to look casual and resist the temptation to run. Before turning the corner, he glanced over his shoulder to see the two policemen entering the guest-house. Oh shit, he thought. 'Oh shit!' he exclaimed, as he bumped into Terry. 'What the hell!!'

Terry smiled and shook his hand. 'Welcome back, Robbie. Thanks for stalling them while we got down the fire-escape. Think we may be in even more trouble as we had to leave without paying the bill. And talking of the Bill, it won't take them long to find out we've done a bunk. Come on, we need to get as far away from here as possible and quickly.'

'Hello, mate,' laughed Robbie. 'You won't believe the conversation I've just had.'

He spied Gemma and Kim-Ly waiting at the end of the street and he and Terry both ran to meet them. 'Hi, Sis,' said Robbie. 'Ouch! What was that for?'

'You bloody fool!' cried Gemma. 'What the hell do you think you're doing, getting involved in this?'

'Seems to me we're all involved,' replied Robbie, rubbing his cheek, 'otherwise you wouldn't still be here.'

'I hate to interrupt this little reunion,' said Terry, 'but I think it might be a good idea if we get going. I think maybe we should head for Rotterdam as soon as we can get a train. The others can join us there later.'

'Sounds like a plan,' agreed Robbie.

'You love all this, don't you?' said Gemma, as they walked briskly in the vague direction of the train station. 'The thrill of the chase and all that.'

'Most fun I've had since we used to play cops and robbers as kids,' said Robbie; 'you were always the law-abiding one, even then. There's still nothing like the buzz of staying one step ahead of the law.'

'I'll remember that buzz when we all get arrested,' said Gemma, breathing heavily from trying to keep up with the pace. 'Don't forget that I work for a law firm and will be struck off when they find out how I've spent my holiday. How come they didn't find the fake passports?'

'They're hidden in the lining of my bag. Easy to find for someone who's looking, but I must have thrown them off the scent with my somewhat dubious story.'

Upon reaching the station, Kim-Ly, as the only Dutch-speaking member of the party, was despatched to enquire about train times and tickets. She returned two minutes later, in a rather distressed condition. 'We must go, now' she panted, grabbing Terry's arm. 'It is Emre; he has just got off the train from Amsterdam. Please, he cannot see me or we are dead.'

'Is he alone?' asked Robbie. 'I'm sure Terry and I can deal with him.'

'No, he is too dangerous,' said Kim-Ly. 'He will be carrying a gun or a knife. I have seen for myself when they threatened to kill me if I made any more trouble. Oh no, he is coming this way.'

Terry winced in pain as Kim-Ly dug her fingers into his arm and dragged him firmly into the shadows. Robbie and Gemma concealed their hiding place and shuddered as Emre passed without a glance and headed for the station exit.

'Phew, that was close,' said Kim-Ly. 'Please, can we leave here?'

'My God, he even looks evil,' exclaimed Robbie; 'proper pantomime villain with authentic hook-nose and beard.'

'He's behind you,' said Terry.

Robbie jumped and turned. 'Bastard! That's not funny, Terry.'

'Our train leaves in fifteen minutes,' said Kim-Ly. 'The sooner we are out of here the better.'

Sandra was on tenterhooks; they hadn't heard from Terry and the others for twenty-four hours and she was getting very nervous about being in the same place for too long. The hotel was basic, to say the least, and they were itching to move on and avoid detection. She knew that the longer they stayed the more chance there was of being apprehended and brought to justice; whatever that was. Still, they were afraid to venture outside for fear of encountering policemen or pimps. Sandra had assertively marked the hotel manager's card by notifying him that she would have no hesitation in informing his wife if he didn't cease his lecherous pursuit of Celina. Thereafter, their stay had been quiet and uneventful.

Suddenly, the silence was shattered by her phone reverberating around the rudimentary, peeling yellow-walled lounge. It was Terry. Sandra searched the room for inquisitive ears and concluded that they were alone. Pete and Celina looked on in anticipation as she answered. 'Yes, we're still in Gouda; where did you think we'd be. ...? No, we haven't seen two policemen. ... Emre's in town too? Oh, no. ... Rotterdam, yes, OK, as soon as we can, yes. ... By bus, OK. ... And how's Gemma. ...? Well, what did you expect. ...? Yes, we'll call you when we get there. ... Of course we'll be careful. ... Bye.'

Celina had frozen on the mention of Emre's name and she was visibly shaking as Sandra conveyed her conversation with Terry. 'Time to pack and leave quickly, I think. We are to travel by bus to Rotterdam and inform Terry when we get there; he has booked us all onto the 8.30 p.m. ferry to England. As we expected, the police and Emre are on the case and it won't take long for them to track us down. I suggest that Celina and I walk together and Pete, you keep a discreet distance behind us and sit in a different place on the bus. Robbie has got a passport for Celina.'

'Robbie,' said Celina, 'is he a good man?' She looked pensive and alone, as if she were searching for someone to hold on to, someone to take care of her.

'No idea,' replied Sandra. 'Only met him myself yesterday. Comes across as a bit of a rogue, but seems like a nice guy; and he's sure gone to a lot of trouble on our behalf. Why do you ask; do you like him?'

Celina blushed. 'No, just curious, that is all.'

'Well, save your curiosity for another day. This is no game and we can't have any distractions. When we are safe in England, that will be the time to speculate as to whether or not Robbie is a good man.'

Pete looked at the twitchy Celina with concern and asked, 'Are you OK? It's been quite a few days since your last fix. Can you handle all this pressure?'

'It is always there, the need for the heroin. I could not do it vithout your help. Please, promise that you vill not leave me alone.'

'We cannot stay with you forever,' said Sandra. 'Sooner or later you will have to face the demon on your own; but for now we will look after you. When we get to England we will try to get some professional assistance.'

Upon leaving the lounge, they were oblivious as the hotel manager shrank back into the shadows of an alcove. He rubbed his chin in thought and considered the convoluted conversation he'd overheard.

The memories were unbearable and an unwelcome tear ran down his cheek. Emre only had time to kill until there was more information available from his contact in the police and he'd wandered aimlessly among the tourists, before ending up in the municipal park. The sparrows didn't seem to understand that he was a dangerous man and they pecked irritatingly around his feet at the crumbs dropping from his pitta bread. The sky was grey and a gentle breeze carried the shouts and merriment of a group of children, immersed in a boisterous game of football. Three of the boys appeared to be from the same family and he immediately picked out the competitive one, the winner; nothing but victory would suffice for this physical young man, and he cared little about tackling the smaller boys hard. They too would become tougher if they learnt early how to deal with the knocks and bruises that would inevitably come their way in life.

Distant reminiscences resonated around his head and, no matter how he tried to think of other things, they would not go away. He drifted back to his childhood when he, his friends and brothers had played football in the streets of Istanbul, surrounded by gecekondular (the squatter's shacks they called home), built by their fathers on public land at the periphery of the city. They were rural migrants, forced out of their homes by the poverty brought about by an increased mechanisation of agriculture, and there was no option but to adapt quickly to their new environment. Only Arhan could recall a little of their previous life in the country; Emre and Doruk were too young to remember anything but the dust and delinquency of the urban sprawl.

Their father had worked hard in small-scale industry whenever he could and, though their shoes pinched their feet because they were generally two sizes too small and were stuffed with cardboard to cover the holes, there was usually food on the table. As time took its toll and their father increasingly had to turn down physical work, the brothers grew adept at surviving on the streets and fighting for their territory. Petty theft soon followed, leading to extortion and dealing in stolen goods. With scant parental control, the boys ran wild and vowed to escape their insufficiency

141

through foul means or fair; no longer would they cower and scrimp for morsels in the slums.

Their childhood had been too short; they'd had no choice but to grow up rapidly in order to endure, and Emre listened enviously to the carefree laughter of the budding footballers before him. He'd give anything to go back to those days of kicking a ball around the streets of Istanbul with his brothers. But things were as they were, and a passing couple quickened their pace as an involuntary growl emanated from the depths of Emre's throat; they would die for what they have done – these people who dared to break up the terrible trilogy of Arhan, Emre and Doruk. Make no mistake; someone would pay for this disrespect to his family.

15.

It was only a matter of time before Bomkamp and Van Otterloo happened upon Sandra, Pete and Celina's recent accommodation. Their feet were sore with traipsing from dump to dive and they'd almost given up hope of picking up the trail. If they hadn't wasted time stopping that dubious-looking travelling sex-toy salesman, then they would have apprehended the suspects in that guest-house on Lage Gouwe, but they were long gone before they'd questioned the fuming owner. 'What are the police for if you cannot catch criminals like this who do not pay their bills? I am an honest citizen and demand justice.'

Now, as they entered the sleazy-looking hotel, Bomkamp took an immediate dislike to the manager. 'What do you make of this character, then?' he whispered as they approached.

'He is like an oily cross between Rigsby and Count Dracula,' answered Van Otterloo.

Deriving great pleasure in keeping them in suspense about his lately departed guests, this slimy fellow seemed to revel in the power of his knowledge.

'Yes, there was an English couple here, along with another, um, lady. They left about four hours ago. I thought there was something suspicious about them; on edge all the time and they accused me of lechery. Can you imagine such a thing?'

'Not for a moment,' said Bomkamp. 'Did they happen to

mention where they were going?'

'Not directly, but I may have overheard something if you would care to lubricate my memory.'

Bomkamp pulled a wad of notes from his back pocket and held them tightly beneath the hotel manager's nose. 'Look, we have no time to play games; tell us what you heard.'

'No need for that tone of voice, officer. I am happy to help the constabulary. They received a phone call and, from their side of the conversation, I ascertained that they were to go to Rotterdam by bus and thereafter there was talk of a ferry. That is all I can tell you, honest.'

Bomkamp peeled one note from the wad and smiled through gritted teeth. 'Thank you for your assistance. How would we ever catch criminals were it not for fine, upstanding members of the public like yourself? Come on, Van Otterloo, we have a train to catch.'

Bomkamp looked puzzled as they left the hotel and began their brisk walk to the station. 'So, who is Rigsby?'

'Rigsby?'

'Rigsby, yes. You mentioned him in your description of the hotel manager; you said he was like a cross between Rigsby and Dracula.'

Van Otterloo furrowed his brow. 'I have absolutely no idea, sir. These words are not my own; they are put into my mouth by the Creator.'

'What, you mean God?'

'Well, in a way I suppose he is as far as we are concerned. The creator of this book has given us life and he can just as easily take it away.'

'And do you think he will, take it away, I mean?' asked Bomkamp.

'Who knows? He has already killed off two peripheral characters and I suspect there will be more to come. We must continue to keep him amused; then I think we will be OK.'

'Do you think he is a good god?'

'The jury is still out on that one. It remains to be seen whether or not the good guys win. We must thank God that it is only us in his charge and not the rest of the world; then we would be in real trouble.'

'But which God should we thank?'

'The real one, of course; this guy is just an imposter.'

Bomkamp nodded in agreement. 'It looks like the story may be heading for England. Do you think he will take us too?'

'Perhaps he will find a way. Have you ever been before, sir?'

'No, but I would like to see London. I understand that their policemen wear boob-shaped helmets.'

'So I believe. Perchance there we will find out who Rigsby is.'

As their train left the station, Bomkamp reported back to base, leaving only the information that he wanted Emre to know and nothing more.

'You want to go shopping at a time like this?' exclaimed Terry in disbelief.

'Yeah; why not?' answered Gemma. 'The boat doesn't sail for hours yet and we'll be more likely to blend in with crowds of shoppers, than if we hang around at the docks looking suspicious. Besides, I have to get a present for Daniel; it's his birthday next week.'

'Hmm, what do you get for the boy who has everything?'

'What do you mean by that?'

'Well, you can't deny that he's a little spoilt. I know he's your Godson, but he's a pain in the butt at the best of times and he always gets his own way. What are you going to get him; have you got any ideas?'

'He likes ball games and Frisbees; thought I'd get him something he can throw.'

'What, like a tantrum?'

Kim-Ly stood back and observed the exchange of banter, borne of a familiarity that could only be derived from many years of bonding and intimacy. She felt uncomfortable, like an outsider eavesdropping on a private conversation. It was obvious that nobody on this planet knew Terry better than Gemma; it was a friendship that could never be replaced. Despite Terry's reassurances, Kim-Ly still had her doubts about their long-term prospects. When would Terry begin to question her about her past, about how many men she had been with? At the moment he seemed to be blind: he saw only the good in her and would not contemplate that she was anything less than perfect. She owed Terry everything and for the first time since her childhood she had hope for the future; with the courage to dream again, to consider the prospect of home and a reunion with her family. Would Terry want her to stay with him in London or would he come with her if she returned to Vietnam, to a culture and language he knew nothing about? It was too much to ask, wasn't it?

Preoccupied with her speculations, she looked up to see Terry's smiling face before her. 'You OK?' he asked. 'Not long before we get on that boat, you know, and you can leave your old life behind forever.'

Kim-Ly kept her thoughts to herself and smiled back. 'I know, but I will not feel safe until we get to England and maybe not even there; the police, they co-operate internationally and Emre, he will not stand for the death of his brothers. It would be no surprise if he followed us too.'

'When we get home I will ensure that we sort out this mess,' answered Terry. 'I don't know how yet, but I will keep you safe. Perhaps we can ask for police protection in the UK.'

He called it home, but could it ever be her home too? 'But Terry, you have killed someone and so has Celina; how can we go to the police?'

'Yeah, guess you have a point there. I just know that we can't stay in Holland; things will be better back home.'

Home, there was that word again.

Gemma was right: the shops were buzzing and cosmopolitan, and they could hide more effectively here until boarding time.

Boutiques of all colours and varieties flaunted designer gear and taunted them with their ridiculous prices. Kim-Ly was seduced by a sensory style overload of Gucci, Armani, Yves Saint Laurent and there, in the arcade, they found a shop that filled Robbie with excitement.

'Hey, look at all those Fred Perry's!' he exclaimed. 'I've got to take a look in there.' Kim-Ly, Terry and Gemma followed reluctantly. 'Now this is real style,' continued Robbie, as happy as a pig in the proverbial. 'I want to buy the whole rack.'

'Pick one and I'll get it for you,' offered Terry. 'Least I can do after what you've done for us. Then let's move on; we shouldn't linger in one place too long.'

'Cheers, mate, I'll take this one,' smiled Robbie, holding up a black number with purple and yellow trimming, the familiar emblem picked out in purple on the left breast. Still he stared with eyes agape, sighing in fiscal resignation at each store they passed. 'Bloody hell, you need to be a millionaire to shop here, although there are some good bargains on shoes; they're all buy-one-get-one-free.'

Terry insisted on buying Kim-Ly some new clothes too. 'You only have a few bits and pieces,' he said, 'pick another outfit at least.' They wandered from shop to shop, before she decided upon a pair of faded blue jeans and a couple of plain white t-shirts. As far as she could see, it was only the labels that made them more expensive and she was sure that Terry flinched as he settled the bill.

Kim-Ly kept a watchful eye on the passing punters outside the window, imagining paranoiac visions of Emre with his face pressed against the glass. If it were a choice between being arrested by those two clowns masquerading as policemen, as Robbie had described them, or encountering Emre again, then she would choose arrest every time. Then back among the crowds she assessed every transient stranger, whilst trying to keep her head down and remain anonymous. Again she took in all the beautiful clothes, shoes and bags that festooned each display and her head span with the temptation of it all. She could be a classy lady in that dress; she could be comfortable in any company with that handbag; and those high-heels were the perfect match. Fluorescence here, pastels there, the serene expressions of shop window dummies, as each delicately placed outfit seamlessly hugged their perfect figures in a never-ending parade of lights and logos. Where would life's breeze blow Kim-Ly; to Western commercialisation or to Eastern simplicity? A jumbled confusion filled her head as she followed the others aimlessly through the buffeting crowds.

The bustling bus station was the ideal place to slip the leash and Celina had planned her escape long before they got there. Maybe Sandra and Pete had grown to trust her, to believe that she was over the worst of the withdrawal and that she would not betray their faith. It was far too easy to make her excuses and visit the bathroom, then to slip out the back entrance and disappear into the multitude of commuters and tourists. It was too easy to drift into the less salubrious part of town and to recognise the girl on the corner as a like-minded soul, on the game and dependent on her lord and master. It was too easy to extract the information she required, to find the place to score and to leap from the frying pan into the fire. Yes, she felt a tinge of guilt at leaving her newfound friends in the lurch, but she was in desperate need of a fix and nobody was going to stand in her way.

The barman looked her up and down with an expression of both admiration and suspicion as he smiled crookedly and pointed the way to the back of the bar. 'Ask for Mijnheer Angenent; he may be able to help you.'

Dark and dingy, this was an establishment built on dodgy dealings, with an abundance of cobweb-infested shadowy nooks in which to tender illicit trade. Stale sweat and sour alcohol filled the stagnant air and every fake mahogany surface was covered in dust. Celina knew what she had to do and, as much as it felt wrong, the desire for heroin was overbearing all other thoughts. Heads turned in instant appraisal as she passed the bar's motley customers and employees; an appreciative growl from a grubby, unshaven old punter, a nod of recognition from a hard-faced, but attractive girl in black hot-pants and skimpy bra; and there, holding counsel with a group of hangers-on, stood the ample frame of the owner. Ice rattled in his tumbler as he took a swig of amber liquid and his conversation stopped in its tracks at the approach of Celina.

'Can I be of assistance, young lady?'

'Mijnheer Angenent?'

'It depends who is asking.'

'My name is Celina. Can ve talk in private?'

'This way,' he indicated, with a barely noticeable nod towards the rear exit.

Celina shivered as they emerged through a creaky door, into the cool air of an enclosed and cluttered yard. Mijnheer Angenent undressed her with his eyes and enquired, 'And what do you want of me?'

The flush of a nearby toilet delayed her reply and a young man leered as he passed them and returned to the bar. Celina's attention reverted to the matter in hand and she came straight to the point. 'I am told that you can obtain drugs here; vill you sell some to me?'

Mijnheer Angenent took her left hand in his clammy palm and rolled up her sleeve. 'I assume that heroin is your poison; and can you afford my prices?'

Celina hung her head and her voice emanated as a husky whisper. 'I have no money, but there are other vays in vhich I can pay.'

Mijnheer Angenent licked his lips lecherously and, breathing heavily, he led her to the back of the outhouse. 'I am sure we can come to some arrangement. Wait here and I will return in five minutes.'

As she listened to his retreating footsteps and the creak of the door, Celina took in her surroundings: the weeds growing through cracked flagstones, the tall brick walls that seemed to be coming closer each time she blinked, the broken glass swept into the corner, along with discarded Shiraz wine boxes. A tear came to her eye as she realised once more what she had become; soon he would return with all the familiar paraphernalia required to feed her addiction. Should she run now, back to the sanctuary of her friends; to the promised new life in England; to Robbie, Sandra, Pete, Terry, Gemma and to her dearest friend, Kim-Ly?

Too late, Mijnheer Angenent stood before her with a grubby cloth for a tourniquet, a loaded syringe and a benevolent smile. 'Just to prove that I am an honourable man, I will give you your shot before I take payment; that way, perhaps, you will be more relaxed in my company.'

Shuddering at the thought of what she would have to do for this fix, Celina proffered her arm and closed her eyes. What was one more fuck, after all? She felt the tourniquet tighten and his sausage-like fingers searching for an undamaged vein, the accustomed sharp prick of the needle and the pressure as the venom coursed through her blood and her whole body shook with relief. She had little time to enjoy the experience before he was upon her; his fat gut overhanging his belt; his unshaven face on her neck; the stench of whisky, halitosis and perspiration combined nauseously with the pungent urine from the drains; one hand pummelling her breast and the other up her skirt; her back scraping painfully against the rough brick wall as he entered. Celina barely felt a thing as the thin rubber prevented a second injection of poison. At least it was over quickly, she thought, as she whimpered and slid down the wall, her head in her hands.

Mijnheer Angenent stood above her with a satisfied grin and wiped the sweat from his brow. 'Now, that wasn't so bad, was it?' he laughed, as he pulled up his pants. 'You are very good and have passed the audition; how would you like to work for me? You can earn good money and I look after my girls.'

'Thank you for the offer,' sobbed Celina, 'but I have friends to meet and a boat to catch.'

'That is a real shame; we could make a great team and become rich together. You are one of the best and obviously very experienced; we could charge high for your services.'

Celina sank back into the shadows as she heard that door creaking once more and footsteps on the flagstones. An apologetic head poked round the corner. 'Sorry to interrupt, Boss' said the barman, 'but there is a man in the bar who wants to speak to you. He looks like trouble.'

Mijnheer Angenent stared down at Celina. 'Nothing to do with you, I hope.'

The heroin-induced paranoia kicked in and Celina cried, 'No, no, he could not find me here. Please, please, don't let him take me back there.'

'So who is he, this man that you are so scared of?'

Her fear was inexorable. 'His name is Emre, my old pimp from Amsterdam. I have run away and he is looking for me; but how vould he know that I am here?'

'Well, presumably he knows that you are an addict. Perhaps he simply asked where to score, as you did, and is visiting all the likely places. What does he look like?'

Shaking with fear, Celina gave them a comprehensive description, painting him in an evil light and leaving no doubt as to his reputation.

'That sounds like our man,' said the barman; 'just from your portrayal of his prominent proboscis I would have recognised him.'

'Please, do not tell him that I am here,' pleaded Celina; 'he vill kill me if he finds me. I promise, if you get rid of him, then I vill vork for you.'

'And what is the worth of a junkie's promise?' sneered Mijnheer Angenent. 'If I take the property of a fellow businessman, then he will be very angry with me. How do I know you are worth the trouble?'

'You already know how good I am,' reasoned Celina. 'I promise that I vill make it vorth your vhile to help me. You vill not regret it, honestly.'

Mijnheer Angenent considered her words and her beauty and, fresh from the satisfaction of copulation, conceded, 'OK, OK, I will speak with him and hear his side of the story; I do not make any promises.' He spun and made his way back to the bar, closely followed by the barman.

'Please, I beg you, do not betray me,' pleaded Celina once more as they disappeared and she was left pathetically at their mercy.

Through the crack in the door she watched nervously as Mijnheer Angenent shook hands with the unmistakable figure of Emre. The barman proffered a generous glass of whisky, which Emre downed in one and slammed down on the bar. Celina shuddered as Emre depicted an hour-glass figure with both hands, then raised one hand above his head to indicate her height. Celina turned and regarded the yard, desperate for any possible means of escape; there was no way out. Returning her gaze to the drama before her, she observed the angry gesticulations of Emre and the sympathetic ear of Mijnheer Angenent, as the conversation continued unabated to its conclusion. The suspense was killing her, until Mijnheer Angenent hesitated and, eventually, shook his head. Emre cursed in frustration and handed over his card. Mijnheer Angenent nodded seriously and led Emre to the exit with a friendly arm around his shoulder. She had escaped his clutches once more. How many lives did she have left?

Celina considered her situation through a drug-induced haze, then gasped in disbelief as a sheepish-looking Pete entered the bar. Mijnheer Angenent greeted him curiously. Obviously out of place and nervous, Pete's eyes darted from one punter to another and his expression showed distaste at the dubious nature of this slovenly saloon. Unconsciously, he mimicked Emre's picture by outlining Celina's hourglass figure with both hands then, with one hand above his head, he too indicated her uncommon height.

Again a vacant shake of the head from Mijnheer Angenent, an arm around the shoulder and Pete was gently shown the way out.

The tears ran like rain; tears of relief, of desperation, of regret, of sadness. How had she been so easily trapped again; would she ever have another chance of escape from this degenerate life? Celina felt helpless; she thought about running after Pete, but that would put him in danger; and besides, Emre would still be in the vicinity. Her legs were barely functioning as she tried to stand up straight to face her new owner, as he stood smugly before her.

'It seems that you are a very popular young lady,' observed Mijnheer Angenent, once the coast was clear. 'And who was the second man?'

Celina hung her head in shame. 'Pete is a good man. He and his vife have helped me to stay clean and now their efforts have been vasted. I vill never forgive myself for letting them down.'

'That is what junkies do, isn't it? Let people down. Now, I have done you not one, but two very big favours and, from this moment on you are beholden to me. Let us discuss how you will repay the debt. I am sure that this is just the beginning of a beautiful and prosperous relationship.'

Early evening drizzle dampened their clothes and their spirits. Robbie looked at his watch and turned to Terry as they checked the glum ferry queue once more. 'They're cutting it a bit fine, aren't they; are you sure they know where to come?'

'Yes, I gave Sandra all the details and the boarding deadline. Don't worry, they'll be here.'

Kim-Ly looked unconvinced. 'Something has happened to Celina; I can feel it. Please, call Sandra and find out what is wrong.' Terry nodded, removed his phone from his pocket and began to dial.

'Wait, there they are,' pointed Gemma, 'but there are only two of them.' She waved and a dejected Sandra and Pete joined them at the dockside.

'I'm sorry, but we lost her,' said Sandra. 'We should have known she would try to get away, but we thought we'd gained her trust. She must have been desperate. Pete has been to all the dodgy places in town, but no-one is admitting to seeing her.'

'I can honestly say that I have been to the kind of bars and taverns that I never want to frequent again,' confirmed Pete. 'I feel even more grubby than usual. I'm truly sorry, Kim-Ly, but I have looked everywhere.'

Dozens of seagulls cried plaintively above their heads as if lamenting the loss of another soul.

'I must go,' sobbed Kim-Ly. 'I will find where she is.'

Terry looked on in amazement as Gemma placed a gentle arm around her shoulder and reasoned. 'No, she is a grown woman and there comes a time when people must be responsible for their own actions. Sandra and Pete have done their best, at no small risk and inconvenience to themselves. Celina has been given the opportunity to escape and has chosen to go back to her old lifestyle. What would be the benefit of you going back too? You would simply become trapped with her; different city, different pimp, but the same despairing results. Then everything we have all gone through will be to no avail. Please, we are almost on the boat; don't leave now.'

Kim-Ly hesitated as she reflected on Gemma's words, then sighed. 'I guess you are right; we cannot watch over her forever. But why are you persuading me to stay? This was your opportunity to be rid of me forever and have Terry to yourself again.'

'No, the stupid fool would have gone with you. At least this way I can keep an eye on him.'

Terry looked Gemma in the eye. 'Thanks.'

'Don't mention it. Now we'd best get in that queue before she changes her mind – we have a ferry to catch.'

They waited in silence, shuffling forward each time the line made progress towards their transport to salvation, looking nervously over their shoulders for evidence of pimp or police. The huge white ship, with P&O picked out in blue, filled their vision. Soon it would take them away from Holland; a land of sexual liberty for some, but of enslavement for others. In fact, no different from any other country in that respect; it was simply a question of degree. So much could still go wrong: they could be stopped at Customs and Kim-Ly's fake passport detected; the police could have alerted the ports to apprehend this motley crew of fugitives; Emre or the comedy cop duo could have picked up their trail from Gouda and would scupper their escape at the last minute.

Now that they were close to boarding, their breathing grew heavier, a restless anxiety prevailed and they just wanted to be away from here, attempting to remain anonymous, just another bunch of travellers, no different from anyone else in the line; then, without warning, the peace and their anonymity was shattered by a cry of 'Hey, vait for me!'

'Celina!' cried Kim-Ly. All heads turned to view the ever-striking figure striding along the gangway towards them.

'That's it,' exclaimed an exasperated Pete, 'we're bound to be stopped now.'

With a relieved smile, Sandra grabbed Celina as she approached and whispered through gritted teeth. 'For God's sake, stop making such a scene; we're trying to remain inconspicuous here. I think you may have blown our cover.'

To their amazement, the young Customs officer blushed bright red as Kim-Ly and Celina hugged; instantly smitten, he took a cursory glance at their passports and waved them all through.

'Jesus, that was close,' grinned Sandra. 'Where the hell have you been?'

'I am sorry, I just got a little lost for a vhile,' replied Celina, as she pulled a wad of notes from her pocket. 'Now, I believe there is a casino on this boat.'

'So I'm told,' said Robbie, linking arms with Celina to a disapproving glare from Gemma. 'We may as well make use of the amenities.'

155

They arrived at the dock within minutes of each other: Bomkamp and Van Otterloo first, closely followed by Emre; and then, breathing heavily from the exertion of running from the bus, Mijnheer Angenent. They all cursed in frustration as the ferry pulled away from the quay.

A fuming Emre addressed Bomkamp first – 'Does your incompetence know no bounds? How could you let them get away? You will pay for this; your reputation will lie in ruins. I have protected you for too long; now it is time to let your wife and colleagues know the kind of man you are.'

There was disappointment in Van Otterloo's eyes, the implications of Emre's utterances hitting home and deflating his estimation of his boss; a man he'd always looked up to. Bomkamp appeared to shrink before his eyes.

Emre directed his attention to Mijnheer Angenent. 'And what the hell are you doing here if, as you assured me, you know nothing of the minx Celina?'

'I too have been duped,' gasped Mijnheer Angenent. 'I am sorry; if I had known of her duplicitous nature, then I would have turned her over to you. I have been fooled by her dubious charms; she has robbed and made a clown of me. I left her to wash glasses behind the bar while my barman ran an errand, I turned my back for a minute and she was gone with all the cash from the register.'

Emre raged and shook his fists at the departing ferry. Was that Celina he saw through the mist, smiling through a window and with her middle finger raised in defiance? 'This is not over,' he seethed, as he addressed Bomkamp. 'You are no longer any use to me. From now on I will work alone; and they best hope that you get to them before I do.'

Emre turned and, in one movement, slammed his knuckles into the surprised face of Mijnheer Angenent, the blood spurting profusely from his nose as he fell heavily to the floor. A foghorn hooted derisorily through the gloom, as Emre strode resolutely away and vanished into the recently disembarked crowd. As he walked, he pulled his phone from the depths of his inside pocket and called his cousin in England.

Mesmerised as the roulette wheel rotated before her, Celina's vision was blurred and the clatter of the little metal ball echoed noisily between her ears. The busy casino was buzzing with anticipation and suspense as an array of predominantly inebriated punters placed their bets. She wobbled slightly as the croupier spun the wheel of hope once more and groaned as, again, the ball fell into the wrong number. The room seemed to be closing in around her and, in the stifling body-heat, she was overcome by a feeling of claustrophobic anxiety.

'You OK?' asked Robbie, taking a sip of his Courvoisier. 'You look a bit pale.'

'Please, excuse me,' answered Celina, 'I must get some air.'

Without waiting for Robbie's answer, she staggered erratically towards the exit, bumping against the shoulder of a large, indignant man in her hurry. Robbie apologised on her behalf as he rushed to follow.

Inhaling deep gulps of cool air as she gratefully reached the deck, Celina held on to the rail for support and gazed with vacant eyes at the full moon, darting between the clouds above the horizon. She stood for a few minutes as relative calm filled her senses, thankful for Robbie's supportive arm. Then, without warning, an excruciating pain in her chest bent her double as her body protested at the unrelenting abuse it had been subjected to; and she slipped slowly to the floor in unbearable agony. The last thing she saw was Robbie's panic-stricken face as she drifted gradually from consciousness.

No nightmares this time; no more silent screams, no floating, diving, thrashing around among desperate corpses as she sunk into a watery abyss. Gone were the evil expressions of Emre and

157

his brothers; gone was the revolting figure of Mijnheer Angenent and all of the other disgusting devils disguised as human beings. No longer would they stand over her with their self-satisfied grins as they wiped themselves down, pulled up their pants and left without so much as a thank you. No; this time she was at peace as she prepared for perpetual sleep and whatever lay beyond. The timeworn fog lifted from her soul and her entire being filled with harmony and tranquillity. Life could hurt her no more.

At first the jolts didn't register and she was blissfully oblivious to the cruel intrusion on her serenity. Semi-conscious sounds interrupted her sleep and someone was throwing her a line, a way back to reality, to an unkind, unrelenting world. Did she want to return; was there any point; any purpose to her existence?

'Stand back! Shock!' she heard, and her whole body jerked once more; a flicker of recognition of where she was, of what had happened. 'Stand back! Shock!' Blurred outlines of faces began to take focus and she gasped as she felt the blood coursing through her veins and her heart beating once more. It was Robbie's concerned face that she saw first, before Kim-Ly rushed to her side with tears of rage in her eyes.

'You stupid girl!' she shouted. 'I thought we had lost you. What have you put into your body now that causes this? Do you not know that there are people who care about you? You must stop now or there may not be anyone to save you next time.' Kim-Ly turned to the relieved lady who was packing away the defibrillator. 'Thank you so much. I do not know if my friend deserves your act of mercy, but you have given her yet another chance to live; we can only hope that she uses it wisely this time.'

'That's what I'm here for. I will ensure that there is an ambulance waiting when we dock and, in the meantime, I suggest your friend spends the remainder of the trip in the first-aid room, so that I can monitor her recovery. I have to complete a report and I will need some details.'

'No ambulances, please,' pleaded Celina, in fear of the

inevitable questions that would follow. 'I vill be fine. I thank you for saving my life, but I vill take responsibility from now on.'

'I would strongly recommend that you get to a hospital as soon as possible. They will undertake tests to discover the cause of your collapse.'

'She's right,' said Robbie, 'you should get yourself checked out; this isn't a game, you know, and we'll all come with you.'

'I said no ambulances and no hospitals. I know vhat is wrong and I promise this vill not happen again.'

'I have heard it before,' sneered Kim-Ly. 'What is the worth of your promises?'

Overwhelmed, Celina burst into uncontrollable tears and held her friend tightly. 'I mean it, Kim-Ly. It has never been this bad before; the heroin must have been contaminated. I *vill* change, I promise.'

16.

They all slept fitfully for the remainder of the journey, with the unfamiliar gentle swell of the ship and the not-too-distant nightmares of recent events fresh in their minds; each had a different perspective and each had their own fears and hopes.

And what of Hull? A fleeting visit, taking in the port and the bus station. They knew that their pursuers were likely to be on their tail at the earliest opportunity, so they didn't hang around to take in the local culture. And a weak and sunken-cheeked Celina still stubbornly refused to visit the hospital.

A six-and-a-half hour National Express trip was to follow, spent deep in thought and in watching the world flash past; by all but Terry. The bus was about half-full and he found himself a seat on his own near the back, not daring to sit with either Gemma or Kim-Ly for fear of upsetting either one. Kim-Ly sat beside an anxious and withdrawn Celina; occasionally she would turn and smile at him, causing his heart to melt anew. Gemma stubbornly ignored Robbie's efforts to cheer her up and simply stared straight ahead in a seething silence. Sandra rested her head on Pete's shoulder and they both looked lost, as if it were dawning that they could never return to their beloved home in Amsterdam.

Terry watched them all and contemplated once more the damage he'd caused by caring about a complete stranger. Did he regret coming to Kim-Ly's rescue? Could he have predicted what had transpired? How could he ever hope to repay the kindness and loyalty shown by these good people; not least Gemma, who'd been wonderful throughout? His heart was torn in two as he remembered why he had fallen in love with her in the first place. How could he be so cruel as to repay her devotion with rejection and heartbreak?

Despairingly, he focused his mind on the practicalities by calling ahead to make some temporary arrangements; the hapless Barry's friendship not the first to be exploited during this extraordinary escapade. 'Hello, mate,' said Terry, as if nothing had happened and he was phoning to invite him for a beer. 'How are you?'

'On the mend, thanks, and mobile again; back at work part-time. They've given me a few jobs with Charlie, the ambulance chaser, but it's not the same; hate to say it, in case your head gets too big, but I'm missing our old assignments. Where are you?'

'We're on the way home; should be in London this afternoon. Listen, mate, I need a few favours.' Terry thought that if he used the word 'mate' enough times then Barry would be more accommodating.

'That sounds ominous,' replied Barry. 'The last time I saw you, you'd upset some particularly nasty individuals and were striding off into the sunset for a new life on the Orient, as it were. OK, how can I be of assistance?'

'Well, you know you were telling me that you were sick and tired of living alone.'

'I know what you're going to say: that you've found me that Halle Berry lookalike and she's feeling lonely too.'

'Er, not exactly,' said Terry. 'I need some short-term accommodation for a few friends. Do you still have your spare room and sofa-bed?'

'Yes, the last time I looked, the spare room was uninhabited and the sofa-bed is still where I fall asleep in front of the TV every evening. How many friends, who are they and how long do you consider to be short-term?' asked a sceptical-sounding Barry.

'Well, you remember that I told you about Sandra and Pete, lovely couple and completely house-trained; and then there's Celina, a friend of Kim-Ly's.'

'When you say a friend of Kim-Ly's, do you mean from the same profession?'

'I can't deny that she has a similar background, but she's a reformed character; I think. It's just until we can sort out more permanent digs for them all. Please, mate, I'm desperate.' There was that word 'mate' again.

Barry sighed. 'OK, but no longer than a week and you can underwrite any costs, or disruption to my humble home.'

'Barry, I've been round to your place, remember. No-one would notice any disruption.'

'Don't push it. I've said yes, haven't I? Against my better judgement.'

'Thanks, mate, I really appreciate it.'

'Don't mention it; and you can stop calling me mate now you've got what you want.'

'OK, mate. Are you going in to the office today?'

'Yes I am, as it happens; have to see Chris to get my next assignment. Why, do you have a message for him?'

'No, not yet,' said Terry. 'I'll come in and face the music in the next few days. Could you look something up in the archives for me?'

'I guess so. What is it?'

'Do you remember that scandal of the English professor and the prostitute a few years ago?'

'Yeah, I think so. What was the headline? "Professor Prefers Prostitute to Proust"?'

'Hmm, I'd forgotten that. Well, I need to track down our disgraced don. A name would be a good start, but if you can find out what happened to him, where he disappeared to; that would be even better.'

'You don't want much, do you? Look, I'll see what I can do,

162

but Chris might start asking questions. I'm a photographer, not a journalist.'

'Thanks, mate, really appreciate it. I'll see you later with your new guests.'

'Can't wait,' said Barry.

Terry made his way along the bus to impart the good news and was surprised by the lack of gratitude. Now that there was a lull in proceedings, it appeared that the individual consequences of their adventure were sinking in. 'It'll do for now,' said Pete, 'and we will be thankful to Barry for his hospitality; but we've lost our home and our belongings, Terry, probably for good. Where do we go from here?'

Terry had no answer, and Kim-Ly hung her head.

After a while, Kim-Ly drifted off to sleep and Gemma asked to speak with him alone. They made their way to the back seat, the other passengers turning in curiosity. 'So, this is it then,' she said. 'When we get off this bus and go our separate ways, there's no turning back. Are you sure you're doing the right thing?'

'Oh, Gemma, I don't know. Pete told me to follow my heart, but it's split down the middle.'

'Well, you can't have us both,' decreed Gemma. 'It's final decision time.'

'And how do you feel?' asked Terry, trying to delay the inevitable.

'I think you know how I feel. I came all the way to Holland to get you back. I've suffered the humiliation of watching you together and I've even become friends with Kim-Ly. It tears me apart to think of you with another.'

'Now you know how it was for me, when you ran off with Sam,' replied Terry, immediately regretting the cheap shot.

'So, is that what this is all about: revenge?'

'Definitely not. You know I'm not a vindictive person.'

'Yeah, I guess so,' conceded Gemma. 'Is it because she is younger than me?'

'No, I don't think of you as any older than when we first met; but neither of us are the same person as we were in Cedarwood Comprehensive. Why does life have to be so complicated? It all seemed so black and white back then; we both knew what we wanted and where we were going.'

Gemma looked him in the eye and all their history flashed before him. 'It's still black and white for me. I have to admit that it turned a few shades of grey for a while, but now I'm certain that I know what I want.'

'How many shades of grey?'

'Oh, a lot less than forty,' smiled Gemma, then her expression hardened. 'It's me or her, Terry; simple as that. You have until the end of this journey to make up your mind.' And, without further ado and with head held high, she made her way back to her seat. Terry watched his first love attempt to stride with dignity down the aisle; until the bus swerved to the left and she landed in a stranger's lap. She stood apologetically, brushed herself down and continued less confidently. Terry would have sniggered were it not for the seriousness of the situation and, with her ultimatum still ringing in his ears, he curled up in a ball in an effort to shut out the world.

Before he knew it, they'd arrived and the mid-afternoon melee of Victoria Coach Station battered his senses. All kinds of people were moving in all manner of directions, some alone, some in couples, some in groups; each going about their daily business, apparently deciding upon their course with little consideration. A young man kissed his girl goodbye as she boarded her bus; it could have been Gemma and him when she'd left for University a lifetime ago.

Terry stood alone and looked from Kim-Ly to Gemma, from Gemma to Kim-Ly; and the others observed silently, curious as to which way he would jump. He felt paralysed in body and mind, not even noticing as a fly buzzed erratically around his head. He swept his hair from his eye and scratched his nose; he put his hand in his pocket and rattled his change; and all the time his brain barely functioned, not a rational thought to be had. All noise was reduced to a dull background hum and thud, unintelligible, as if he were awaking slowly from a bad dream; and in such a state he was expected to make the most important choice of his life. It was impossible.

Then suddenly it was all over, taken out of his hands. In the end, Terry didn't make the decision; it was made for him as Kim-Ly could stand it no longer and rushed to be by his side. Gemma simply tugged at Robbie's sleeve and they both turned away without spotting the tear in Terry's eye. He stared sadly after them, Gemma sullenly shaking off Robbie's arm of comfort. There was no turning back.

'Been on holiday?' asked the back of the taxi-driver's head.

'Yeah, kind of,' answered Sandra, 'a holiday we'll never forget; now it's back to reality and England.'

'Nothing wrong with England,' declared the taxi-driver; 'best country in the world.'

Sandra was in the mood for a petty argument and this hackneyed old cabbie was as good a victim as any. 'I assume from the fact that you appear to know where you are going that you have done the Knowledge, but may I ask what knowledge you have of the rest of the globe, to be so confident about proclaiming England to be the best?'

'Hey, I've been abroad: Spain, Tenerife and Calais. No place like home, though.'

Home; where was that? Sandra stared through the window as the familiar trappings of suburbia flashed by; a place she thought she'd escaped forever. There were the semi-detached mock-Tudor houses with the immaculate Audis and BMWs in the drive, the pristine white nets in the windows and symmetrical gardens, the nanny looking after the kids while the occupants were at work. Oh, how she regretted those lost years that could never be reclaimed;

when work and social progress had seemed more important than time to spend with her son. She gripped Pete's hand a little too tight and he flinched in pain.

'You OK?' he asked. He seemed to sense her thoughts as he said softly, 'We will get out of here, you know; there's no way you're going to be entrapped in the trappings of your old life again. I know how much you loved living on that boat and so did I; maybe we can never return to Amsterdam, but there are other places yet to be discovered. Look upon it as a chance to try somewhere new.'

Terry and Kim-Ly looked suitably guilty at being the cause of her unhappiness and said nothing. Celina shivered in the corner, a manic and desperate look in her eye. Sandra had no doubt as to the reason for her brief disappearance and it was obvious that she was in withdrawal again. Sandra resolved to forget her own problems for a while and concentrate on sorting out this unholy mess.

The cab weaved past the stylish part of the urban sprawl and into a slightly less salubrious area: Barry's neighbourhood; still pretty posh, but just a few steps away from squatter territory. It never ceased to amaze Sandra that, in any half-a-mile of London, you were as close to poverty as to prosperity.

Nobody paid them any mind as they disembarked, bade the cabbie good day and approached Barry's door; no answer. A quick call from Terry determined that their host was still at work and would be with them in about an hour; in the meantime, he could recommend the Spotted Dog: fine ale and good pub grub at reasonable prices.

Having availed themselves of the cordiality of the local hostelry, where they'd been viewed with curiosity by the regulars, they returned to Barry's in time for his arrival. 'You took your time,' said Terry.

'Good to see you too,' replied Barry. 'I've been looking through the archives as you requested. No pleasing some people.'

Terry grabbed his hand and shook it vigorously. 'Great to be back; and thanks for helping out. Promise I'll make it up to you.'

After brief introductions, they made their way inside, Sandra recoiling at the disarray before her. Discarded takeaway containers, beer bottles and socks adorned every available surface and cobwebs hung from every lampshade. 'Please accept my apologies for the state of the place,' said Barry, as he discreetly shoved a pair of underpants behind a cushion. 'I wasn't expecting guests.'

Sandra took a deep breath and immediately regretted it, as the stale air caught the back of her throat. Even Celina and Kim-Ly, who were used to the slovenly nature of some men, wrinkled their noses in distaste.

'I'll do a deal with you, Barry,' offered Sandra. 'In return for your hospitality, we'll attempt to make this place habitable again. What do you say?'

'Fine by me,' said Barry; 'that's what this place has always lacked: a woman's touch.'

'Oh, it'll have that alright,' replied Sandra, 'but you can help too. What good will it do if we spend the week renovating the place, if you simply return it to its current state as soon as we're gone? I consider it my mission to teach you to look after yourself before we depart.'

Barry looked apprehensively at Terry. 'Thanks, mate, that's just what I need: a mother figure.'

'It'll do you good,' laughed Terry. 'Pete will testify to the soul-saving qualities of Sandra, the Patron Saint of Hopeless Cases. He tells me he was almost beyond redemption before they met. Now look at him; did you ever see such a clean-living and wholesome specimen?'

'I survived the exorcism,' said Pete, 'but it does get a little tiresome, polishing Sandra's halo.' He ducked just in time, as Sandra aimed a playful swipe at his left ear.

'Now make yourselves scarce the three of you,' demanded

Sandra. 'I want to talk to Kim-Ly and Celina alone. I'm sure Barry has some beer in the kitchen.'

'It comes to something, when you're being ordered about in your own home,' complained Barry, as he handed both Terry and Pete a bottle of San Miguel.

'You'll get used to it,' said Pete. 'I had to.'

'So, what did you find out?' asked Terry, taking a grateful swig from his bottle.

'His name was Professor Julian Nutt,' replied Barry, referring to his notebook, 'and he was a highly esteemed Professor of Science, Literature and Language at Westminster College, specialising in Modernism and Politics, Fiction and Ethnicity, not to mention Literary Criticism and Theory.'

'Julian Nutt,' repeated Terry. 'No wonder he changed it to Higgins. So, what happened to him after the press hounded him out of his job?'

'Well, it appears that he accepted early retirement. Although the stories in the papers were pretty damning, there was never any proof as to their validity. However, due to the adverse publicity, his position at the College became untenable and he took a pay-off and disappeared.'

'Disappeared? And we don't know where to?' asked Terry.

'No, the trail goes cold after he sold his house in Kensington. You know how things are: the tabloids moved on to the next scandal and Professor Nutt was able to fade away. He's probably enjoying his retirement somewhere nice, where the vultures can't be bothered to go.'

'Should be easy enough to trace, with a name like that,' said Terry. 'I'll get onto it tomorrow.'

'What's so important about our errant professor?' asked Barry. 'Is Kim-Ly the other half of the story?'

'Yes,' admitted Terry, 'but she says he was a good man and only wanted to help her to pass her English exam. I believe he

168

may have been the victim of a set-up and that someone was out to discredit him.'

'So where will you and Kim-Ly go tonight?' asked Barry. 'There's not enough room for all of you here.'

'Back to my flat, I guess. This is the first night of our future together.'

'Well, I for one hope you'll be very happy,' said Pete. 'I know how hard it must have been to see Gemma walk away like that.'

'Not as hard as it was for Gemma,' said Terry. 'I can't imagine how she must be feeling. I'm not worthy of such devotion.'

'That's true,' observed Pete. 'What do you think, Barry? How does an ugly sod like that earn the adulation of not one, but two stunning women?'

'Beats me,' said Barry, 'but let me know when you find out the secret.'

Pete adopted his most serious expression and addressed Terry. 'I think it only fair that Barry should know that we've made some serious enemies. He may wish to reconsider his offer of accommodation if he knew that Emre and the Dutch police are likely to follow us to the UK.'

'And how could they track us to here?' asked Terry.

'I don't know,' replied Pete, 'but I'm just saying that if Barry is going to put us up, then he should be brought up to date with the facts.'

'What, all of them?' Terry protested.

'Yes, all of them,' insisted Pete.

Barry listened intently as the whole sorry story was told in full by Terry, with the odd interjection from Pete. 'Bloody hell!' he exclaimed at the culmination of the tale. 'You'll be looking over your shoulders wherever you go.'

'We have been for the last few weeks,' said Terry. 'It's getting late; Kim-Ly and I should get home. What do you say, Barry? Are you in or out?'

'You know me, Terry; I'm on the side of the good guys. I'm in, without a doubt.'

'Thanks, mate,' said Terry, as he firmly shook Barry's hand. 'Now, let's find out what the girls have been talking about.'

Returning to the living room, they saw a contrite, silent Celina, seated and with head bowed. Sandra and Kim-Ly stood over her, as if delivering an admonishing lecture of grave importance.

'What's happening?' asked Terry. 'You all look very serious.'

'We were just discussing recent indiscretions with Celina,' answered Sandra, 'and how we're going to change things for the better.'

'And have you reached a conclusion?' asked Pete.

'For now, yes,' said Sandra, 'but I doubt that this is the end of the conversation.'

Terry nodded sagely and addressed Celina. 'It will be a long battle, but you have some good people on your side.' He turned his attention to Kim-Ly. 'We should be making tracks; my place is about half-an-hour from here by taxi. We'll catch up with everyone tomorrow.'

They made the short journey in near-silence. Kim-Ly snuggled against Terry's chest as his arms held her tight. It felt so strange, as she approached Terry's flat and he turned the key in the lock. The area was called Notting Hill and Terry had told her of the amazing carnival that filled the streets with vibrant colours, magical music and multicultural revellers each August. Tonight, though, all was quiet, and Kim-Ly sensed danger in the myriad shadows and hidden recesses around this modern housing complex.

With palpable relief, she watched Terry close and lock the door behind them and she followed him up the stairs to an alien but comforting sanctuary. A large poster adorned the wall before her, depicting four sullen young men in front of an arched brick building named Salford Lads' Club; "The Queen Is Dead" it proclaimed with some certainty. The opposite wall featured another moody young man, staring back at them from a bygone era; "James Dean in 'Rebel

Without a Cause'" it stated simply, "Also Starring Natalie Wood".
Kim-Ly knew none of these people, but could see they were important
to Terry. Why else would they have such a prominent position in his
home?

   Terry kissed her tenderly, then, in estate agent mode, commenced
a short tour of her new abode: the small, but stylish kitchen; the
bathroom in cold blue and white; and the bedroom, sporting a bouncy,
cushioned double bed and yet more posters covering the walls. I guess it
is cheaper than wallpaper, she thought, as she studied her opposition:
Marilyn Monroe on one side and an unknown, curvaceous young
lady on the other; both blondes, she observed with unease. Was she
expected to sleep in here with Terry's ivory-skinned fantasies staring
contemptuously down at her, mocking her black hair and oriental
features? This was every inch a bachelor pad, with no evidence of a
female touch, and she felt so out of place.

   Who was she to complain, though? It was infinitely superior to any
other accommodation that she'd had in recent years. She kissed Terry
once more and placed her bag at the foot of the bed, resolving to make
every effort to adapt to this new territory. Then Terry climbed up onto
the bed and carefully removed the posters from each wall. 'I won't be
needing these any more.' He smiled as he rolled them up. 'Not now
that I have you to look at.'

   Kim-Ly smiled back and wondered again at this strange man
who'd plucked her from captivity and set her free; never before had
she encountered such sensitivity in the masculine gender. She yawned
in comfortable contentment and suddenly realised how shattered she
was, the travails of her previous life and the adventure of the last few
weeks overwhelming all her senses. As she began to relax, all she could
think of was the healing qualities of sleep and the dawning of the new
day to follow; when she could dare to hope again for a better future.

   It took ten minutes for her to wash and prepare for bed; and two
minutes after her head hit the pillow to fall into a deep and peaceful
sleep. Tomorrow would have to wait for her to catch up.

* * *

Meanwhile, on the North Sea, a ferry was transporting another group of disparate passengers from Rotterdam to Hull. One man stood alone and stared forlornly at the horizon, until the moon disappeared behind the clouds and he could see it no more. The swell of the ship was making him nauseous, adding to his already dark mood. He let out an involuntary growl, attracting fearful glances from his fellow travellers, and retired restlessly to his cabin.

Not far away, two men sat deep in serious conversation. 'Sir, what did Emre mean when he said it was time to let your wife and colleagues know the kind of man you are?' asked Van Otterloo.

Bomkamp hung his head, then took a deep breath. He looked up to face his Hoofdagent and reluctantly began to speak. 'OK, I will tell you how it was and hope you will understand. Back when I was a young officer just like you, I succumbed to temptation on one occasion. I was not married then, and Aline and I had only been together for a few months, but I have been ashamed of my weakness ever since. It happened when I was assigned to a case to investigate the rise of drug trafficking in Amsterdam; we caught Emre and Arhan red-handed. Doruk was too young then and was not involved. We had them right there: they would have had no defence; then they brought out two beautiful young ladies and my boss and I were persuaded to turn a blind eye in return for sexual favours. My boss has long since retired, but ever since then the Loverboy Brothers have been on my case; the minute I step out of line, they threaten to tell Aline. I know I am not the only one and there are others in authority who have succumbed. I have told the ones I thought I could trust and they say it is too big, that it could blow the department apart and to keep it to myself. And that is how Emre and his gang have been allowed to get away with murder ever since; until now, that is. I don't mourn the passing of Emre's bastard brothers; and it would be convenient if he disappeared too. Whoever they are, this rival gang, they must be serious villains to mess with the Loverboy Brothers. If we can lead Emre to them, then perhaps I can be free of his blackmail for good.'

Van Otterloo considered the words of his mentor, a man he'd always respected, and wondered what he would do if thrust into a similar situation. Would he be able to resist? His job had brought him into close proximity to some of the ladies controlled by the Loverboy Brothers and he, like Bomkamp, was only human. Perhaps it was just a matter of time before they had him over the same barrel, so to speak. Let he who is without sin cast the first stone, he thought. Who was he to judge the man who'd shown nothing but faith in him, guided him through his formative years in the force?

'Your secret will be safe with me, sir. I will assist you as best I can in engineering the downfall of Emre.'

'Thank you, Van Otterloo. I will not forget your loyalty.'

17.

An early morning mist hung over Notting Hill, as Terry sat on the window-sill and watched the city awake. The familiar sounds of stirring London were both reassuring and an unwelcome call back to reality. Slamming doors, spluttering cars, the whistling paper-boy and the whining bus; all were reminders that he had to get back to work and earn a living. There wasn't just an emotional cost to the exploits of the last few weeks; his bank account was practically cleaned out too. He would have to crawl back to Chris today and grovel for the resurrection of his old job.

He sighed and turned to the sleeping beauty that was Kim-Ly, still snuggled contentedly beneath his covers. How could he be there to protect her and work at the same time? How could they survive if Chris failed to see reason and allow him back into the fold? His rent would be due next week and his landlord was not known for his patience and generosity. Terry had been fortunate to afford and land this dwelling in a sought-after area, and a long waiting list existed for these state-of-the-art and luxurious flats. There would be no hesitation in turning him out onto the streets if payment was late.

Kim-Ly began to stir and he observed besotted as the eyes that had entrapped him tried to take in the unfamiliar surroundings. A look of panic passed across her features, until Terry perched on the bed and offered a reassuring hand. 'Sleep well?' he asked, though he already knew the answer.

A yawn and a seductive stretch. 'Yes, thank you; the best sleep I have had for many years.'

'I have nothing in the flat for breakfast,' said Terry, attempting to keep his mind on practicalities, 'but there is a good place a few streets away; finest eggs benedict for miles.'

Kim-Ly smiled. 'OK, you are in charge.'

'But we don't have to go just yet,' said Terry, as he joined her beneath the covers and felt the warmth of her body against his. Each time he had any doubt about the wisdom of his recent decisions, he only had to close his eyes and his senses would take over.

The next bit is best left to the reader's imagination, as each of us has their own vision of this magical moment. Suffice it to say that, one hour later, as the sun began to burn away the mist, a thoroughly contented couple sat down for breakfast at Raoul's Cafe to discuss the plans for the day ahead.

'But what shall I do while you are at work?' asked Kim-Ly, after she'd taken in the gravity of their financial situation. 'I am too scared to be left alone in your flat.'

'I'll take you back to Barry's to meet up with the others,' said Terry. 'I will need some time to convince Chris that it's in his best interests to take me back; and I also want to do some research into our missing professor.'

'Yes, I feel safe with Sandra and Pete; and I should help them with Celina.'

'That's settled then,' said Terry. 'Come on, the day has long since dawned and I have much to do.'

"Associated British Ports Welcomes You to the Port of Hull", it stated, in large blue lettering on the side of a warehouse: Emre's first sight of England; twenty-four hours behind his quarry and as angry as ever, he was unimpressed with the greeting. He had but a vague idea of the whereabouts of the murderers, due to the bungling work of Cousin Mesud. Perhaps he was being somewhat hard on him, though, as he'd probably gone beyond the call of duty. Spurred on by the promise of financial reward, his loyal relative had driven through the night to Hull to arrive the previous day at dawn. From there Mesud had followed the bus to London, whilst battling fatigue and fighting to avoid falling asleep at the wheel. He'd decided upon tracking the larger of the two groups when they split at Victoria station and had kept them in sight; until a combination of a minibus full of Christians and some traffic lights had ended his pursuit in Fulham Broadway.

As he took his seat on the bus (unbeknown to him the very seat that Celina had occupied the day before), Emre sneered and resisted the temptation to spit as Bomkamp and Van Otterloo passed him and made their way to the rear. The sky, the landscape, the roads; everything took on a grey hue and he stared sadly through the condensation-covered window; the setting doing little to lift his dark demeanour. For now he would rest to compensate for his fitful sleep on the ferry, before a reunion with his uncle and cousins in London; in more convivial circumstances than the recent funerals of his beloved brothers. The London branch of the family had done well and they were restaurant owners of some repute, all above board and legitimate. Emre would enjoy the traditional welcome for kin returning to the fold. For the first time in many years, a little warmth entered his soul, as he drifted off to sleep; a sleep occupied by all kinds of demons.

Interview nerves, the only way to explain the butterflies that inhabited Terry's stomach as he approached Chris's office; he felt just as he did the first time around, a rookie journalist, fresh out of media studies and looking for a break. It had been Chris's predecessor that had grilled him that day and Terry had left deflated and beaten; instinctively he knew that he'd screwed up his big chance and that the beads of sweat and trembling hands must have been clearly visible throughout. He was amazed and elated when, two days later, he'd received the call offering him the job. Surely this time around he should be more confident; older and wiser, a seasoned and hardened hack with many a scoop to his name.

With all the trepidation of a wayward lad sent to face the wrath of the headmaster, he knocked on the door and awaited the invitation to enter. 'Hi, Terry,' smiled Chris; 'how are things? We've been worried about you.'

Terry breathed a sigh of relief; it was a better reception than he'd expected. 'I'm really sorry for leaving you in the lurch, Chris, but things got a little out of hand. I guess it's too late to submit my copy.'

"fraid so. I got John to write it in the end; all researched online and without your insightful, hands-on style, but a reasonable piece nonetheless. I take it you won't be claiming any expenses for this one.'

'I wouldn't dare. Look, Chris, I know I've cocked-up; but I've never let you down before, have I? Give me another chance; I need to work and I'm raring to go.'

'And what about your personal life?' asked Chris. 'I understand it's somewhat volatile at the moment. Can you promise me that it won't affect your work?'

Terry tried to summon up the necessary self-assured answer, but his hesitation said it all.

'No, I thought not,' said Chris. 'Look, you're one of the best there is, Terry, but the only thing I can offer you is some freelance work. It's the way the business is going anyway and there aren't many of the old staff writers left.'

Terry knew the score. 'Chris, you know as well as I do, you can call it freelance, you can call it casual or zero hours; it's just an excuse to lose people from the payroll, so they no longer have to pay benefits, pensions, sick pay, etc.'

'That may be so, but I have an ever-decreasing budget to work to and I don't make the rules.'

'I'm not in any position to argue, am I?' said Terry. 'OK, what do you have?'

'How about I give you a couple of covert jobs in the UK to start with? Give you a chance to get your life sorted. We'll see how it goes and build from there. You've heard of Sir Nigel Shelby; well, there have been allegations of corruption in his department and rumour has it that he's in it up to his neck. We have nothing that we can print, so I want you to go digging without attracting attention; find me something that will stick without landing us in court.'

'You know that's not my style, Chris,' protested Terry, 'creeping around rubbish-bins, looking for dirt on people. It's a bit beneath the paper too, isn't it; or have we gone down-market since I've been away?'

'Trust me, if the stories are true, then it's in the public interest that we expose them. Now, do you want the work or not?'

'I guess I have no choice. Where do I get the gen?'

'Charlie will bring you up to speed. Don't let me down again, Terry.'

'I won't; and thanks, Chris. It may not sound like it, but I am grateful that you haven't thrown me out.'

'Don't mention it. You bring me results and there's no reason why things can't return to something like normal, whatever that was.'

Terry left Chris's office half deflated and half hopeful. He felt down that he'd effectively lost the kudos that his previous position had carried, but he was confident that he could rebuild his reputation with a few good pieces. At least he was working again and he would also have access to the paper's resources to pursue the mysterious 'Professor Higgins'. His freelance status now meant that he was at liberty to submit his work to other publications; and he had a number of articles already written that would attract attention. All in all, he told himself, things could be a lot worse.

But first he would seek out Charlie, the ambulance chaser, to check out the case of Sir Nigel Shelby; a brigand and a cad if ever he saw one.

'So you're back then,' said Charlie, barely glancing up from his PC.

'Evidently,' replied Terry. 'I see you haven't lost your powers of observation.'

'And I suppose the golden boy has been received without even a bollocking and given the juiciest stories, as usual.'

Terry was well aware of how much joy his perceived demotion would give Charlie, so he attempted to put a positive slant on things. 'Chris and I have reached agreement that I become self-employed and we are both very happy with the arrangement.'

Charlie smiled. 'So the great Terry Logan is just another freelance hack. A lot of competition out there, you know.'

Becoming increasingly bored with the banter, Terry came straight to the point. 'Chris has asked me to work on Sir Nigel Shelby's story. What do you have?'

'Not much, just a bunch of anecdotes and gossip; it's a libel case waiting to happen. The word is that he has pushed through cutbacks to the funding for colleges, whilst simultaneously sanctioning private contractors to take up the slack in return for substantial donations to the party coffers; a sadly not uncommon tale these days.'

'And we have no proof,' said Terry, 'just speculation and rumour.'

'Oh, our sources are reliable and I have no doubt as to the validity of the story; but absolute proof, not yet, no.'

'OK, can I have your contacts then? Presumably they are people with a vested interest in the downfall of Sir Nigel.'

'Be my guest,' sighed Charlie, handing Terry his notes to date. 'I'm getting nowhere and they won't go to print until there is conclusive evidence.'

'Thanks,' said Terry, 'and if I can make it stick I'll make sure you are credited too; after all, you've done all the leg work.'

Charlie took on a more acquiescent demeanour and shook Terry's hand. 'Cheers; and welcome back.'

'Welcome back, Gemma' said Karen. 'Have a good holiday?'

A few miles away, Gemma, too, was reluctantly returning to work. Defeated and empty, she believed that routine was the only way to overcome her heartbreak; and anyway, she had to get out of the house to escape the cloying, condescending sympathy of Mum, Dad and Robbie. She would embroil herself in toil to take her mind off things; then search for a small flat in which to rebuild her life, to establish some independence and freedom. This was her opportunity to make a fresh start, to shake off the shackles of love and live as she pleased; beholden to no-one but herself.

Gemma turned to her colleague, Karen. 'Sorry, what did you say?

'I said, have a good holiday?'

'Holiday? Oh yeah, holiday; let's just say it was different, but enlightening,' replied Gemma. 'What's been happening while I've been away?'

'Oh, nothing much. Bardsley's still a bastard and Cavendish, well, you know what he is. Jim has announced his retirement and the party's on Saturday. He's hired a boat on the Thames and he's really pushing the boat out, if you'll pardon the pun. It'll be a great night and you can't possibly miss it.'

Gemma looked around the office, taking in all the familiar faces and the staid old décor; this place hadn't changed since long before she'd joined the practice and it reeked of privilege and outmoded values. The sepia atmosphere stifled what little spirit she had left as she considered Karen's proposition. 'I don't think so. Not much in the mood for parties at the moment.'

'Oh, come on, Gemma. Jim will be really upset if you don't come. He's one of life's good guys and deserves a good turn-out for his departure.'

Karen was right. Jim was one of those rare beasts, a gentleman and a thoroughly decent chap. Gemma had worked alongside him since she'd first turned up as a fresh-faced junior and he would be deeply offended if she declined to participate in his send-off. Jim had done more than anyone to fight her corner, to get people to take her talents seriously, to see beyond the beautiful blonde façade. But the thought of socialising filled her with dread; she could hear the inevitable, incessant questions about her love-life, the false empathy, the offers of shoulders to cry on and the hopelessness and despair attacked her senses. 'I'll think about it, OK?' she snapped. 'Now, who's hidden my mug; can't start the day without a coffee.'

The coffee was just how Emre liked it, strong and plentiful, a refill miraculously appearing each time he emptied his small, ornate cup, decorated with traditional elaborate blue and brown swirls. The family welcome had been as warm as he expected and, as he basked in the cosiness of a corner table in his Uncle Saglam's restaurant, the russet wallpaper, with minimal highlights in indigo and red, was a poignant reminder of how far he'd strayed from his roots. Laid back in the plush mock-leather chair, he admired the lavish lampshades above his head; but his comfort was soon disturbed by the inescapable inquisition.

'So, why are you here, Emre?' asked his uncle. 'What do you hope to gain from your visit to London? You are family and, as such, will be always welcome in our home; but tell me, why have you never visited before?'

'I have been busy with my business, just as you have here. You know as well as I how much hard work it takes to run a successful enterprise.'

'How dare you compare your business to mine,' shouted his uncle, as he slammed his fist on the table. Despite his advancing years he was still a strong man, in both body and spirit. The lines, etched deep into his face, spoke of struggle and survival, the greying beard a testament to his wisdom and age. 'This restaurant runs on honesty, respect and cordiality,' he continued, as a globule of indignant spittle landed on the table-cloth; 'we do not exploit people and we treat all who work for us as family. You and I, our paths are as far apart as Turkey and Greece. On the rare occasions that I have been in your company, your brow has been furrowed and your expression bitter; it is no way to live, Emre. Remember, that a vinegar seller with a smiling face commands more respect than a honey seller with a sour face. And tell me also, what do you know of hard work?'

Emre sneered. 'I saw what hard work did to my father. I watched him shrink before my very eyes as each day he would come home from working in their factories, diminished some more. I swore then that I would never be downtrodden like him; and that is why we left, Arhan, Doruk and I, to seek our fortunes elsewhere and to be the ones who are in charge.'

'And to become like the men who killed your father: ruthless, without compassion, using others for your own financial gain until they outlive their usefulness; and so it perpetuates and the world remains a miserable place. I was there too, remember; I too bore witness to what they did to my only brother, and yes, I was angry, with the same intensity that you have now. But just because you have known pain and injustice, it is no excuse to inflict it upon others. Revenge is not the answer; it only serves to create antagonism among your victims and they, in turn, will exact revenge upon you. In the end, an eye for an eye will only serve to make the whole world blind. Do you not see how the circle joins together; how your behaviour towards the people you abused has brought this punishment? I ask again, why are you here, Emre?'

Emre's voice was quiet, but unwavering, as he stared straight ahead. 'They are here, in London, the people who killed Arhan and Doruk, your nephews. Will you not help me to find them?'

Uncle Saglam thought for a moment; then, in a steady,

considered voice, replied, 'No, I will not, as I suspect they may have had good reason for what they did. I know it sounds harsh, but I will not risk my liberty and that of my offspring to service your vendetta. I feel grief for Arhan and Doruk, sure I do; I remember you and they as children, as mischievous and boisterous as children will be, running through the streets of Istanbul and playing with my own boys. But boys become men and, therefore, must become responsible for their own actions. You have taken the wrong path, Emre, but there is a way back. I will make this offer only once: relinquish your resentment, leave behind your immoral life and stay here with us, your family, and I will treat you as one of my own sons.'

For a moment Emre wavered as he considered his uncle's words. He took another sip of coffee and took in his surroundings: a simple, homely eatery where people could come to enjoy each other's company, whist indulging in fine food and wine. Perhaps he could be happy in this environment, where his cousins appeared to live in contentment, earning an honest but modest living until the day that they would inherit the business; and so it would continue, with their own children taking up the baton when the time came. Family, family, family; his uncle spoke of little else and Emre wondered if he could indeed adapt to a lifestyle without power, without conflict, without odium. He returned his uncle's unerring gaze and felt the tears welling as his father's resemblance sat before him; the father he had barely known. All he had were fleeting memories of rare visits at the dinner table, when his father had snatched some passing time between shifts. Perhaps, if the wise words now spoken by his uncle had been uttered by his father all those years ago, then Emre's life may have taken a more honourable track. But there was no use pretending to be someone he was not; it had taken him years to cultivate this evil and feared persona. How could he change now?

'Uncle, I thank you for your welcome and for your kind offer of kinship, but I must think of Arhan and Doruk. Am I to forget what was done to them and leave their deaths un-avenged?'

'But whatever you do now will not bring them back; you must break the circle of hatred, or live the rest of your life in bitterness. The choice is yours and yours alone.'

Surprised to discover a long-lost conscience, Emre felt confused as the arguments ricocheted around his brain. 'Will you allow me to take a few days' sleep on it, Uncle? I will give you my answer by the end of the week. This evening we should take solace in each other's company and my cousins and I have much time to make up.'

'Very well, we have few bookings tonight, so maybe we can close early; but please have respect for my sons and do not lead them astray.'

'You have my word,' nodded Emre, as his attention was diverted by Fazilet, his only female cousin.

'I have made up the spare room for Emre, Father,' she said. 'What will we be eating tonight?'

'I think Emre should savour some of our specialities, don't you? There is a possibility that the lost sheep may return.'

'And he will be very welcome.'

'Thank you, Fazilet,' said Emre. 'The last time I saw you, you were a chubby, spotty teenager and look at you now: a truly beautiful woman.'

Fazilet blushed and replied. 'And when we last met you were making your fortune in Amsterdam. Tell me, what became of that ambitious young man?'

'Ambition can be a cruel master, Fazilet. What worth is a fortune when you lose your soul?'

The revelry grew louder in laughter and conversation as the evening and alcohol consumption wore on, two of Emre's cousins, Vahit and Kadri, proving to be convivial hosts. Fazilet joined them for a short while, until their talk of girls and other supposed exploits became too lewd and vulgar. She made her excuses and left, shaking her head as she went. His Uncle Saglam, too, retired to bed and left the youngsters to it, making a comment about the topic of discussion being no different to when he was their age.

'Where is Mesud?' asked Emre. His cousins had been reticent when asked the same question earlier.

'He will be back soon,' answered Vahit. 'He has some business to attend to in town. We will continue to enjoy our happy reunion while we await his return.'

The wine flowed copiously and the mood mellowed concomitantly, Emre's speech slurring and his vision blurring further with each sip. He barely registered Mesud's entrance, until he stood before him with a proud and serious expression, holding up a piece of paper. 'I know where they are. The taxi driver they used yesterday, his tongue was loosened by a twenty-pound note. I have the address.'

Emre and his cousins sobered up immediately, the significance of the news stifling their merriment. Silence followed as all eyes awaited Emre's reaction. 'Thank you, Mesud,' he said at last, 'you have done well and I will repay your endeavour. I have been in long discussions with your father this afternoon; he wants me to come to live with you here on the condition that I give up my pursuit. It is a generous offer and one that I must consider. With Arhan and Doruk gone, you are my only family, apart from my poor ageing mother who has disowned me. I am truly grateful for your concern.'

'And as family we will assist you in your quest to avenge their deaths,' declared Kadri. 'We cannot simply forget what they did, can we?'

Emre looked him in the eye. 'Whatever I decide I will decide alone; this is not your battle and I will not disrespect your father by getting you involved. It was wrong of me to enlist your assistance, Mesud. Your father has opened my mind and now I must consider whether my duty lies in retribution or forgiveness. I told your father I would give my answer by the end of the week; I will sleep on it and I think we should all do the same. The dawn will bring with it clearer thought.'

18.

Dawn had barely broken in London Town as a shady brace of characters loitered with intent opposite *Turkuaz*. One of them leaned nonchalantly against a lamp-post, as if in casual conversation, his breath visible in the cool of morning; whilst the other had his eye on the restaurant entrance. Bomkamp and Van Otterloo's presence outside the restaurant had been a long-shot; their bumbling pursuit had led them nowhere and they'd lost Emre the minute he'd disembarked from the bus and merged into the crowd. Hence, Bomkamp had reluctantly made the call back to base to ask for assistance in locating the Loverboy Brothers' London family ties; and here they were, far away from home and scratching around for something to further their investigation. To be fair, *Turkuaz* wasn't the sleazy kebab shop they were expecting and it appeared to be a classy joint, with an eye-catching sign in turquoise and gold, its windows without a stain and dark-wood tables in neat, symmetrical rows.

'Do you think this is the base for the UK branch of "Loverboy Brothers Incorporated"?' asked Van Otterloo. 'Could be a front for trafficking and associated criminal activity.'

'It is possible,' replied Bomkamp, 'but that is not our concern. We are here to get to the bottom of two murders on our home soil, to bring the perpetrators back to face justice and, hopefully, to purge Emre's powers over our turf. If we can only achieve the latter, I will be happy.'

They didn't cater for the breakfast market at *Turkuaz*, so all was quiet; until a mumbling, bald-headed drunk emerged from a nearby doorway with bottle in hand. His tattered suit, complete with waistcoat, was testament to somewhat better days. A faded claret and blue scarf dangled at half-mast, a washed-out tribute to the long-lost days of Moore and Peters and the glories of '66. He stumbled past, swearing beneath his breath at the world's injustices.

'Look at me now, look at me now,' he shouted suddenly. 'As soon as that silly moo passed away, that was it; couldn't afford to live in the 'ouse any more once they took 'er benefit away. And that bleedin' Scouse git; turned my own daughter against me with his bloody communist propaganda, 'e did, and then she didn't want to know. I would have fought in the war for this country I would, if I wasn't in a reserved occupation; and look at me now, look at me now: out on the streets with no-one to care for an old man in his dotage. That Marigold, you know, 'e 'elped out for a while and, give 'im 'is due, 'e did a pretty good job for a poof; now even 'e's deserted me. Bloody foreigners, though, they're OK, ain't they, with their 'ousing all paid for from our taxes. What's the world coming to when a man who could've been a war hero 'as to live like this?'

'Poignant stuff,' observed Van Otterloo, as the drunk disappeared around the corner.

'Could be the local UKIP candidate,' said Bomkamp.

'No, I think that was Alf Garnett, you know.'

'Alf Garnett?'

'Yes. He was the satirical lead character from *Till Death Us Do Part*, played by a brilliant actor named Warren Mitchell. And, in one of life's strange ironies, the Scouse git to whom he refers actually transpired to be Tony Blair's real-life father-in-law. The writer, Johnny Speight, had intended Alf to be a subject of ridicule by mimicking and exposing the bigoted attitudes that prevailed in certain circles at the time, but some people didn't understand the satirical element and took Alf's views seriously, holding him up as a role model. Sadly, his opinions remain manifesto for particular parties and, no matter how often they are revealed to be the ravings of the uninformed, these narrow-minded attitudes endure to this day. Still, it is sad to see old Alf in such a wretched state.'

'I suppose any one of us could suffer such a fate if circumstances were to turn against us,' mused Bomkamp. He looked at Van Otterloo, not for the first time, with a confused expression. 'How do you know of this man, Alf Garnett?'

'I have absolutely no idea, sir. Perhaps the Creator is testing the boundaries of belief once more. I do not know how he gets away with it.'

'We must stake-out the place until we learn if Emre is there and then follow if he leaves,' said Bomkamp, returning his attention to the threshold of *Turkuaz*. 'We have no idea as to the whereabouts of our fugitives; we can only bide our time and hope that Emre has a few clues.'

'Hang on, there he is,' whispered Van Otterloo. They stepped back into the shadows as Emre emerged, accompanied by another younger man with similar physiology. Keeping a discreet distance, they followed, with little cover on the sparsely populated early morning streets. Each time Emre or his companion glanced over their shoulders, Bomkamp pulled Van Otterloo into a shop entrance or recess; their efforts to remain inconspicuous hindered by a tendency to keep bumping into each other. Eventually, their quarry turned right and descended the steps of Paddington underground station, deep in animated conversation as they went.

'Come on,' encouraged Bomkamp; 'we will lose them if we are not quick.'

Sleepy commuters were beginning to converge as they entered the station just in time to see Emre and his cohort at the ticket machine, before boarding the escalator to the District Line; a dash to follow suit and Bomkamp and Van Otterloo, too, burrowed beneath the city towards ageing tunnels and soulless trains. Down, down they went, past posters advertising the latest West End shows, past Wonderbras and exotic holidays, on the way to labyrinthine underground warrens. The wind, caused by the pressure of an approaching train, hit their faces as they continued their descent; and they quickened their pace to reach the platform and witness the rear of Emre boarding a middle carriage. Bomkamp pulled Van Otterloo to the back of the train and they climbed aboard just as the doors closed. 'Phew, that was close,' he panted, as the whine grew louder and the rattle faster. 'We must sit on opposite sides; then we will see when they get off.'

They sat in silence as the clatter of wheels on tracks and the buffeting motion lessened at the forthcoming stop. Both peered through the dirty windows at the cosmopolitan disembarking travellers at the start of their daily routine; they were ready to jump at the first sight of Emre. Wimbledon, the sign had said above the driver's windscreen; but, on inspecting the colour-coded tube map, they could see many stations between.

'The home of the Wombles,' stated Van Otterloo.

'What?' said Bomkamp.

'Wimbledon, the home of the Wombles; strange-looking furry creatures with pointy noses. It was a kids' TV show and they used to pick up, hoard and recycle litter and live in burrows. Haven't you heard the song, sir – *"Underground, over-ground, wombling free, the Wombles of Wimbledon Common are we ..."*?' The other passengers stared, as if some ancient etiquette had been breached; singing on the tube: who ever heard of such a thing?

'For God's sake, stop,' pleaded Bomkamp through gritted teeth; 'you are drawing attention to us.'

'You know, I've always wondered where the inflection should be,' Van Otterloo went on unabated. 'Is it *"the Wombles of Wimbledon Common are we"*, indicating that they reside on Wimbledon Common, or *"the Wombles of Wimbledon, common are we"*, which would imply that they are of humble origin? I think I prefer the latter.'

The man in the pinstriped suit looked at the cool dude with the headphones; they both raised their eyebrows and shook their heads.

It was the end of the line before Emre and his buddy disembarked and Bomkamp and Van Otterloo left it as long as possible before pursuing at unnoticeable length. They followed from the main drag to suburban streets, the houses growing more salubrious with each step. Eventually, their targets stopped opposite a house typical of the area, but with flagstones cracked and paint crumbling, noticeably not as well maintained as its immediate neighbours. Emre scrutinised the property pointed out by his companion and nodded sagely; the two of them shook hands and hugged farewell, then Emre sat alone upon a wall and folded his arms, as if preparing for a lengthy stake-out.

'Could be a long day,' observed Bomkamp, hiding his face as Emre's guide and another man passed each other on the other side of the road. 'I am sure all these comings and goings will attract the attention of the Neighbourhood Watch.'

'Hey, is that not our travelling sex-toy salesman?' observed Van Otterloo, as the other man approached the house. 'You remember, the guy we stopped by the canal.'

'You know, I think you are right. What the hell is he doing here?'

'I think we may have been hoodwinked, sir,' said Van Otterloo. 'I will wager that man is in cahoots with our murderers. You see how slyly he knocks upon that yellow door.'

'It's a lemon entry, my dear Watson,' observed Bomkamp.

Van Otterloo groaned. 'Sir, that joke is older than my grandfather.'

Robbie stood nervously on the step and awaited an answer to the doorbell. Through the ornately patterned glass he could see the shadow of a figure making its way slowly along the hall towards him, before the door opened slightly on the chain. 'Who is it; what do you want?' asked a voice that he didn't recognise.

'It's Robbie, Gemma's brother; hope you don't mind, but she gave me your address. Can I come in?'

Through the crack in the door, Robbie could just make out Pete immediately behind the man he assumed to be Barry. Pete nodded his ascent and Barry released the chain from the door.

'To what do we owe the pleasure?' smiled Pete; 'as if I didn't know.'

'Thought I'd pop by and see how things were going,' answered Robbie.

'And Gemma knows you are here?'

'Kind of. She said, "Do whatever the hell you want; I don't give a shit any more".'

'You'd better come through,' said Barry, 'one more guest won't make any difference. Coffee?'

'Yeah, cheers,' answered Robbie, distracted by Celina's beguiling smile.

'Hi, Robbie,' said Sandra, with tray of croissants in hand; 'come for breakfast?'

Robbie glanced at Celina again. 'Something like that, yeah. Where are Terry and Kim-Ly?'

'At Terry's place,' answered Barry. 'He's dropping Kim-Ly round soon, while he and I go to work.'

'I'll make myself scarce when they turn up,' said Robbie. 'Terry's not exactly my favourite person at the moment; Gemma's heartbroken.'

'I know,' sympathised Sandra. 'I'll give her a call later.'

'So where do we all go from here?' asked Robbie, flinching from the heat of his coffee. 'I take it you've been discussing your next steps.'

'Pete and I have been looking for boats on the internet,' answered Sandra. 'Pete still has some of the money left from the sale of the *Drifter* and we're going to look at one this afternoon in a place called Aylesbury, about forty miles away. Looks like Pete's going to get his old lifestyle back after all.'

'What about Celina?'

'Celina is welcome to stay with us temporarily, or she can go and live with Terry and Kim-Ly; it's her choice. If we do buy this boat, it'll take a week or so for the deal to go through; in the meantime, Barry has kindly offered us accommodation.'

Celina said nothing, but looked disconcerted about discussions of her future continuing as if she weren't there.

'And there's no way you can be traced here?' asked Robbie.

'None that I can think of,' said Pete. 'The Dutch police have been in touch with my friend Martin as the registered owner of the *Christina*, but, as it was the first he'd heard about our disappearance, he couldn't tell them anything. Wasn't too happy when I spoke to him yesterday, though; wanted to know what the hell was going on and why the police were pestering him for information. He told me that it's best he doesn't know where we are and that he'd be renting the boat to someone else at the earliest opportunity. Sad, but understandable, I suppose. I'll make it up to him if we ever get to clear our names.'

At the sound of the doorbell, Robbie retired to the garden while Barry let in Terry and Kim-Ly. He lit a cigarette, took a deep drag and leaned against the garden wall. A beam of sunlight broke the clouds and illuminated the bright yellow of a Laburnum tree and Robbie admired the colourful wildness of the garden, as if someone had scattered seeds at random and let nature take its erratic course.

'Hello, Robbie.' He jumped and turned as the Amazonian figure of Celina emerged from the suburban jungle and the flowers faded insignificantly into the background.

Robbie tried to appear nonchalant and extinguished his cigarette beneath his shoe. 'Hi, there; welcome to London,' he smiled; 'what do you think of it so far?'

'I have seen only through bus and taxi vindows and the inside of Barry's house.'

'We can soon fix that,' said Robbie. 'I can take you to see all the attractions: Tower of London, Buckingham Palace, Stamford Bridge.'

'Vhy are you here, Robbie? Do your loyalties not lie with your sister?'

'Isn't it obvious? I am here to see you.'

'But you know vhat I am, Robbie: nothing but a hooker and a junkie. Surely you can do better than that. Vhat is it about you Englishmen that you have such low standards?'

Robbie considered Celina's question and chose his words carefully. 'You know, the one thing that the last few weeks have taught me is that nobody has to remain what they have always been. Most of us are who we are and where we are through circumstance, but we also have the power of choice; you don't have to be a hooker and a junkie, and I don't have to be a petty criminal. I'll make a deal with you: I'll help you to change if you help me. I think we could make a great team; and what have we got to lose?'

Celina smiled. 'OK, Robbie the Englishman, vhen you put it like that I guess it makes sense. You know that you, Pete and Terry have made me realise that not all men are bastards.'

'I think we've had entirely the opposite effect on Gemma,' pointed out Robbie, 'but our hearts are in the right place.'

'Yes, you have a good heart,' agreed Celina, and moved towards him.

Robbie closed his eyes in anticipation of their first kiss, of those full, voluptuous lips on his; and was rewarded only by a blood-curdling scream. 'What the fuck?' he cried.

'He vas there,' sobbed Celina, hyperventilating; 'it vas Emre, looking over that vall.'

Robbie held her close in an attempt to calm her down and, despite the perceived imminent danger, was aroused by her hysterical body quivering against his. 'Are you sure? You're not hallucinating again, are you?'

The back door swung open and Terry emerged, closely followed by the others. He took in the scene of Celina trembling with fear in Robbie's arms. 'For God's sake, Robbie, can't you control yourself?' he said. 'Hasn't the poor girl been through enough already?'

'Emre vas there,' pointed Celina, still sobbing uncontrollably. 'His evil eyes vere staring right into mine. I svear it vas him.'

'No, it could not be,' said Kim-Ly. 'How could he have found us?'

'I don't know,' said Sandra, 'but we can't stay here. We must split up again to throw him off the trail.'

'And go where?' asked Kim-Ly. 'I am sick of running away. He is one man against seven of us; why can we not stay and fight?'

'Now, hang on,' said Barry; 'are you including me in your magnificent seven?'

Terry gingerly opened the back gate and peered up and down the alley. 'No sign of anyone,' he said, as he re-joined the group. 'I think Sandra is right; he cannot chase us all at once. If we move in different directions he will not know which way to turn. You're good at this kind of thing, Sandra; who goes where and with whom?'

'Well, Pete and I have our boat viewing appointment this afternoon, so we'll be heading for Aylesbury; he's not likely to follow us there. What were your plans for today?'

'I have some more research to do on the piece I am writing, but I can work from home. I have also discovered the whereabouts of Professor Nutt, a.k.a. Higgins, Kim-Ly's errant English tutor. I have his address and had planned to visit him later today; might make it interesting if Kim-Ly were to come with me.'

'And what about you, Celina,' asked Sandra, 'who do you want to go with?'

'Celina can come home with me, if she wants,' offered a chivalrous Robbie.

'And what will your parents think of that?' asked Terry.

'I'm a grown man,' said an indignant Robbie. 'I can bring home whoever I choose.'

'Hmm,' said Terry, looking somewhat sceptical. 'Your call, Celina; you have people fighting for the pleasure of your company.'

Celina, still held firmly in Robbie's arms, looked from one to the other. 'I vould like to go vith Robbie,' she concluded; 've have made a deal to help each other.'

'That's settled then,' said Terry. 'I suggest we all travel in public places as much as possible and disappear into crowds at every opportunity, to throw any pursuer off the scent.'

'We should leave here together,' said Sandra; 'safety in numbers in case he's still around, then we go our separate ways on the tube.'

'Agreed,' said Robbie, as he considered what he was going to tell his mum and dad about Celina.

19.

Had Emre seen enough to make up his mind? The sight of Celina had brought his blood back to the boil, but his uncle's words still resonated. He needed more time to clear his head and make the decision that was right for him; but time was something he had little of. His business in Amsterdam had been left in the hands of two of his lecherous lieutenants; an arrangement that he would prefer to be on a very temporary basis. With Arhan and Doruk gone, there was no-one he could trust to maintain a tight ship in his absence, no-one to rule through fear and to keep their grubby hands off the merchandise. If he did not return soon, then he would have no business to go back to; but then again, he still had business to attend to here. No, he would continue his quest for revenge until he could decide upon his life's direction.

He took a deep breath and hid behind a tree with a full view of the front of the house. Soon they would emerge, the fear instilled by his appearance sufficient to scare the rats from their cage. Sure enough, twenty minutes later they appeared, one by one, each looking fearfully in every direction. This was the first time that Emre had seen the murderous gang at relatively close quarters and he had to admit that they didn't look dangerous; apart from the ever-striking figure of Celina, they could have been any normal bunch of residents or tourists. As they made their way cautiously along the street, Emre began to follow at a discreet distance.

Understandably spooked, they glanced over their shoulders at each turn and Emre had to dart behind parked cars, dustbins, trees, any cover available. A sudden turn by Kim-Ly and he jumped behind a hedge, only to bump painfully into Bomkamp and Van Otterloo.

'Ouch!' exclaimed Emre. 'You pair of fools! What purpose are you serving exactly? You have added nothing of value to the proceedings so far.'

'Oh, I don't know,' replied Van Otterloo. 'I think we have contributed some levity and light relief to what is a very serious subject. Without us the tale would be dark indeed.'

Emre thought quickly. 'OK, you may come in useful after all. They know now that I am here, so I suspect they will split up to throw me off the trail. If that happens, I will follow Celina and whoever she is with, whilst you two clowns keep track of Kim-Ly; remember the consequences if you do not do as I say. Now, we have no time to lose; we can exchange numbers on the way and I will call you at 6 p.m. to trade information.'

And so it came to pass that the murderous gang went their separate ways and trod their own paths once more. First, we will join Sandra and Pete on their journey to find a new place to live, to obtain a boat with an even keel and to draw some crumb of comfort from their sacrifices. Pete held Sandra's hand as they stood beneath the steel-structured, pigeon's-paradise-roof of Marylebone station, awaiting their train to Aylesbury. The aroma of diesel trains mixed pungently with the smell of fresh coffee and pasties as they gazed up at the departures information, waiting for their cue to board.

'Any regrets?' asked Pete.

There was a crack in her voice as Sandra replied. 'We've lost everything, Pete; our life is back on the *Christina* in Amsterdam. All our possessions are there, my paintings, your guitar, our clothes, shoes, trinkets and dreams, all gone forever; and you ask me if I have any regrets?'

'Yeah, we were happy there,' agreed Pete, 'but consider the difference you've made to the lives of Kim-Ly and Celina; they were enslaved before you decided to help and you've made a major contribution to setting them free. Surely that is worth more than possessions.'

'It wasn't only me.' Sandra grasped Pete's other hand and looked him in the eye. 'We've all done our bit and you've lost just as much.'

'Not as much, no. I'm a man of simple needs and can adapt to any accommodation. I lived on that crappy old barge for years remember, before you came along and reintroduced me to civilisation. And that old guitar; all I hope is that someone picks it up and makes better music on it than I could. You never know, could be the next *Townshend* or *Springsteen*.'

'What, in Holland?' Sandra questioned.

'Good point; but they did produce *Golden Earring*.'

'I rest my case.'

'Look, all I'm trying to say is that possessions can be replaced,' continued Pete. 'People's lives, however, are far more valuable. You've been the driving force behind this whole escapade and you've given a few people hope for a better future.'

'Hmm, I don't think Gemma will agree with your prognosis,' said Sandra.

'You can't concoct a happy ending for everyone,' said Pete, 'but I'm determined there will be a happy ending for us. I'm so proud to be your partner and, so long as we are together, I don't care where we live.'

She kissed Pete and smiled. 'I guess the two of us get along OK. I'm proud to be with you too. But I don't want to spend the rest of our lives on the run, looking over our shoulders for cops or pimps wherever we go. Do you think that Emre will follow us?'

'I doubt it, no; it will be Celina or Kim-Ly that he'll be after.'

'Perhaps Kim-Ly was right and we should have stuck together and faced up to him; seven to one.'

'Maybe, but it's too late now,' reasoned Pete. 'We'll contact them all when we get back.'

The fifty-five-minute train journey was uneventful, with suburban stops evolving into the rolling greenery of the Chiltern hills: Amersham, Missenden, Wendover to the Vale of Aylesbury. Then the short walk from the station to what was left of the canal basin. Pete had been here a few times before, when a thriving boating community had joined the locals in The Ship, long since demolished to make way for the building site that stood beside an architecturally imposing new theatre that advertised all the usual post-West-End shows and little else.

A solitary sorry barge was tethered at the water's edge and Pete took in the death of a way of life; the tragic demise of what was once a place of tranquillity, but a stone's throw from the centre of town. Faceless concrete walls, the exposed rear-end of a hotel, supermarket and multi-storey car park, stood opposite the boat they'd come to view and the imposing neon-lit supermarket sign reflected green in the rippling water. Pete rapped sadly on the door.

A weathered man emerged, a trifle older than Pete, his wrinkled skin etched deep with oil and his hair apparently full of thick black grease. He wiped his hand on a filthy pair of dungarees and shook Pete's hand before turning to Sandra. 'Pleasure to meet you, ma'am,' he rasped. 'Malcolm Smith at your service. Come on board and I'll put the kettle on, or would you prefer something a little stronger?'

'Tea will be fine, thanks,' answered Sandra, as she viewed their potential new home with some doubt. Pete had told her that, based on the price, it might need some work, and he was not mistaken. A polite assessment in estate-agent language would have been "rustic, has great potential".

'Thanks,' said Pete, as he accepted a mug containing a dark brown liquid bearing scant resemblance to tea. 'I think I know the answer, but why are you moving on?'

'Well, take a look outside,' seethed Malcolm; 'it's a bloody travesty, that's what it is. They even called the theatre the *Waterside*, then they built these monstrosities alongside it; and I wouldn't be surprised if they go on to fill the canal with concrete. I hope they bury the bleedin' town-planners there while they're about it.'

'And where will you go?'

'My brother has a barge up north; I'm going to buy something near him. They've built a marina about a mile upstream from here, you know; it's not too bad and there's some decent places further along, but I just want out after what they've done to the old place. What do you think of my humble home, then; think you might be interested?'

Pete looked at Sandra and raised his eyebrows.

'Does it go?' asked Sandra. 'I'll want proof that it can convey us away from here before we think about it.'

'Yeah, of course it goes,' answered Malcolm. 'How do you think I got to look like this? Been messing around with boat engines since I was a kid and this'll take you as far away from here as you want to be. Finish your tea and we'll go for a spin.'

Pete surreptitiously tipped his tea into a plant pot and they climbed apprehensively from cabin to deck.

'Well, what do you think?' Pete asked Sandra, as they chugged under a footbridge, scattering a raft of ducks as they went. 'The engine is sound and we could make it our own with a bit of graft.'

Sandra smiled. 'You love it, don't you; the simplicity, the challenge, the back to basics. Go on, admit it: the *Christina* was far too bourgeois for you, wasn't it. You're itching to get your teeth into this old wreck.'

'Only if you're happy too,' said Pete.

Sandra hesitated, looked around again, shook her head and sighed. 'Go on then. Guess I haven't got so many shoes to accommodate any more. But you'll have to take me out somewhere nice sometimes; maybe the occasional night in a hotel to remind me of civilisation.'

Pete spat into his hand and held it out. 'It's a deal, partner.'
Sandra reciprocated. 'I hope I'm not going to regret this.'

Meanwhile, a nervous Robbie was introducing Celina to his parents. They'd successfully negotiated the suspicious glances of Mrs Jones next door and the twitching curtains of the Neighbourhood Watch; and now stood nervously before Mum and Dad, furtively seeking approval. 'We met when Gemma and I were in Holland; is it OK if Celina stays for a while until she finds a place to live?'

Robbie's mother looked Celina up and down in disbelief, whilst his father stood with mouth agape and a "that's my boy" expression.

'You could have given us some warning,' said his Mum. 'I would have prepared the spare room.'

'Oh, no need to go to all that trouble,' replied a hopeful Robbie; 'plenty of room in mine.'

'It's no trouble at all; just got to move out a few boxes of junk,' said Mum, effectively drawing the boundaries. 'How long do you think you'll be staying, Celina?'

'I am not sure. This is my first time in England and I do not know yet if I vill return home.'

'And where is home?' asked Robbie's father.

'Originally Poland, but for the last ten years Amsterdam; I think maybe I vill try to contact my parents. I have not seen them for a very long time.'

'Well, you will be welcome here until you get sorted out; won't she, dear?'

Robbie's Mum looked with an air of some scepticism at her all-but-drooling husband and concluded, 'Celina can be our guest for a short time. Robbie and Gemma's friends have always been welcome in our home, so long as they don't abuse our hospitality.' She turned to Celina. 'Now, get your things and I'll show you to your room.'

Celina pointed to the small bag over her shoulder. 'These *are* my things; it is all I have.'

'But where is your luggage?'

'Er, we had to leave in a bit of a hurry,' said Robbie. 'Celina had no time to collect her belongings.'

'Robbie, what's going on here; you're not in any trouble, are you?'

'It's nothing to worry about, Mum, honest. All we need is somewhere for Celina to crash and you won't even know we're here. I'll take her to get some new clothes tomorrow; as it's a Saturday, perhaps Gemma can come too, in an advisory capacity.'

Robbie's Mum looked unconvinced. 'I don't know what you're up to or what went on in Holland, but you're old enough to make your own decisions and live by the consequences. All I know is that we've barely been able to get a word out of Gemma since she returned and that her trip, at least, was an unmitigated disaster.'

'Yeah, I know,' said Robbie; 'she couldn't patch things up with Terry. Think it might take a while for her to get over it.'

'Has Terry found someone else?'

'You could say that.' Robbie shot a warning glance at Celina to prevent the addition of more detail. 'Early days, but I think it's serious.'

'And have you offered your sister support?'

'Of course, but you know what she's like when she's down; she won't accept help from anyone.'

'That's true,' agreed Mum. 'I'll try again this evening; she's insisted on going back to work, you know. I suppose the routine will take her mind off things. Now, you show Celina to her room and I'll put the kettle on.'

Robbie led Celina into the spare room, full of all the things that nobody could bring themselves to throw away: his box of old *Shoot* magazines, Gemma's collection of *Barbies*, his Dad's old vinyl LPs; a testament to their stereotypical upbringing, hidden away in a space that could barely accommodate a child, let alone someone of Celina's physique. Robbie peeked through the window and looked up and down the length of the street outside: the passing be-suited banker, the obligatory backwards-baseball-capped skateboarder, the two old ladies chatting opposite. 'I can't see anyone out there. Do you think we may have lost him?'

'I hope so; or he may have followed Kim-Ly and Terry.' Celina took Robbie's hands. 'Your parents are very kind and I am thankful to you and them, but I vill not stay for long. I am too much trouble, Robbie; I do not belong in a nice house like this.'

'And I am too much trouble too. I'm no guardian angel, Celina; I'm just a slightly reformed petty-villain with no money and no prospects. I'm surprised that Mum and Dad haven't kicked me out years ago, what with some of the stuff I've been involved in. I don't plan on sticking around too long either; let's go and see the world, you and me and no-one to tell us what to do. What have we got to lose?'

'But you hardly know me, Robbie. I have many problems and things I find hard to control.'

'OK, so let's get to know each other better then; you never know, it might be good for us both.'

'And how vill ve pay for our trip around the vorld? You said you have no money and I have lost my only vay of making any; unless you are like the others and vant to live off the proceeds of my body.'

'How could you suggest such a thing after the risks we've taken to get you and Kim-Ly out of there? No, we can find a way; I don't know what it is yet, but I'll think of something.'

Celina's countenance was thoughtful as she casually announced, 'Robbie, I have been thinking about vhat I should do next: there are many like me and Kim-Ly, trapped and unable to escape from those bastard pimps. I vant to do for them vhat you have done for us; to set them free and help them to live a better life. I can vork undercover and you can be my partner. Vhat do you think? Ve could travel as you vish, but use our experience for good.'

Robbie considered her words and looked incredulous. 'And would this plan involve murder, like the last time?'

'If necessary, yes, but ve vill be of more use if ve can remain un-noticed; get the girl and go.'

'Hm, "Get the girl and go"; that was always Jimmy One-Note's philosophy. Never got *him* very far though.'

'I mean it, Robbie. I nearly died on the ferry and I do not vant to go back there again. If I am to change my life, give up drugs and prostitution, then I must have something good to vork for.'

'You've been giving this some serious thought, haven't you? I like the concept, but we would need somewhere safe to run to after we have liberated our ladies of the night; we can't just leave them on the streets to fend for themselves.'

'I agree that ve must vork out the details, but it could be vhat we both need; a purpose, a reason to be on this earth.'

Robbie considered the stunning lady before him and for the first time he could see a woman with strength and determination, no longer the victim he'd encountered barely five days ago. Was that all it was? The intensity of their brief time together was such that a lifetime of emotions had flashed before his eyes, the physical attraction evolving rapidly into feelings more uncomfortable and unfamiliar, yet filled with warmth and hope. He recalled how he'd felt when they'd nearly lost her on the ferry and realised that Celina was right; what is the point of being on this planet if you don't make some kind of difference?

'OK, I'm in,' he smiled, 'so long as we do it properly and work as a team.'

'It is a deal, partner,' Celina laughed.

'I hope I'm not going to regret this,' said Robbie.

"Welcome to the Royal Borough of Berkshire" greeted the roadside sign, as the sparsely populated bus transported Terry and Kim-Ly towards a potentially fateful meeting with Professor Nutt (a.k.a. Higgins).

'And you are sure he has agreed to meet us?' asked a nervous Kim-Ly for the tenth time.

'Yes, I think I aroused his curiosity when I gave him the abridged version of what had become of you; must have forgotten to mention that I am a journalist.'

'Did he sound angry? It is because of me that he lost his job and his life was ruined.'

'On the contrary; he was very suspicious at first and took some convincing that we were on the level, but once I'd won him over he was fine. Said he remembered his brief time teaching you with great fondness and was looking forward to seeing you again. This is the village; we get off at the next stop.'

A fine drizzle covered everything in a dew-like film and Terry caught a slipping Kim-Ly as they stepped down from the bus. He glanced back at the only two passengers left that had boarded in London and was reassured that they didn't follow. 'You OK?' he asked.

'Yes, but I am not sure if this is a good idea after all. I have been the cause of many problems for this man, whatever his real name is; why should he welcome us?'

'I have been doing a little research and, as far as I can tell, he just seems like a thoroughly decent bloke. Apart from your little scandal, I can't find a word said against him; and even then he had a lot of support from his colleagues and students. The only people that wanted him out were the college management because of the bad publicity and, I'm not sure yet whether this is relevant, a few politicians, whom he'd upset because of his outspoken opinions on education cutbacks.'

Kim-Ly looked in awe at the posh houses set back in substantial grounds, with immaculate lawns and neatly trimmed colourful borders beneath ancient oaks. 'Wow, I have never been to a place such as this; the people that live here must have a lot of money.'

A squirrel skipped in front of them and effortlessly shinned up a tree, to a soundtrack of birdsong and crickets. Then, from around a corner, a man's bellow shattered the tranquillity: 'SON OF A BITCH, SON OF A BITCH!'

Terry and Kim-Ly stopped in their tracks as the sound came closer: 'SON OF A BITCH, SON OF A BITCH!'

Kim-Ly gripped Terry's hand tightly as they sank back into the shadows of a thicket, before a character resembling an off-duty *Ministry of Silly Walks*-era John Cleese hove into view. Tall and gangly, in brown tweed and wax, he almost strode past without noticing the cowering couple, but the snap of a twig as Terry shifted his weight gave them away. The man turned and appraised them with curiosity. 'Good afternoon,' he boomed at last. 'Awfully sorry, I'm just calling my dog. Bloody thing keeps running off.'

'You named your dog Son of a Bitch?' asked Terry.

'Well you have to admit that it's a technically accurate description; and it's more original than Fido. And what, may I ask, are you doing in these parts? Not seen you around here before.'

'We're looking for the home of Professor Julian Nutt,' answered Terry. 'Hedgerow Lane, I think it is.'

'You're not the bloody press, are you? Couldn't move for the bastards when that scandal hit; they wouldn't leave the poor chap alone. Always liked him myself, perfectly amenable fellow, invariably stopped for a chat; been a bit of a recluse since all that fuss, though.'

'No, we're not journalists,' lied Terry, 'we're ex-students. He is expecting us.'

'Down there and take the first right.' The man pointed towards a single-track road covered by an arch of trees.

'Thank you,' said Terry, 'and I hope you find your dog.'

'My pleasure. Give my regards to the professor; Bagshot's the name.' The man strode purposefully away: 'SON OF A BITCH, SON OF A BITCH!'

Terry shook his head and smiled at the bemused Kim-Ly. 'That's what I love about places like this,' he said; 'full of eccentrics and you never know who's round the next corner.'

Professor Nutt's house proved to be somewhat smaller and different from those of his neighbours; unkempt and rambling, ivy covered every wall and the garden could only be described as wild. The bell jangled noisily as an apprehensive Kim-Ly hid slightly behind Terry. She needn't have worried, as the door creaked open to reveal the convivial features of a small, bespectacled, balding man who seemed in the best of health as he revelled in the freedom of his early sixties. He looked beyond them, as if to reassure himself that they were alone; then, satisfied, he opened the door wider.

'How good to see you,' he smiled, and showed them into an ornate hallway, adorned with decorative vases and stunning oil paintings; the home of a man with immaculate taste. 'I hope you had a good journey. We're a bit out of the way here; did you have any trouble finding us?'

'One of your neighbours pointed us in the right direction,' answered Terry, 'a man named Bagshot; sends his regards.'

'Ah, Bagshot, yes; wasn't searching for his dog by any chance, was he?'

'Yes, he was as it happens.'

The professor laughed. 'Never did see that dog, but I'm glad that Bagshot's still out there looking. A Great Dane, he told me, so it shouldn't be hard to find. Some of the residents tried to get him sectioned, you know, bad for the image of the neighbourhood and all that, but he's perfectly harmless. Come on through and we'll have some tea.'

The living room proved to be just as welcoming and, with its plush leather sofas and deep red design, the place simply oozed warmth. Books of all shapes, sizes and genres adorned a multitude of shelves and the *Guardian* lay open on the coffee table. A large, kindly-looking lady entered, along with a waft of home-baked bread, and the professor made the necessary introductions. 'Kim-Ly, I'd like you to meet my wife, Bunty; she's been very much looking forward to making your acquaintance. And what was your name, young man? Terry wasn't it?'

Kim-Ly began to relax. She was expecting a much frostier greeting and Bunty felt warm and soft as she shook her hand. During their lessons the professor had often spoken of his wife and partner of many years, probably to put her at ease and to demonstrate the lack of an ulterior motive. Bunty retired to fetch their tea and it shortly arrived in an authentic Five-Blessings Chinese blue and white porcelain tea pot, surrounded by matching cups on saucers and accompanied by an array of biscuits on a side plate.

Professor Nutt sipped his tea noisily then turned to Terry. 'I must say that your call came as something of a surprise. How on earth did you find me?'

'Oh, I have my sources,' replied Terry, 'but I'd rather not reveal them.'

'A man of mystery, ay? No matter, at least you have brought Kim-Ly to safety. Your story was a little sketchy on the phone; perhaps you would be so kind as to fill in the gaps.'

Kim-Ly took up the tale and left little to the imagination. She told of her enslavement and of her friend who had escaped to England too; she told of the bravery of Terry and of the others who had helped them to flee, against the backdrop of the Loverboy Brothers' tyranny. She recounted the tragic saga of sleaze that had seen her transported from one city to another to practise the same trade, but with differing degrees of legality. She failed to mention the blood on their hands and the recent sighting of Emre. 'I am so sorry for what happened to you,' added Kim-Ly, 'but Terry says your real name is not Higgins and that you only taught me for a bet.'

An embarrassed silence ensued, before Bunty spoke on the professor's behalf. 'You *have* been busy with the detective work. The damn fool told me all about it; after the whole sorry mess was out in the open and it was too late to do anything about it. I suppose it was the name Higgins that gave it away.'

'Yes,' answered Terry, 'there were too many similarities to *Pygmalion* for it to be coincidence.'

A somewhat sheepish Professor Nutt tried to explain. 'It was Sir Nigel that started the whole thing off. We were at a conference to discuss the future of education and, in the bar afterwards, he was wittering on in his usual boorish manner about natural selection; arguing that he and his kind resided at the top of the food chain for a reason. His argument revolved around the theory that the plebs are where they belong on the social ladder and that any money spent on cultivating the masses is a waste of resources. I'd been fighting against cutbacks for years and, inevitably, I took the bait, citing numerous examples of how social status is no measure of intellect; but he wouldn't have it. The damned fellow only attends these events on the pretence that he is engaged in the democratic process; in reality the man's a bully and doesn't care who he treads on to serve his agenda. From the point-of-view of enhancing the advancement of education, he's as much use as tits on a boar-hog. Anyway, after a few too many brandies, we ended up with a small wager. I challenged him to send me anyone he wished and I would get them through their GCSE English. "I know just the girl," he retorted. Sorry to be indelicate, but these were his exact words: "Lovely little filly, bloody good ride too, but she barely speaks a word of the lingo". And that's how it began. Kim-Ly turned out to be one of my best students and was well on the way to the standard required to pass with flying colours. Then you know the rest; the press got wind of it – I have my suspicions how – and that was the end of that. It is I that should be apologising to you, young lady; I had no right to raise your hopes, without delivering the goods.'

Kim-Ly looked crestfallen. 'Can I ask how much the bet was worth?'

'On his part, he was to exempt my college from the budget cuts; and if I lost I was to withdraw my opposition. Damned stupid in retrospect; but I was close to retirement anyway and wanted to secure the future of the department before I left. Fortunately, Bunty has stuck by me, God knows why; and we have retreated here a little earlier than intended. This is the ancestral home, you know; it was bequeathed to me when my parents passed on. The college has honoured my pension in recognition of services rendered, so I suppose I can't complain. All I can say in my defence is that, once we'd commenced our lessons, I genuinely believed in my argument and in you. I have no doubt whatsoever that you would have passed. You're actually close to A Level standard, but the powers-that-be insist that you take the GCSE first.'

'OK, then finish what you started,' said Kim-Ly. 'I still wish to take my exam and you no longer have anyone else to teach.'

The professor considered this proposal, looked to his wife and raised his eyebrows.

'It's the least you can do,' Bunty proclaimed without hesitation, 'after what this poor girl has been through. She must be our guest until it is done.'

'Do you think that's a good idea, dear? The papers would have a field day if they got hold of that one. Why can't I go to London and teach her there?'

'Because you are known in London and that's where the papers are. They soon got fed up with pestering us once we'd battened down the hatches; and they've not been back since. There is no reason for anyone to suspect that Kim-Ly is here and part of me thinks sod the papers. What more can be done to your reputation that hasn't been done already? Besides, it gets a bit lonely here with just the two of us driving each other round the bend; it would be nice to have some company for a change.'

'But I do not want to be a burden,' said Kim-Ly, 'and I have no things with me.'

'Our daughter, Shelly, has some bits and bobs here for the rare occasions that she visits,' said Bunty. 'She's not much bigger than you and I'm sure she wouldn't mind if you borrowed a few outfits.'

'What do you think, Terry?' asked Kim-Ly.

'I'm thinking that I don't want to leave you, but I guess it makes sense; and you'll be safer here than in London. Can I come and visit?'

'You may,' said Bunty, 'and you will be very welcome. The other characters in your story sound intriguing too, so please feel free to invite them to the party; just give me a little warning so that I can prepare.'

'Now, hang on dear,' the professor protested, 'bit risky, isn't it? Sounds like these fellows have a proclivity for attracting attention. We've not long been out of the public eye and I'd rather not open up that can of worms again, if it's all the same to you.'

'Yes, but I'm bored, Julian. I need more social interaction; a lady can only take so many WI meetings and I'm convinced that they gossip behind my back the minute I'm gone. What do you want us to do; spend the rest of our lives in hiding? You've done nothing wrong apart from make a fool of yourself and, let's face it, you're not the first man to do that.'

The professor took another sip of tea and appraised Kim-Ly and Terry. 'Very well, my love,' he said at last; 'you're in charge, as always.'

'That's settled then,' Bunty smiled. 'You must stay for as long as it takes.'

Kim-Ly beamed and expressed her gratitude. Terry looked concerned. 'Professor, you said that the bet was with Sir Nigel. It wasn't Sir Nigel Shelby by any chance, was it?'

'The very chap. Why, do you know him?'

'I know of him,' answered Terry; 'nasty piece of work, from what I've heard.'

'He is that; reactionary policies that pander to the lowest common denominator, delivered with all the subtlety of Prince Philip. Unfortunately, he has gained some popularity among the xenophobic of the populace and it would seem that he and his ilk are on the rise.'

Bunty and the professor retired to the kitchen to wash up and left Terry and Kim-Ly alone to say their goodbyes.

'You were right; he is a nice man,' said Terry, as he held her tight.

'And Bunty, she is nice too,' said Kim-Ly. 'Are you going to be honest and tell them how you earn your money?'

'Not yet; they are understandably distrustful of journalists and may change their mind if they knew. Are you sure that you want to stay?'

'Yes; it is my best chance of passing. I will have one-to-one lessons with the top teacher and I like it here.'

'I'm not sure about this. We were just getting to know each other and I want to be there for you.'

'It will not be for long and you said I would be safer here.'

Terry sighed. 'OK then, but on one condition: you don't get too comfortable and forget to come back.'

'It is a deal, partner,' said Kim-Ly.

'I hope I'm not going to regret this,' replied Terry.

Van Otterloo was decidedly damp, in both body and spirit. 'It is that fine rain that soaks everything,' he complained. 'I understand that it is a regular feature of rural England. Should we not have disembarked at the same stop as them, sir? How will we find them now?'

Bomkamp shook his head. 'I don't know, my loyal Hoofdagent, but we would have aroused suspicion had we followed them off the bus. This is a small village; it should not be hard to find out what they are up to. Come, we should return to their stop and watch from a place of concealment; preferably one that shelters us from this damn drizzle.'

Down-hearted and homesick, they trudged back up the road from whence they came; no footpath to keep them safe. Suffering the hoots and splashes of passing 4x4s, they kept close to the roadside and took cover among thickets and bushes whenever necessary; where thorns scratched and twigs poked at every protruding body-part. Thoroughly pissed-off and muddyshoed, they found a disused allotment shed from which to view the bus-stop.

'Sir, what are we doing here?' asked Van Otterloo, once they'd been ensconced there for half-an-hour. 'Does Emre really have that much of a hold over you? Why can we not simply arrest him for his many misdemeanours and let him face justice?'

'Because he would bring me, and probably many others within the force, down with him,' answered Bomkamp. 'I have no choice but to do as he asks until such time as the game turns in our favour. My plan to lure him into the snare of a dangerous gang of rival criminals is not working. I am beginning to think that the people responsible for the murders of his brothers are relatively innocent and were just good guys inadvertently caught up in circumstances beyond their control. Having viewed their movements and behaviour since we have been in the UK, all of my instincts lead me to conclude that they are a bunch of damp squibs.'

'I doubt that they are as damp as us, sir,' shivered Van Otterloo. 'I suspect that, as we speak, they are cocooned in the heart of *Good Life* country, enjoying the delights of tea and biscuits.'

'SON OF A BITCH, SON OF A BITCH.'

'What was that, sir?' asked Van Otterloo.

'SON OF A BITCH, SON OF A BITCH.'

'Well, if I am not mistaken, it sounds like a man shouting "SON OF A BITCH, SON OF A BITCH" to me. Could be normal practice in this part of the world for all we know.'

'SON OF A BITCH, SON OF A BITCH.' The voice grew louder and Bomkamp and Van Otterloo attempted to keep to the meagre shadows in the small shed, before a large head poked round the door. 'I say, you haven't seen a large dog pass this way by any chance, have you?'

'Sorry, no,' answered Bomkamp. 'Son of a Bitch; it is a good name for a dog.'

'Thank you, I think so too. Bloody village is full of strangers today. May I ask what your business is here?'

Bomkamp flashed his badge, hoping that its Dutch origin would go unnoticed. 'We are police officers on surveillance and would be grateful for any information you can offer. Have you seen a tall man bearing a vague resemblance to Elvis and a woman of oriental origin?'

'I may have. Seemed like decent chaps to me; of what heinous crime are they accused?'

'I am not at liberty to divulge that, sir; but suffice it to say that this is a sensitive operation and we would appreciate your co-operation.'

'Strange business, all this; nothing ever happens here and one day is much the same as another. Will there be guns involved?'

'It is unlikely, sir. We simply wish to establish the whereabouts of two suspects in a crime. Are you able to assist us?'

'Very well; they were asking for directions to the professor's place, Hedgerow Lane, down that way.'

'Thank you, sir; and may I commend your good citizenship.'

'My pleasure; always happy to assist the constabulary. Bagshot's the name when you're handing out the medals. I bid you good day.'

'Good day, sir; and we'll keep our eyes peeled for your dog,' said Bomkamp.

Bagshot turned and, once again, strode purposefully away in search of his enigmatic pooch. 'SON OF A BITCH, SON OF A BITCH.'

Van Otterloo watched as Bagshot disappeared from the unkempt allotment. 'And from such unconventionality, comedy is born,' he mused. 'What now, sir? Should we try to find this Hedgerow Lane?'

'Absolutely. We will find a concealed place from which to observe the property.'

They were about to leave the shed, when Bomkamp pulled Van Otterloo back and pointed towards the bus stop. 'Wait, look!'

'Interesting,' said Van Otterloo; 'he is alone, which means he must have left the lovely Kim-Ly with the professor.'

'Then we must separate,' concluded Bomkamp. 'I will stay and ascertain what is occurring here, whilst you follow our mystery man back to London.'

'Do you think that's wise, sir? We will be like Morecambe without Wise, Little without Large, Hinge without Bracket. Besides, he may recognise me if I board the same bus.'

'Then you must wear this,' said Bomkamp, as he pulled an old moth-eaten, brown gardener's coat from a hook on the door. 'How about that hat and those wellies too; they will complete the disguise.'

'But there could be all kinds of lice and bugs residing in that coat, sir,' protested Van Otterloo.

Bomkamp shook it vigorously and handed it to his despondent subordinate. 'There, that's better; good as new.'

Van Otterloo reluctantly donned the decrepit garment and placed his right foot in the first discarded welly. Bomkamp supported him as he attempted to insert his other foot in the left boot. 'Wait, sir; there is something in here.' As Van Otterloo upended and shook the unwanted footwear, a bemused frog leapt out and, with an indignant 'ribbit', hopped away.

'That's better,' said Bomkamp, 'it should fit now.'

With a shudder, Van Otterloo tried again and complained that the outfit did little to enhance his street-cred.

'All in the name of duty,' declared Bomkamp. 'Now, you best hurry, before the bus arrives.'

He approached the bus stop nervously, keeping his head down to avoid the curious gaze of the tall man who, in the premature dusk, looked a bit like Elvis.

'Good afternoon,' said the man; 'pretty unpleasant weather we're having.'

'That it be, that it be,' agreed Van Otterloo, attempting to get into character and embrace the yokel vernacular.

'Yes it is, not that it be,' corrected the man as the bus approached.

Van Otterloo attempted to disguise his recognition of the

215

iconic exchange from *Blackadder*, but he couldn't resist a wry smile. Thankfully, the conversation ended there as they boarded and he made his way to the back, ignoring the probing glances of the other passengers. As the bus trundled away he looked back to see Bomkamp crossing the road. Van Otterloo shivered from the damp, but also in the realisation that he was alone in a strange country, probably wearing the cast-offs of some long-dead horticulturist and, on top of that, the less than elegant coat was emitting a rather unusual odour. He stared sadly through the window as a green and pleasant land rolled by and made a promise to himself that justice would be done.

20.

Buses came and buses went, each carrying a multitude of sin and virtue in countless human shells; each with their own hopes and fears. Lonely, that was the only word for it; Terry had been apart from Kim-Ly for a mere one-and-a-half hours, but already he was missing her and questioning the wisdom of leaving her behind. He was looking forward to meeting-up with the others at Spaghetti House in Covent Garden, for updates on their day and to plan their strategy; as well as to indulge in a little pasta and wine. He'd chosen the venue for its very public location, which would hopefully act as a deterrent to Emre; the place would be heaving on a Friday night and there would be no opportunity for him to go unnoticed if he had any mischief in mind.

Terry paused to button his jacket against the elements and almost retched as the smell of the country bumpkin in the brown coat caught his throat. The man glanced sideways at him as he passed, then disappeared behind another bus in the busy terminal. There was something not quite right about that guy. Terry shrugged and made his way towards the taxi rank, but stopped in his tracks as he caught the reflection in a shelter of the man discarding his coat and wellies. He circled round to get a better view, until he was immediately behind this shady character; and then he recognised him as one of the two passengers who had been on the bus to Berkshire. How could he have been so blind?

If this man was here, then his associate must be shadowing Kim-Ly and she may be in peril. Thinking quickly, he grabbed a half-full Coke bottle from his bag, crept up behind his pursuer and rammed it hard into his back.

'OK, what's the game?' growled Terry, attempting to sound mean, but secretly shaking inside. 'Why have you and your friend been following us?' The man winced and endeavoured to look back at his assailant. 'Keep looking straight ahead,' ordered Terry, thinking that his captive may not be quite so scared if he knew the gun was actually a bottle of pop.

'I am a police officer,' the man said at last, 'investigating a double murder in Amsterdam; and I have reason to believe that you may be able to help us with our enquiries. Please take that gun out of my back and I will show you my badge; then I will explain over a coffee. If you have nothing to hide, then you have no reason not to speak with me.'

Terry hesitated. 'I'll take a look at that badge before I put the gun away, if you don't mind,' said Terry. 'Put your hand in your pocket slowly and put your badge where your mouth is.'

'That is a very corny line, if you do not mind me saying so.'

'Just show me the badge and cut the critique.'

Without sudden movement, the proof was held before Terry's eyes. 'But you are Dutch police,' he observed; 'surely you have no jurisdiction here.'

'It is true that I am working undercover and we have no power. If it would help to convince, I can tell you that I am also an enemy of Emre. Now, please take that thing out of my back.'

'Very well,' said Terry, and held up the Coke bottle with a wry smile. 'Sorry about that. What is your name?'

'Hoofdagent Van Otterloo at your service. I thought it may not have been a gun, but I could not take any chances. After all, we have a hunch that you and your companions have already killed twice.'

Terry ignored the casual accusation and asked, 'And what of

your associate? Don't try to deny it; there were two of you on the way to Berkshire.'

'He is still there. When you and Kim-Ly split up, we had no choice but to separate too.'

'Kim-Ly; is she in any danger?' asked Terry.

'No, just under surveillance at the moment; she is in safe hands with my boss around and Emre is nowhere near.'

'Then where is he?'

'Come, let us have that coffee,' suggested Van Otterloo. 'Can we not hold this conversation in a more agreeable location?'

Terry considered their surroundings and had to concur that diesel fumes, among damp and mud-splattered buses did not constitute the most congenial of settings for a tête-à-tête.

Rendezvous was the name of the small French coffee bar, the mock-sophisticated décor in blue and white endeavouring, but failing miserably, to engender the romance of Paris. Terry held the door open for Van Otterloo and they made their way to a secluded table in the corner. The waiter eyed them with an aloof expression, then sauntered over with open pad to take their order. ''ow may I 'elp you, gentlemen?' The words were polite enough, but Terry had never heard anyone inject the word 'gentlemen' with such contempt; and the tone conveyed a very different message: ''ow dare you sully my classy establishment.'

'Have you got frogs' legs?' asked Van Otterloo.

'Inevitably,' replied the waiter.

'Well, hop over there and get us two lattes, will you.'

'Very amusing, sir, albeit somewhat stereotypical.'

'Tommy Cooper,' exclaimed Terry, as the waiter looked down his nose, then turned to fetch their coffee. 'The frogs' legs joke; it's classic Tommy Cooper.'

'Indeed it is,' said Van Otterloo. 'Are you a fan too?'

'The man was a genius. He only had to walk on stage to get the audience laughing; they'd be eating out of his hand before he'd even uttered a word.'

'That is true; but enough reminiscing,' said Van Otterloo. 'What can you tell me about the deaths of Emre's brothers?'

'Why should I trust you?' asked Terry. 'We've only just met and you flash a Micky Mouse badge and expect me to tell you everything. How do I know you are not working with the British police and we'd be under arrest as soon as you say the word?'

'You have my word that we are working alone. The British police do not know we are here and anything you say to me will be in the strictest confidence.'

The rattle of coffee cups interrupted the discussion and the waiter slammed down their drinks with disdain, before moving on to his next victims. Terry looked Van Otterloo in the eye and considered his pledge. He looked an honest enough chap and Terry was utterly sick of carrying around the burden of those unintentional manslaughters; he almost welcomed the liberation of confession.

'OK, here goes. I would argue self-defence in a court of law,' he said. 'We didn't mean to kill them, but they would have had no hesitation in killing us. It all started like this. ...'

Van Otterloo listened in disbelief as the whole intriguing tale was laid bare before him; from Terry's reason for being in Amsterdam, to his obsession with Kim-Ly; from Sandra and Pete's inadvertent involvement and support, to the loss of their home; from the method of murder, to the disposal of the bodies and weapons; from Robbie's assistance, to his unlikely alliance with Celina; concluding with Terry's transformation from journalist to killer, from free man to fugitive, all in the space of two weeks.

'Phew! So you are not part of an international drugs and prostitution cartel, then?' said Van Otterloo. 'And you were not trying to muscle in on Emre's patch.'

'Do I look like a drugs baron?' protested Terry. 'Nothing could be further from the truth; we just stood on some dangerous toes and things have somewhat snowballed from there.'

'Then I am willing to assist you,' said Van Otterloo. 'I, too, have a vested interest in accommodating the demise of Emre. I am not at liberty to say why, but it would be in all of our interests if he were to disappear.'

'Are you suggesting what I think you are?' asked Terry. 'His brothers' unfortunate deaths were not premeditated, you know; we had no option but to render them incapacitated. We didn't intend to kill anyone.' Terry recalled the fury on Celina's face as she'd finished off the second sibling and shuddered at the thought; there was no doubting *her* intent. 'Besides,' he continued, attempting to eradicate the memory, 'we are on English soil now; what's the old adage about not shitting on your own doorstep?'

'Another one of your quaint English sayings, no doubt,' said Van Otterloo. 'I am not necessarily proposing that we kill him, just that we prevent him from continuing his vendettas against you and my superior.'

'Ah, he has something on your boss, does he? Think I'm getting the picture now. That's why you are working alone and have not enlisted the assistance of your UK counterparts. So, where is Emre now?'

'He has followed Celina and he thinks we are complicit in his plans. He will call Hoofdinspecteur Bomkamp at 6 p.m. to exchange information.' Van Otterloo looked at his watch. 'Hey, it is 6.30 p.m. now; I did not realise how the time had gone by. I will call the Hoofdinspecteur now to find out the lie of the land.'

Terry sat in silence and listened, fascinated, to Van Otterloo's side of the conversation: ... 'So you are still watching the house ... yes, it will be cold and wet. They are unlikely to go anywhere tonight, sir; why do you not find somewhere to stay and resume your surveillance in the morning? ... Have you spoken with Emre? ... Ah, so he lost them in the underground melee; interesting ... yes, I am still following the Englishman; he is in a pseudo-French café at the moment. ... Yes, OK, I will call you in the morning. Sleep well, sir.'

'Why didn't you tell him you'd caught up with me?' asked Terry.

'Because I do not want him to know about our conversation and that I am going after Emre. He would get nervous if he suspected that I am a maverick cop with a mind of my own.'

'Am I to understand that Emre is no longer tailing Celina and Robbie?'

'So it seems. The London Underground is a confusing place for us foreigners, you know.'

'That's a big relief,' said Terry. 'It was only going to be a matter of time before he took a pop at Celina.' Terry thought for a moment. 'Are you sure I can trust you?'

'Absolutely. As I said before, Emre is our mutual enemy and we should join together to defeat him.'

'OK then. I am meeting the others this evening. You must join us for some Italian food, while we discuss our next move.'

'Thank you; it will be an honour. I can guarantee that you will not regret this.'

Emre had allowed himself the luxury of an evil grin after completing his conversation with Bomkamp. It suited his purpose for them to believe that he'd lost sight of his quarry; he did not trust the police and was well aware that they would betray him at the earliest opportunity. The chill in the evening air impregnated his bones and he was utterly fed-up with staking out Celina and her new companion. For a while he'd started to believe in his uncle's words that encouraged forgiveness, a new path to honesty and a clear conscience; to the extent that he'd even tried being nice to people.

He was sure that the old lady wished to cross the road and, as he'd taken her arm to help, was rewarded only by painful blows from her walking stick, raining down upon his head, to the amusement of onlookers. The resultant black eye made him look even more evil than usual, but no-one would ever believe how he came by it.

The *Big Issue* salesman had cowered back in the doorway, seeming certain that this foul-looking man was about to relieve him of his takings. Emre had thrown him twice the cover-price and muttered something about not judging people by their appearance.

He'd tried smiling at passers-by and wishing them good-day, but his fearsome fizzog was poorly designed for such facial gymnastics and his row of misshapen teeth manifested in an uncomfortable grimace. How could he pretend to be something he was not?

Ultimately, the pull of retribution had won. What had he been thinking of, listening to his conscientious uncle, the voice of the past and of a downtrodden generation? Every tale needs its villain and he was more than qualified for the part; he was Emre, feared and loathed by all, and he had not gone soft after all. He would have to bide his time and pick the right moment, but his resolve had returned and he was on the war-path once more.

At last they emerged and stood beneath the street light, looking nervously up and down the road: Celina, as provocative as ever in short skirt and figure-hugging jacket; and her chaperone dressed to impress, like an extra from some retro-movie, all sharp lines and checks in blue and black, with pointy shoes and a boastful expression. 'She is with me' it seemed to say, provoking yet more wrath in Emre's troubled soul. He waited for them to decide which way to go, then followed, keeping to the shadows, ducking and diving each time Robbie looked uneasily over his shoulder. Emre's chance would come soon, he was sure. Then he would return to tend to his business and things could go back to normal; but he knew that his life could never be as it was. With his brothers gone, he was alone, with no-one to care for or to care for him. Sure, he'd had women on tap for as long as he could remember, with no qualms about taking full advantage of the power he wielded mercilessly; but, although some pretended, deep down he sensed that none felt anything but contempt for him. The bitterness welled up inside and once more he vowed vengeance on all who had shown disrespect.

Sandra and Pete got there first. They weaved their way to the table booked by Terry and made themselves comfortable; Pete, as he invariably did, chose a seat that took in the panorama of the rest of the restaurant and the outside hustle and bustle, while Sandra contented herself with facing the wall, a small romantic portrayal of Venice her only window to the world. She thought about how things had changed since that chance meeting with Pete, of how the canals had become her home too. She studied the Venetian vista before her and promised herself that, one day, they would visit; of all the exotic holidays she'd endured with her ex-husband, the beauty of Venice had somehow passed them by.

'Bloody hell, Kim-Ly's changed,' exclaimed Pete, puncturing her dreams. Sandra turned to see Terry entering with a strange, lean young man. She gave Terry her best quizzical look that asked without the need for words: 'What the hell's going on?'

'Sandra, Pete, I'd like you to meet Hoofdagent Van Otterloo from the Dutch police force. Don't worry, he's on our side,' Terry added quickly, upon viewing Sandra's apprehensive expression. 'He and his boss have been tracking us since Gouda.'

Pete stood and shook Van Otterloo's hand, while Sandra asked, 'What have you done with Kim-Ly?'

'She's perfectly safe,' said Terry. 'The professor turned out to be a nice guy and his wife's an angel. Kim-Ly is out of harm's way with them.'

Sandra was unconvinced. 'Terry, I'm a bit concerned that we're all doing our own thing here. Emre is still at large and we haven't a clue where he is or who he's following. In case it has escaped your notice, he's a dangerous man with good reason to despise us all.'

'You are very astute,' observed Van Otterloo. 'He should not be underestimated and I will do all I can to bring him to justice. I know we have just met, but I will prove that I am your ally.'

It was obvious that Celina recognised Van Otterloo as soon as she crossed the threshold, cowering behind Robbie; a futile gesture, as it would require a far more imposing figure than Robbie to conceal Celina. 'V-vhat is he doing here?' she snarled.

'He is police and not to be trusted; they are as bad as the pimps, some of them vorse. They hide behind a mask of respectability, but treat us just the same. I have lost count of the times I have been let off a drugs charge in return for sex.'

'It is a pleasure to see you again too, Celina,' said Van Otterloo. 'Do not worry; you cannot be busted this time, as I have no power here. And please do not include me in your lazy generalisations. Yes, there are some bad apples in every police force, but I am not one of them. My only interest is to prevent Emre from doing you or us any harm.'

'Are you alone?' asked Celina.

'No, Hoofdinspecteur Bomkamp is here too; well, not here exactly, but in the country.'

'Hoofdinspecteur Bomkamp!' sneered Celina. 'Is that supposed to be reassuring? That lowlife is in Emre's pocket and he vill do vhatever he is told.' She turned to Terry. 'Vhat are you thinking of, bringing him here? Kim-Ly and I have lived among these vermin, remember; all they vill do is lead Emre to us in order to cover their backs and avoid his blackmail.'

Van Otterloo looked defiant. He thought for a moment, then spoke in measured terms. 'OK, I will be entirely honest with you all. Emre does have some influence over Hoofdinspecteur Bomkamp. My mentor did succumb to temptation once and has been reluctantly susceptible to the whims of Emre ever since; but I, I will not tolerate his skulduggery and, with or without your assistance, I intend to destroy him and his empire.'

Sandra could see that everyone but Celina looked impressed with this declaration: Terry, already convinced as to Van Otterloo's intentions; Pete, seeing the good in everyone, as usual; and Robbie, willing to cut him some slack. She stood and put her arm around Celina's waist, inviting her to sit down. 'What do we have to lose by listening to what he has to say?' she reasoned. 'Let's just enjoy the meal and each other's company, shall we? Then we can decide who are the good guys.'

225

Celina reluctantly sat down beside Sandra and proceeded to scowl at Van Otterloo throughout the antipasto. By the time dessert had been served, however, Van Otterloo had won them all over, aided by an abundance of alcohol and bonhomie. Celina smiled at Robbie whilst seductively sucking her panna-cotta and, for a while, all seemed well with her world. Reassured that Emre had lost the scent and that Kim-Ly was safe, she began to relax and enjoy the evening.

The banter and vino flowed in copious quantities, Terry and Robbie exchanging good-natured acidic asides. 'I'm not trying to be clever …,' began Robbie.

'Good, because it doesn't suit you,' replied Terry.

'… but, if you know the way, it's just as quick to walk from here as it is to get the tube or a taxi.'

'Yeah, but my bladder wouldn't last the journey,' said Terry. 'I suppose I could pee behind a bush in the park on the way home, but the steam tends to give it away this time of night and, knowing my luck, I'd inadvertently piss on a tramp; then where would I be? I can just see me dashing through the park pursued by an irate itinerant, who, no doubt, will be able to run faster than me. No, I'll get a cab if it's all the same to you.'

Barry, exhausted after his first full day's work for some time, joined them in time for coffee and the inevitable question of sleeping arrangements reared its head. After much slurred discourse, it was agreed that Sandra and Pete would go back to Barry's; Robbie and Celina to Robbie's parents; and Terry would extend his hospitality to Van Otterloo.

Sobering thoughts concluded a pleasant evening and, as Celina retired to the bathroom, the others took the opportunity to plan their strategy. 'If Emre has lost the trail, then the only place he knows where to pick it up again is at Barry's house,' reasoned Robbie. 'He won't be interested in you, Barry, or Sandra and Pete. No, it will be Celina and Kim-Ly he'll want. It's time to get mean and play him at his own game. I suggest that tomorrow we lay a trap for him and scare him off for good. Anyone have any ideas?'

'But do you think any of us are scary enough to frighten him away?' asked a sceptical Terry. 'He'll laugh in our faces.'

'Maybe not us,' replied Robbie, 'but I know some men who can put on a pretty good front. Why don't we lead him to the Capital? A Saturday night, the place will be packed and I can enlist the assistance of some mates. You remember Stevie Reece, Joey Sullivan and Jimmy One-Note? They'll be well up for it if they think someone's looking for trouble on our manor.'

'What is the Capital?' asked Van Otterloo.

'It's a nightclub,' replied Robbie. 'There's some kind of altercation there most weekends, so no-one will suspect a thing if it all kicks-off. Someone could watch the place from the outside, so we'll know when he enters. We can communicate by text and be ready for him.'

'I've not been to a nightclub for years,' said Sandra. 'Won't we look a bit out of place?'

'Nah, they let anyone in and you get all sorts there.'

'The Capital, one of London's classiest establishments,' laughed Terry. 'It could be a plan; unless anyone has any other suggestions.'

Robbie took the ensuing silence as agreement. 'That's settled then. I'll alert the lads and we'll all meet there at eight. Now, let's change the subject. Celina is returning and she'll get nervous if she knows what we're up to.'

'Time to go our separate ways again, I think,' said Terry. 'We'll reconvene tomorrow.'

Sandra, Pete and Barry watched as Terry and Van Otterloo, then Robbie and Celina, climbed into different cabs and headed off in opposite directions. They were about to turn and make their way to the underground, when a loud bang made Sandra jump. 'Was that a gunshot?' she gasped.

'Probably just a car backfiring,' reassured Pete, as he put his arm around her shoulder. 'You're jumping at every sound. Lead the way, Barry.'

21.

Hoofdinspecteur Bomkamp shed tears of rage and regret as he watched the news in disbelief. The homely guesthouse boasted all mod-cons (even a kettle with tea, coffee and biscuits), and the small TV on the wall above his bed was coldly broadcasting the chilling headlines, "Dutch policeman murdered in London", "Mystery as to why he was in UK", "Police looking for man who shared taxi".

He glared up from the pages of the book and sobbed. 'You bastard. You had to do it, didn't you? You call yourself the Creator, but all you do is destroy. Has there not been enough murder and misery already? Van Otterloo was a good, loyal man and the only one injecting any wit into this wretched tale. Where are your lame jokes going to come from now, ay? Why could you not take me instead? I am the one responsible for bringing him here, for leading him to his lonely death; but you, you are the one creating this senseless destruction, pulling randomly upon our strings before you discard us once you've had your amusement. Who will be the next to satisfy your bloodlust? Yes, it is clear that you will lay the blame at Emre's feet, but we all know who the real killer is, don't we? Please, I beg of you, take me next. I have brought shame upon my family and the force and now my only true comrade has gone. If the good guys are to triumph in this inexplicable saga, which, I hasten to add, is not a foregone conclusion with you in charge, then you can find someone else to be your hero. I am no longer prepared to play your puppet.'

In uncontrollable anger, he thrust his fists repeatedly into the pillow, before an insistent banging on the paper-thin, damp-infested wall prompted him to stop. 'Hey, keep it down, buddy. I'm trying to wank in here and you're disturbing the ambience.'

Bomkamp looked up again and sneered. 'You see, already the humour has hit the gutter. Where will you take us next; to *Benidorm?*' In an effort to share Van Otterloo's interests, he'd been watching this highly amusing and gaudy show the previous night, whilst attempting in vain to get to sleep.

A new determination overcame him as he dressed quickly and brushed his hair and teeth with vigour. Eschewing the obviously offended landlady's offer of breakfast, he settled the bill and headed for the door. Taking a deep breath of fresh morning air, he walked briskly back along the main road before turning down the lane towards the professor's house. He was sick of subterfuge and deceit. He would take the bull by the horns and confront Kim-Ly.

'SON OF A BITCH, SON OF A BITCH.'

Bomkamp raised his eyes to the heavens once more. 'For God's sake, have you not done that joke to death?'

Regardless, Bagshot stood before him, with no sign of his permanently wayward hound. 'Ah, good morning, officer; a fine day for a stroll, don't you think. Haven't seen a dog on your travels by any chance, have you?'

'No, I have not seen your bloody dog,' shouted Bomkamp, rapidly losing what little patience he had left. 'Now, will you kindly get out of my way and allow me to continue my mission.'

'I say, there's no need for that tone of voice, old fellow. I suggest that you calm down before you get to the professor's house. I'm sure he will not welcome such an ill-mannered intrusion.'

'Thank you for your unsolicited advice,' snapped Bomkamp, as he turned and strode away, to the fading sound of 'SON OF A BITCH, SON OF A BITCH.'

'Aagghh!!' he screamed, before turning purposefully into the professor's drive. Taking a deep breath, he approached the door, rapped loudly and awaited a response. After a short while, he could see the silhouette of a small man behind the frosted-glass.

'Who is it?' shouted the shadow. 'What do you want?'

'I am a police officer, sir. I am investigating a very serious crime and have reason to believe that you are sheltering someone who may be able to help me. Do you have a young lady by the name of Kim-Ly on the premises?' Bomkamp could just make out the outline of someone shuffling in the shadows behind. A muffled, urgent conversation ensued, before the letterbox opened slightly.

'Slowly place your badge through the letterbox, then stand back,' said the voice on the other side. 'I would like to see some ID before I allow you access.'

Bomkamp impatiently did as instructed and, after more muffled dialogue, the door opened slightly and a studious-looking man poked his head round and appraised him suspiciously. 'I suppose you'd better come in,' he said.

As he entered, the undeniably sexy Kim-Ly stood insolently before him. 'Hoofdinspecteur Bomkamp, what a pleasant surprise. Please come through; this way.' Kim-Ly stood aside, with her arm indicating the way, and he seethed silently at her nonchalance as he made his way along the hall to the kitchen. His vision was filled by an array of copper kettles and pans that hung from the ceiling and he was temporarily blinded as the morning sun reflected dazzlingly into his eyes. Disorientated, he noticed not the open hatchway at his feet and, before he could recover, he was falling fast, his head banging painfully against a beam as he descended into a dark abyss. An excruciating pain shot up his leg as he landed awkwardly, his ankle twisted beneath him. Then darkness, as the hatch slammed shut, his screams of agony and anger unheeded. 'HELP, LET ME OUT. YOU WILL PAY FOR THIS.' No answer, as he heard the chilling sound of the bolts slamming home.

Professor Nutt was not a happy man. 'What the hell do you mean, you planned it,' he shouted at his wife, who stood in front of the fireplace looking rather proud of herself.

'Terry called last night, while you were incommunicado in your study, as usual,' replied Bunty. 'He said that the Dutch police were watching the place and that we may be getting a visit. Kim-Ly and I came up with this little plan just in case.'

'You damned fools. Do you know what kind of trouble we could be in? And what, pray, do you intend to do with him now that you have him locked in our cellar? We can't leave him there indefinitely. Or did you intend to starve the poor chap to death as well?'

'I just thought that he couldn't do anything while he's incapacitated down there, that's all,' said Bunty. 'It will buy us some time until we decide what is to be done.'

Professor Nutt pulled fretfully at what was left of his unkempt hair. 'This isn't a game, you know. You can't simply imprison policemen on a whim. Kim-Ly, I don't believe that you have told us everything. A very serious crime, he said; what exactly are we talking about here? You have accepted our hospitality and you should be straight with us.'

Kim-Ly sat beside Bunty for reassurance, then reluctantly recounted the story so far, culminating in Bomkamp's interest in keeping it under wraps. 'Everybody knows that he and half of the force are being blackmailed by Emre. How else could the Loverboy Brothers get away with the things they do?'

'So, let us review the situation,' the professor sighed, when she had finished. 'Terry and your friend Celina are both the subjects of a murder enquiry, whilst the rest of you are, at best, accessories. We have drugs, prostitution and passport fraud, not to mention the latest development: kidnap and imprisonment. What do you do for an encore?'

Kim-Ly sobbed. 'Do you think I wanted all this? I was perfectly happy at home in Vietnam. Yes, we were poor, but we were strong together as a family and community.' She paused in thought for a moment, before declaring, 'I cannot stand this any more. Let me go home; I do not belong here and I am not a pawn, to be used for sex or for a bet. I will go to the Vietnamese Embassy and rely on their mercy. As for Bomkamp, all I ask is that you let me get far enough away before you let him go. Your Western ways and attitudes have destroyed me; now I must try to get home and rebuild my life. I have met some good people here and I want to thank all of you for what you have done for me: you, Bunty, Sandra, Pete, Robbie, my best friend Celina; even Gemma was kind to me. Tell Terry that he is the only man I have ever felt any love for.'

'The only man for whom you have ever felt any love,' corrected the professor.

'Yes, yes, OK. But now, it is time for me to go and leave you all in peace. I have caused more than enough trouble for one small girl.'

Bunty put a comforting arm around her shoulder and addressed her cantankerous spouse. 'Julian, please show a little compassion. Can you not see that Kim-Ly is upset?'

'She's upset!! How do you think I feel? You conspire, behind my back, to plunge an unsuspecting police officer into our wine cellar and leave him, probably badly injured, in total darkness. The poor man must be terrified. Before we do anything else, I intend to check that he is, at least, still breathing.'

The professor stood defiantly and strode to the kitchen, followed by a silent Bunty and Kim-Ly. Slowly, he lifted the cellar door and peered into the darkness. 'I say, are you OK down there?'

'No, I am not OK. I think my ankle may be broken and I have a head injury. I suggest that you call an ambulance to allow a paramedic to assess the extent of my injuries.'

'All in good time,' interrupted Bunty, as she took over and closed the hatch once more. 'Julian, I will take Kim-Ly to London and accompany her to the Embassy. When we are gone for three hours you can attend to our prisoner. Tell him that we know all about his peccadillo and that, if he tries to follow, we will have no hesitation in exposing him for the rogue that he is, or words to that effect.'

The professor turned to Kim-Ly. 'So, you have given up on your dream to pass your exam.'

'Not given up, no; but how can I continue with the world falling to pieces around me? Perhaps, one day, I will get the opportunity, but my English is already very good; you and everyone else say so. A GCSE is just a piece of paper. My qualification is in my speech, my written word. There will be no-one better qualified to teach in my village; that is all I need. Please, let me go home.'

'You don't need our permission; you are free to do as you wish. Very well. Bunty will assist you as best she can, but it may not be wise to convey the whole story to the Embassy. Just tell them you are a victim of human trafficking and request a safe passage home. Now, you'd best be making tracks; our friend below will no doubt be a little angry when he emerges and I will have to come up with a convincing ruse to explain how he got there.'

'Please, do not tell Terry where I have gone,' pleaded Kim-Ly. 'He will only turn up at the Embassy and try to change my mind.'

'I will attempt to stall him, but I don't want to lie to the fellow; he's obviously besotted.'

'I know, but I cannot stand goodbyes. It is better that I slip away quietly.'

Professor Nutt nodded in agreement. 'Maybe it's for the best.'

Kim-Ly hugged the professor and kissed his blushing cheek. 'Thank-you, thank-you, thank-you,' she gushed. 'How can I ever repay your kindness?'

'Just have a happy life; and maybe write occasionally to let us know how you're doing. Now, in the words of the Bard, wilt thou be gone?'

Professor Julian Nutt waved sadly as the taxi pulled out of the drive. He wasn't used to his students flunking their exams, but he knew that Kim-Ly would endure and that his efforts would not be wasted. As he turned back into the house, he found it hard to ignore the angry cries from the cellar, but he stepped carefully over the hatch and retreated to the sanctuary of his study. Three hours, Bunty had said, before he could release the prisoner. It would be a long three hours.

Still shaking with shock, Terry stared straight ahead at his bedroom wall, the blood-splattered clothes on the floor beside his bed belying his hope that it was all a bad dream. He didn't really know what had happened; all he could recall was the gunshot as they'd stopped at the traffic lights, the warm, damp feeling of Van Otterloo's gore spurting all over him; his sheer panic as he'd opened the door and ran without looking back, until he could run no longer. He'd wheezed and coughed and slumped in a back alley, before an indignant vagrant had sent him packing with the gruff advice: 'Bugger off and find your own patch.'

He tried to piece together the events of the previous night, but could only feel the contrast between Van Otterloo's convivial company and the suddenness of his demise. He'd slept some, God knows how, but fitfully and without any consciousness of time or the urgency of his situation. Slowly he regained his senses and a cold shiver overcame him. What was he thinking of? The others could be in peril. Why hadn't he called last night to warn that Emre was very much on their case? At least, he assumed it was Emre that had performed this barbaric execution; he hadn't actually seen the killer in the darkness.

Terry took a deep breath as he dialled Professor Nutt's number. 'Hello, Professor, it's Terry; can I speak to Kim-Ly?' He felt like a teenager, calling to ask Gemma out; he'd always felt uncomfortable when her father answered.

'Kim-Ly's in the bath at the moment. I'll ask her to call you back later.'

In the bath or washing her hair, that was always Gemma's excuse when she fancied a night in by herself. Despite his troubled soul, he couldn't help but close his eyes and picture Kim-Ly in the bath.

'Are you still there?' asked the professor.

'Yes, yes, sorry. Please, ask her to call back quickly; she could be in danger.' He was surprised when the professor asked no more questions, as if he had other things on his mind.

Fumbling with his keypad, he called Robbie. 'P-please be careful. Emre is still at large and on the warpath.'

'I guessed as much,' replied Robbie. 'It's all over the news this morning. I assume that was our friend Van Otterloo who was killed last night. I don't imagine there are too many other Dutch detectives on the loose in London. So, the other passenger that the police are looking for then, that'll be you, presumably.'

'I haven't seen the news. God, Robbie, it was awful; he blew his brains out, right there beside me. His blood is all over my clothes. What should I do?'

'Well, the way I see it, we've got two options: we either go to the police and tell them everything, with the possibility of jail to follow; or we pursue our plan to lure him into the trap at the Capital, on our terms and turf. I suggest the latter. The first thing you must do is to burn whatever you were wearing last night. No offence, but it'll be no great loss to fashion. Then shower and lie low for the rest of the day. Call the others to warn them to be on their guard and not to go anywhere alone. I will contact Stevie and the boys and ask for their help.'

'But what are we to do once we have him there?' asked Terry. 'Are we to beat him to within an inch of his life? I don't think I could, Robbie.'

Robbie's voice was cold and grave. 'Celina has told me of some of the things he did, the way he treated her and Kim-Ly; not to mention all the others he's used and abused. If it comes to it, I think I could add a few strategically placed kicks here and there.'

'But you're not a thug, Robbie. You shouldn't even be involved in all of this.'

'The man is pure evil, Terry. He must be stopped and, if you have any doubts, then last night should tell you that he'd have no hesitation in knocking us off one by one. If it makes you feel better, you can be the man outside who gives the nod when he enters the club. I'll take care of the rest.'

'I don't know, Robbie. We're way out of our depth here.'

'What's the alternative, Terry? We've been out of our depth since this all started. Now it's either sink or swim.'

'OK. What do you want me to do?'

'Firstly, let everyone else know the plan and tell them to be there at eight. This evening you must find somewhere to hide with a full view of the entrance of the Capital. You text me when he comes in, then disappear. I will call you to let you know the outcome.'

'Understood,' said Terry, 'but please be careful; he could be watching you now.'

As Terry hung up, he noticed the missed call from Sandra, his hand shaking as he called her back. 'What the hell's going on, Terry?' she said. 'Every channel has it on a loop. The police are looking for a tall, thin man with an Elvis haircut; that's the description the taxi driver gave them, anyway. They say that the shot came from outside the taxi, so they only want to speak to you as a witness.'

'That's reassuring,' answered Terry. 'I'm still in shock, Sandra. Van Otterloo was laughing, right beside me. Said he'd had a wonderful time and what great company we all were. Then he was gone, just like that, as if he'd been executed by a firing squad.'

'Jesus, it must have been a nightmare. I'm scared, Terry. He could be watching any one of us. So, what happens now?'

'I've spoken to Robbie and he wants to follow the plan we agreed yesterday. We're all to meet at the club at eight. I'm on watch outside and Robbie's setting the trap.'

'Why do we all have to be there?' asked Sandra.

'Because we don't know who he's stalking. As far as we know,

I'm the only one whose address he doesn't know. If you all go, then there's a good chance he'll be there too. I suggest you stay in today, lock everything and don't answer the door to anyone. Tonight's the night he'll get his come-uppance.'

Terry stared at his gaunt face in the mirror. He looked about five years older than he did three weeks ago; bags had developed under his eyes when he wasn't looking and worry lines had appeared on his forehead, his hair a mess from tossing and turning. "The police are looking for a tall, thin man with an Elvis haircut", he recalled Sandra's words. Taking the scissors, he began to cut, almost in tears as his magnificent, thick black quiff fell in clumps to the floor. Snip, snip; he cut miserably to the skull, before a large dollop of shaving foam and his razor finished the job. If he was to spend time in jail, he may as well look like a convict.

The shower revived his senses, the hot water bouncing cruelly off his newly shaven head as the remnants of his hair swirled down the drain. He didn't recognise the emaciated individual in the mirror and it dawned on him that his friends and colleagues wouldn't either. What would Kim-Ly think of him now? She would probably run, all the way back to Vietnam. With resignation, he dried himself and dressed in jeans, t-shirt and his long black coat, felling a little more human again.

Terry picked up the offending blood-stained clothes and placed them in a large carrier bag, along with a box of matches. He descended the stairs, stopping only to don his grey woollen hat. A cool breeze hit his face as he slowly opened the door and, peering up and down the street until the coast was clear, he left the flat, feeling conspicuous and guilt-ridden. "Burn whatever you were wearing last night", Robbie had advised. All well and good, thought Terry, but where? His head down to avoid the inevitable CCTV cameras (a 1984-style intrusion of privacy, or designed to expose people like him?), he walked and walked, until he came upon a deserted service road at the rear of some shops, where someone had conveniently left an empty skip. At least, he thought it was empty. With one final look around, he doused his formerly finest threads in lighter fuel and sparked the match that would destroy any links he had to the crime. Holding the flame to a protruding trouser leg, he ensured that the fire had taken hold, then lobbed the bag into the skip. Walking briskly away, he'd reached the end of the road before a roar indicated that something highly flammable had combusted behind him.

'Shit!' he exclaimed, and quickened his pace, closely followed by a pair of fuming, white-overalled painter and decorators, shaking their fists and shouting obscenities. Fortuitously, they both looked as if they were partial to the odd pie and Terry was able to make his escape, turning the corner and leaving them panting and cursing, doubled over with hands on knees.

How had it come to this, he thought; of what crime could he be accused, to make him run like a fugitive from justice when he'd done nothing wrong? Inside he felt as guilty as hell; as if he were the one who'd pulled the trigger.

Upon his return, he again phoned Professor Nutt; no answer. Perhaps Kim-Ly really didn't want to speak to him. Feeling utterly miserable, he turned on the TV, the news depicting a fairly detailed description of the man that the Met wanted to interview. The reporter at the scene of the crime went on to declare that the police were co-operating with their counterparts in Holland and that they were also very concerned about the disappearance of a second Dutch detective.

The picture skipped to some breaking news concerning a large fire in West London. The fire brigade were in attendance and a nearby parade of shops had been evacuated as a precautionary measure; fortunately there were no casualties. The police are appealing for witnesses and for any information about a tall, thin man observed running from the scene.

Terry put his unfamiliar head in his hands and took a gasp of air. 'Oh, my God!' he sighed; but there was no-one to listen.

* * *

The atmosphere was like ice as Gemma met Celina on the landing and they both reached the bathroom at the same time. 'Please, after you,' said Celina, standing aside.

Gemma nodded, but said nothing. It wasn't her fault, but Celina was a cruel reminder of the trauma of the past few weeks. Gemma splashed cold water on her face in an effort to confront another day; it was mid-morning, and still she felt like going back to bed.

Downstairs, and Gemma caught Robbie at the front window, carefully pulling back the net-curtains and surveying the street outside. 'What's going on, Robbie?' she asked. 'Expecting someone?'

Robbie jumped. 'Do you have to creep around like that? If you must know, Emre is in London and he's not in the best of moods.'

'So we've brought all that crap back with us, have we? And there was me thinking we'd escaped and it was time to move on.' It was in this very room that her gran had uttered the wise words: "You have to look after number one and take control, because no-one else can determine your destiny". Gemma had spent the previous day mulling things over and over and had reached pretty much the same conclusion, albeit at the expense of her busy work schedule; as usual, no-one else had picked up her tasks while she'd been away.

Robbie gave his sister a hug. 'I'm sorry, Gemma; been so preoccupied these past few days that I haven't had time for my big Sis'. How are you coping with the fallout?'

'Guess I'll survive; not got much choice, have I? What about you? Are you sure Celina is the one, or are you just along for the ride, if you'll pardon the expression?'

'Cut her some slack, Gemma, she's had a tough life. I think she's special and, for once, I'm not just talking physically.'

'You know you'll have my support,' said Gemma, 'however

things turn out. So, what about Emre then? Do you think he knows where we are?'

Gemma sat in dismayed silence, as Robbie brought her up to date. 'And that's where we're at,' he concluded. 'Tonight we take charge of the situation. It's the only way we can ever be free of him. Celina knows nothing of our little plan – didn't want her getting frightened – so keep it under your hat.'

'Jesus, Robbie, this is way out of your league. Please don't do it,' pleaded Gemma. 'You're under the influence of a beautiful woman and you're not thinking straight. We should just call the police and ask for protection. I must admit that, if you have to do it anywhere, then the Capital is the very place, but please think; you're risking your life and liberty.'

'And if we call the police, what happens then? We're in this up to our necks and I doubt the rozzers will be particularly understanding about some of the shit we've been up to.'

'But you're only going to exacerbate things if you add another crime to the equation. GBH, that's pretty serious stuff, you know.'

'I know, but he's ruthless, Gemma, and he must be stopped. That Dutch copper was a really nice guy, you know; there was no need to knock him off like that.'

'So, how do you intend to go about it? I hope you're going to be a bit more subtle than bludgeoning him with a blunt instrument like his unfortunate brothers.'

Robbie tapped his nose. 'Leave that to me. It's best you know nothing about it.'

'And how's Terry taking all this?'

Robbie looked her in the eye. 'You still care, don't you?'

'Not at all, just curious, that's all,' snapped Gemma, face red with embarrassment.

'He's absolutely terrified and still in shock from last night. Listen, I don't want you anywhere near him or the Capital. You stay away until this is all over. Agreed?'

'Agreed,' said Gemma. 'Terry's had his chance and you know

how much I hate the Capital. Besides, I'm going to Jim's retirement do tonight; Karen's picking me up at seven.'

'Look, Celina needs something to wear for tonight. Could you come to town with us and help her pick something out. It's not my area of expertise, you know. I'm perfectly capable of dressing myself, but choosing clothes for a lady, that's another matter entirely.'

'A lady?' replied Gemma. 'Hmm, I suppose I could assist. Wouldn't mind purchasing a little number for myself too; might cheer me up a bit. Isn't it a bit risky to leave the house, though, with Emre around?'

'Don't think he'll try anything in broad daylight in a busy shopping centre. Come on, what do you say? I've never known you turn down a shopping trip before.'

Gemma sighed. 'Oh, OK then, but I doubt that Celina and I have the same taste.'

Robbie smiled. 'Thanks, Sis. I'll make it up to you when things are back to normal.'

'Robbie, you know things can never be "normal" again.'

22.

Bomkamp had to admit that the acoustics were superb as he sang the melancholy melody at the top of his voice. A family of mice scurried to their hole, the cobwebs vibrated and spiders were shaken from their slumbers at the boom of his baritone ...

Dans le port d'Amsterdam
Y a des marins qui boivent
Et qui boivent et reboivent
Et qui reboivent encore
Ils boivent à la santé
Des putains d'Amsterdam

... until a ghostly figure in the corner abruptly silenced his dulcet tones. At first it was just a misty glow, before he gradually gained focus and the unmistakable figure of Van Otterloo stood before him and spoke. 'Sir, I think you may have had a little too much wine.'

Bomkamp scrambled back in terror. 'What the hell are you doing here? You are not real; I have had a bang on the head and you are a figment of my imagination; or is it the wine? I only drank so much to numb the pain in my ankle.'

'But how did you see to open the bottles?' asked Van Otterloo. 'It is pitch-black down here and you have no corkscrew.'

'I have a torch on my phone and, to open the wine, I used an old trick demonstrated at a police party several years ago. A man named Frederick Beukham insisted that, if you bang the base of the bottle on the wall for long enough, then the pressure created pops the cork. It works too, although the host was not happy with the dents in his wall. Why am I speaking to you? You are just the cruel after-effects of concussion and vino. You are dead; why have you chosen to come back and haunt me?'

'Many years ago there was a TV detective show, sir, named *Randall and Hopkirk (Deceased)*. The whole plot was based upon the premise that only Randall could see the ghost of his ex-partner Hopkirk, who had been murdered in the line of duty and came back to assist Randall in catching criminals. As you can imagine, his invisibility to others proved to be a great asset in bringing numerous scoundrels to justice. I am here beyond the grave, sir, to offer the same support to you. Bomkamp and Van Otterloo (Deceased); it has a certain ring to it, do you not agree?'

'And do you think the readers, if there are any left, will fall for that one?'

'I do not see why not, sir; it was a very popular show in its day. The characters were latterly resurrected by the brilliant Vic Reeves and Bob Mortimer, so even our younger bookworms might get it. Besides, if the readers have endured thus far, it shows a certain willingness to embrace the absurd, do you not think? Either that or they have got nothing better to do.'

Bomkamp slapped himself round the face and poured wine over his head in a desperate attempt to stimulate clearer thought; but, when he looked up again, the ghost of Van Otterloo was still there. 'I am still at a loss as to how you know all these things – Rigsby, Alf Garnett, the Wombles, to name a few of the unlikely characters that have gate-crashed the party. How do they all fit into your strange world?'

Van Otterloo thought for a moment. 'Sir, I have told no-one else of my heritage but, as you have entrusted your dubious secret to me, I will reciprocate.' He paused for dramatic effect before declaring, 'My grandfather was the famous Dutch detective, Van Der Valk and, when I was but a small boy, he would take me to Simon Park to listen to the orchestra; there he would kneel down until we were at eye level and tell me all about the wonderful performers he'd met when he inhabited the same wavelengths. Since then I have embarked upon an amazing journey, studying everything to do with English culture of that era and beyond.'

Bomkamp looked upon the spectre of his subordinate in a new light. 'Van Der Valk!! Phew!! I can see why you kept it to yourself; that is some act to follow. And now we have Van Otterloo (Deceased) to add to the pantheon.'

'I would not presume to be worthy to walk in their footsteps, sir; and now that I am but a phantom, my influence will be diminished.'

'That is true,' said Bomkamp. 'OK then, until I sober up, I am willing to countenance your existence. Do you have any ideas as to how we can get out of here?'

'Oh, I can come and go as I please,' replied Van Otterloo. 'I am a ghost, remember. You, however, are in a bit of a predicament and will have to rely upon the mercy of your jailer. Having observed him for a little while, I am sure he will release you soon. They are all good people, you know. I was only dining with some of them last night, before my unfortunate and untimely demise. They have a plan to scare off Emre tonight and I intend to be there as a witness. I cannot intervene, though, being no longer of this world, but I am happy to report the events back to you, as they unfold.'

'This is utterly ludicrous,' exclaimed Bomkamp. 'This guy Randall; how long did it take before he realised that Hopkirk was a mere apparition and of no earthly use whatsoever?'

'Oh, he was a little sceptical at first, just as you are, but eventually they made a great team and solved many a mystery together. Ah, here is the professor now, right on cue.'

Bomkamp shielded his eyes from the sudden light as the hatch opened above him. 'OK, I suppose I should let you out now,' conceded his captor. 'I suspect you may be a trifle upset about our poor hospitality, but I can explain everything if you promise not to get too angry.'

Bomkamp was in no position to argue and he involuntarily glanced at Van Otterloo for reassurance, to see nothing but the shadows of the cellar's depths. So, he had imagined it all along. Shaking his head, he returned to reality and addressed the professor. 'I will require assistance to climb the steps, as my ankle is causing me much pain. If you help me out of here, then I am willing to discuss your kidnapping of a police officer in a civilised manner; before we throw the book at you.'

The professor nodded, descended slowly and proffered his hand. 'Professor Julian Nutt at your service, sir; I must apologise for the unwelcoming nature of your entrance to our humble home. I can assure you that we don't usually treat our guests in this way.'

'I am glad to hear it,' replied Bomkamp. 'Now, for God's sake get me out of here.'

Ten minutes later and Bomkamp was settled on the professor's sofa, his throbbing ankle raised up on a foot-rest, with an ice-pack accelerating the inevitable swelling and multi-coloured bruising. 'I'm awfully sorry,' said Professor Nutt. 'This wasn't my idea, you know. I was as surprised as you were when you disappeared down that hole, but it *has* given Kim-Ly the chance to put a few miles between her and you.'

'So, where is she?' asked Bomkamp.

'Now, you don't expect me to answer that, do you? Suffice it to say that she is somewhere safe. I know the whole sorry saga, you know; even about your little secret. If it's any consolation, I do have *some* sympathy; history is littered with men ruined by temptation and you won't be the last. Anyway, I'm sure we can come to some arrangement about this unfortunate accident. I am prepared to forget all I've been told about your, um, indiscretions, if you agree to leave here and return to Holland at the earliest opportunity. I will take you to the hospital to get an X-ray on that ankle and you can recuperate here until you are fit enough to leave. Now, what do you say?'

'But the mystery is unsolved,' protested Bomkamp. 'How can I return to my superiors, minus one very good Hoofdagent and bereft of answers?'

'From what I can gather, Kim-Ly and her associates have done you and some of your superiors a big favour in disposing of two extortionists; and now I think you should act in an honourable manner and cease your blind adherence to Emre's command. Do the right thing, man. Kim-Ly is not your enemy.'

A sudden shiver and Bomkamp sensed movement in front of the fireplace. 'He has a point, sir,' said Van Otterloo. 'Maybe it is time to go home to your wife and family and *que sera sera*, whatever will be will be.'

'Thank you, Doris Day,' snapped Bomkamp. 'When I want your advice I will ask for it. Now, will you stop messing with my head and go away.'

'Hey, I am only trying to help,' said Van Otterloo.

Professor Nutt followed Bomkamp's eye-line to see only companion set and coal scuttle. 'I say, are you OK, old chap? There's no-one there, you know, although I certainly wouldn't object to Doris Day warming her cheeks in front of my fire.'

Bomkamp felt the bump on his head and returned his gaze to the professor. Dazed and confused, he had to admit that the lure of home was becoming more appealing with each bizarre twist in the tale; and he was tired, tired of the chase, tired of the sleaze and tired of hiding the truth. With exasperation, he shook his head and sighed. 'Very well, I give up. I will leave, so long as the doctor says I am fit to travel.'

'A wise decision, sir,' said Van Otterloo. 'I will keep you abreast of events here, while you return and get some rest.' Bomkamp said nothing; the presence of Van Otterloo, whether real or imagined, was at once irritating and reassuring.

'A wise decision,' said Professor Nutt. 'I will fetch the car round to the front door and we can make our way to A&E.'

Glancing over his shoulder as he accepted the professor's offer of support, Bomkamp could swear he saw a smile and a nod of the head before the image of Van Otterloo faded into the ether.

23.

It looked like a normal building, no grandeur or pomp, just a terracotta townhouse with square windows and a balcony. Kim-Ly and Bunty approached the Embassy with trepidation, not knowing what response they would receive. 'It will be OK,' reassured Bunty. 'What is the worst thing they can do; and can it be any worse than you've been through already?'

'I guess you are right,' answered Kim-Ly.

'How may I help you?' asked the somewhat aloof gentleman at the desk.

Kim-Ly stood with head down to avoid his gaze, as Bunty got straight to the point and answered on her behalf. 'We are here to request the repatriation of one of your citizens. My friend here has sadly been mistreated in this country. She has been enslaved and abused by evil men and simply wants to go home to her family. Are you able to help?'

The man appraised Kim-Ly with a curious expression and asked, 'Do you have any proof of identity?'

Kim-Ly handed over her passport and hoped for the best. The man looked from her to her passport photo and back again, before requesting, 'Would you mind taking a seat over there, ladies, while I consult my supervisor? I will not be long.' He disappeared along a short corridor, knocked and entered a room at the end.

'I do not like this,' said Kim-Ly, as they sat down. 'It looked as if *he recognised me when he saw my passport. Why does he have to speak with his supervisor?'*

'Probably just procedure,' reassured Bunty. 'Look, this place is your best chance. Where else can you go for assistance?' She picked up a Vietnamese travel brochure from the small round table and flicked through the pages. 'It looks very beautiful, your country. I can see why you wish to return.'

'They are trying to sell you holidays,' replied Kim-Ly; 'they do not show the poverty and the shacks where the poor people live – but yes, Vietnam is a beautiful place and I miss it so much.'

After a short while a tall, elegant lady emerged and asked if they would enter her office. The man from the desk bowed politely and resumed his reception duties.

'Please, take a seat,' said the lady. 'My name is Hanh and I am here to help. Firstly, will you tell me how you came to be in England and why you have a false passport?'

Kim-Ly flinched. So, she was in trouble already and knew she would not be able to fool Hanh. She glanced at Bunty, whose simple nod was a signal to continue. Taking a deep breath, she began to speak, her heart pouring out details of the London leg of her misfortunes. She made no mention of Amsterdam, preferring to keep it simple and avoid too many questions. It felt good to relieve her burden to someone in authority, to place herself at the mercy of a representative of her country. Hanh said nothing, her face inscrutable and intent. 'My real passport was stolen by the pimps,' concluded Kim-Ly. 'The one you have there was obtained by someone who was trying to assist me to get back home. It was done in an act of kindness, not for criminal gain, so I will not reveal where I got it.'

'A heart-rending story,' said Hanh at last, 'but sadly not unfamiliar. There are many like you in the UK. I only wish that more would come to us for assistance.' She turned to Bunty. 'And can you vouch for Kim-Ly? How does she come to be in your care?'

'She is not in my care,' replied Bunty. 'Kim-Ly has just been staying with us for a short while and I can only speak for her honesty and

character. Please, all she asks is repatriation to her homeland.'

Hanh looked back and forth, from Kim-Ly to the passport photo. 'I think you are known to us. A man who says that he is your brother has been a regular visitor to the Embassy for the last two years. He brings a photograph and tells us each time that his sister would not desert her family and disappear without reason. He is very determined and insists that he will stay in London until he finds her. I tell him that many Vietnamese girls vanish without trace and are working as slaves or prostitutes throughout Europe, but still he persists. I keep telling him that it is like looking for a needle in a haystack, but it appears his patience may be rewarded after all.'

'An Dung is here?' exclaimed Kim-Ly. 'Do you have his contact? Can I speak with him?'

'Hey, one question at a time,' laughed Hanh. 'He did leave a number, yes. I will ask Phuoc Huu to call him. I am sure he will be here as quick as he can.'

'Thank you, thank you,' squeaked Kim-Ly, bouncing in the chair with excitement.

'It is always a pleasure to reunite someone with their family,' smiled Hanh. 'It is one of those rare and rewarding parts of my job. In the meantime, I suggest you fill out one of these "Lost Passport" forms and we can set the wheels in motion. We cannot have you travelling with this counterfeit, even though it is one of the best I have seen. Are you sure you will not tell us how you came by it?'

'I am sorry, but I will not get my friends into trouble.'

'I understand, but I have to ask. There is a lucrative trade in fake passports and many girls are forced to travel from one hell to another.'

'Is it as simple as that?' asked Bunty. 'Kim-Ly just fills out this form, you get her a new passport and she can go home?'

'Subject to some checks with Customs and the British authorities to confirm that Kim-Ly is not wanted in connection with any criminal activity, then yes, it can be that simple. It may take a few weeks, but I will try to expedite the procedures. It will give you a chance to say goodbye to your friends.'

Kim-Ly thought of Terry, of all he'd done for her, of his blind devotion to someone not worthy of his love. She would have liked to thank everyone for their kindness, for the sacrifices they'd made on her and Terry's behalf. She would have liked to say farewell to Celina, her best friend and fellow victim; but she had Robbie to look after her now. She looked sadly at Hanh. 'I think it will be better if I leave quietly, without fuss. I am not good at goodbyes.'

'As you wish. Do you need any protection or a place to stay?' asked Hanh. 'We can find you temporary accommodation until everything is in order. I will leave you to think about it while I ask Phuoc Huu to phone your brother.'

'It may be for the best if you take her up on that offer,' said Bunty, after Hanh had left the room. 'You cannot return to our house because Terry will come looking for you, and our policeman guest is not likely to be too happy with the welcome he received. There is a possibility that he could inform Emre. You should hide out with your brother until arrangements are made for you to return home.'

'I guess I have no alternative. But she said they would check with the British authorities and Customs. What if they are looking for me too?'

'That is a chance you will have to take,' said Bunty. 'There is no reason to believe that they are on to you yet. What other options do you have?'

Hanh re-entered with a beaming smile. 'An Dung will be here in thirty minutes. I think they may have heard his shout of elation back in Vietnam. Now, I am forgetting my manners; I have not offered you ladies any refreshments. I think we have cause for celebration.'

Kim-Ly was too excited to complete the passport form. She tried to focus, to answer the serious questions, but the knowledge that her beloved brother was on his way left her shaking and lacking in concentration. When An Dung entered the room she ran to him and wrapped her arms around his neck, the floodgates opening as the accumulated tears of oppression burst forth in an unstoppable torrent. 'Anh tôi, anh tôi were the only words she could muster: my brother,

251

my brother. Until, finally, his reassuring voice calmed her as he told of his quest to find his long-lost sister.

An Dung had moved to Hanoi in order to work and save sufficient funds to come to London, their mother insisting that Kim-Ly must be in trouble or she would have written. After a year, he still did not have enough and he calculated that it would take a decade on slave wages to accrue the plane fare. Eventually, a work colleague had pointed him in the direction of a charity that helped to search for and repatriate those who had been lost to their families. In return for the price of a ticket, An Dung had promised his services to the charity upon his return, until he'd paid his due. 'They must think that I have deceived them and taken their money and run away,' he said.

'Oh, my brother, you have sacrificed so much on my behalf. What about your life? Do you not wish to marry and raise your own family?'

'I still have time, but I am not sure if my girl will wait. I do not think she expected for me to be away so long.'

'And how is everyone back home?' asked Kim-Ly. 'I am so sorry to have put everyone through this worry.'

The reunion turned bittersweet, as An Dung answered. 'Father passed away before I left. You know he was not strong and his heart was broken when you did not return. He did not blame you, because he knew that you went to make money to send back to the family. I guess the streets here are not paved with gold after all.'

Kim-Ly wept. 'No, the streets are paved with shit. I should never have left; I could have looked after Father in his dying years. That was my duty and now I will never see him again.'

An Dung hugged his sister. 'Father was very ill; not even you could have kept him alive.'

'And Mother, is she OK?' asked Kim-Ly.

'Mother is ageing by the day, but ten years will fall from her face when you come home.'

'Oh, An Dung,' she sobbed, 'thank you, thank you for searching *and never giving up, for believing in me. I will spend the rest of my life making it up to you, I promise.'*

An Dung smiled. 'To know that you are safe is enough. I need no more thanks than that.'

24.

Gemma didn't want to be there, the floating party in full flow as she watched sadly from the periphery. Conversations overlapped in a continuous cacophony and she couldn't concentrate on any one subject-matter. Glasses clinked and laughter resounded; the retiring Jim, jovial to the end and holding court in the centre of the large, spot-lit cabin. Her head was all over the place: one minute insecure and bordering on tears, the next defiant and careless as she railed against rejection. She stared through the window as the boat sailed past the London Eye and recalled the time she'd clung to Terry in terror as the Eye reached its apex, her fear of heights heightened by the clear Perspex bubble and the lack of perspective, seemingly suspended in mid-air with little support. Shuddering at the thought and the fact that there was no longer anyone to hold her when needed, she turned back to the revelry and felt the metronomic beat of the music: 1970s Disco, Jim's era. She vowed to jump ship immediately if they dared to play *I Will Survive*.

Maybe she should have been flattered by the pursuit of Lewis, the infatuated office junior, but she really wasn't in the mood. It was all Celina's fault, mused Gemma. It must have been her subliminal influence that led her to choose this dress on their shopping expedition that afternoon; it was at least two inches shorter than anything else in her wardrobe. She tried to be polite, to let Lewis down gently, but still he persisted. She thought about hiding somewhere when he made his excuses to answer the call of nature, but was stopped by a voice from behind.

'Need rescuing?' asked Colin.

'No thanks, it's nothing I can't handle,' answered Gemma. She was on nodding terms with Colin, the occasional exchange of pleasantries at the coffee machine, a thank you when he held the door for her, the odd few words about matters of work; but she couldn't recall an entire conversation. It was difficult to assess Colin's age, but she suspected from his demeanour and manners that he was older than he looked. Of average height, with dishevelled fair hair and indistinct features, he was the kind of guy that no-one took much notice of. Pleasant enough, but ordinary; yes, that was the word, ordinary.

'You've got to admire that young man's courage,' said Colin, 'and you can't blame him for trying. When I was his age I was a gibbering wreck around women. Now that I have gained a modicum of confidence, I'm far too old and too married to do anything about it.'

'And where is your wife?' asked Gemma.

'At home; she's not one for parties. Nor am I, come to that, but I thought I should make the effort for Jim's retirement. He's one of the best, you know.'

'Yes, that's the only reason I'm here,' agreed Gemma.

Lewis swayed a little as he made his way back, either from the slight swell of the boat, or from the pre-party vodka consumed before he left home. Colin moved closer to Gemma, and Lewis smiled and waved, before changing direction and heading for a group of girls closer to his age.

'Thanks,' said Gemma. 'Think he's got the message.'

'So, what are you doing here on your own?' enquired Colin. 'You can't be short of suitors.'

'It's a long story, but in short, my ex ran off with a hooker.' Gemma felt obliged to fill the awkward silence, as Colin obviously couldn't tell whether or not she was joking. 'And what about you; are you *happily* married?'

'Generally, yes. I love my wife and kids, but I'm not sure that she still loves me. The intimacy went years ago, when the children were small. I don't know if she lost interest in sex or in me – probably both. Sorry, you don't want to know that.'

Gemma knew which way the conversation was going, but couldn't stop herself from asking – 'And aren't you ever tempted to seek intimacy elsewhere?'

'Well, firstly, I'm not vain enough to presume that anyone would be interested, and secondly, I don't think I could take the hassle of an affair. I've seen it happen to friends and colleagues, seen the wreckage it leaves behind, the heartbreak and ramifications. And then there's the lack of opportunity. What was it that the *Bard of Barking* once said? "Virtue never tested is no virtue at all".'

'You don't think I'm going to fall for that one, do you? The old "my wife doesn't understand me" line.'

Colin laughed. 'I expect you've heard all the dodgy chat-up lines there are. Some blokes look upon it as a challenge: how many notches can they add to the bedpost? But that's not me. I don't go out looking for trouble and trouble has done a bloody good job of avoiding me.'

Gemma took another look at Colin through wine-tinted spectacles and saw a kindly face, considerate and gentlemanly. Above all, she needed some comfort, a shoulder to cry on and, in her confused and slightly inebriated state, Colin was starting to fit the bill. 'This could be a long night,' she sighed. 'The last thing I need at the moment is to be among people who have the audacity to have a good time, when my world has fallen apart.'

'Do you want to talk about it?' asked Colin. 'A problem shared is a problem halved and all that.'

'Not really. You wouldn't believe it anyway. Let's get out of here,' suggested Gemma, feeling suddenly impulsive and reckless.

'Take me somewhere seedy and have your wicked way. Looks like you may just have found all the trouble you can take.'

Colin choked on his beer and glanced around in case anyone had overheard. His face was red with embarrassment and ardour. 'What, are you serious?'

'Never been more serious in my life. Come on, what harm can it do? We're both adults and we can be discreet. What's the old saying? While you can you've got to, because one day you won't be able to. I'd go with young Lewis and make his day, but it would be all round the office next week.'

'I'm a little out of practice,' said Colin, looking at once shocked, scared and uncomfortable.

'Then I'll be gentle with you,' said Gemma. 'Look, I don't make offers like this every day, you know. No strings attached; we go our separate ways in the morning and we're back on acquaintance terms on Monday. What do you say?'

'How can I refuse?' said Colin, breathing heavily. 'I must admit to indulging in the odd fantasy featuring you.'

'When you say the *odd* fantasy, what happens exactly?'

'I'll tell you later. It may have escaped your notice, but we're in the middle of the Thames at the moment so, unless you fancy swimming ashore, we'll have to wait till we dock.'

Gemma leant over and whispered in his ear. 'Are you sure you can last that long?'

'Jesus, will you stop that!' Colin shivered. 'I'm not used to this sort of thing.'

'No, me neither,' laughed Gemma. 'I think some of the others are going on to a nightclub after, but we can slip away quietly. Now, I suggest we mingle before people start talking. I'll see you on the quay.'

The remainder of the party drifted by in an impatient blur as Gemma considered what she'd just done. Had she really propositioned a married man and promised to indulge his fantasies? Could she go through with it? Colin returned her gaze and smiled nervously. Was he, too, having doubts?

Karen sauntered over, glowing from the exertion of a night on the dance-floor, as the boat rocked to a halt. 'Are you OK? You seem to be getting on well with Colin.'

'Oh, we were just chatting,' said Gemma.

'Are you coming to the club after?'

'No, I don't think so. I'll have to take this socialising business one step at a time. It has been a while, you know.'

An orderly queue formed as Jim made a point of shaking everyone's hand on their approach to the gangway. It seemed to take forever to get to Gemma's turn and she felt guilty for using his party as an excuse to indulge her insecurities. 'Ah, the beautiful and talented Gemma,' he beamed. 'Never give up, have confidence in your abilities and you will get that promotion. Whatever happens, don't lose your self-esteem; you can knock spots off most of those starchy old toffs. If the bastards overlook you next time, then take them to court for sex discrimination. Give me a call if you need my testimony. It's been an absolute pleasure working with you.'

Gemma smiled and gave him a hug. 'Thanks for everything, Jim; that means a lot. I could do with a bit of self-esteem at the moment. You have a very happy retirement and don't forget that you don't have to come to work on Monday.'

'Oh, you won't see me in that place again. I will be taking an honorary position with the Snuff Sniffers' Symposium and my days will be filled with relaxation. You take care now.'

Jim's words had slightly rekindled the spring in her step and, as she negotiated the rather rickety gangway, a slight breeze blew a little life back into her soul. Surveying the quay in search of Colin, she was buffeted by staggering revellers on their way to more merriment. There he was, leaning on the railings and waving in anticipation. Glancing around for concealment, she joined the back of a crowd and made her way casually in his direction. Grabbing his arm as she passed, they continued behind the throng until they reached a junction and took the opposite direction, disappearing into the neon-lit London night like so many other illicit lovers.

The street outside the Capital was even busier than usual and Robbie jumped at the slightest sound or boisterous holler. With Celina on his arm, he was attracting the accustomed envious glances from all the young studs in the queue and he wondered again at her subliminal talent to draw unwanted attention. He studied every swarthy face in the crowd, fearing a sudden attack like the previous night. Where *was* Emre? For a moment he thought he saw him, the same hooked nose and intense stare, until the man smiled and kissed the mousy girl by his side.

Robbie squeezed Celina's hand and waved as the nervous-looking Sandra, Pete and Barry appeared on the other side of the street. He motioned for them to join the back of the line. Terry's text had confirmed that he was in place and Robbie searched the urban sprawl for any sign of his hiding place. It was of some comfort to know that it would not be hard for him to disappear in such a multitude; but, equally, it served as perfect concealment for Emre.

Charmless as ever, Timmy the enormous doorman greeted him with his usual air of macho authority. Robbie had been frequenting the Capital for years, but still he was subjected to the ritual frisking every week. 'And how are you on this fine evening?' enquired Robbie, as Timmy ran his hand up his inside leg. 'You enjoy this bit, don't you? I'm sure you look upon it as one of the perks of the job. You'd get arrested if you walked up to someone in the street and touched their thigh, you know.'

'Just doing my job,' grunted Timmy, as he turned his attention to Celina.

'Do not even think about it,' scowled Celina, his equal in height in her customary heels.

Timmy stepped back and summoned his stocky female counterpart. 'I wouldn't dare, Miss,' he said. 'Tracey will oblige if you'd be so kind as to open your bag for inspection.'

Celina glared at him defiantly for a moment, before Robbie said, 'No problem, let's get this over with and let us in, will you.'

Once inside, they met up with Stevie, Joey and Jimmy, all inevitably in awe of Celina as they clapped Robbie on the arm and welcomed him back.

'So, where's this guy you want seeing to?' shouted Joey, raising his arms and mock-sparring in boxer fashion. 'Just say the word and I'm ready.'

Robbie grabbed him and took him to one side. 'Will you keep your voice down, you tosser. Firstly, Celina knows nothing about this and I don't want her frightened; and secondly this is no joke – he's a dangerous man and he'll probably be armed.'

'He won't get past Timmy the Bouncer if he's carrying anything,' reasoned Joey. 'He even confiscated Stevie's comb the other week.'

'Maybe so, but we can't take any chances. Has Stevie briefed you on the plan?'

'Yeah, such as it is. Not exactly subtle, is it?'

'We don't need subtle. All we're trying to do is to scare him away and leave him in no doubt as to what would happen if he returned. Now, come and meet some friends of mine. Pete, Sandra, Barry; please allow me to introduce Joey, the brains of the operation.'

As if on cue, he felt the vibration of his phone and, fumbling in his pocket, he read the chilling words from Terry: 'He's here; good luck.'

A thumbs-up to Stevie and their eyes fixed on the entrance, where Emre appeared briefly before ducking out of sight and into the crowd. 'Shit!' exclaimed Robbie. 'We've lost him already; he could be anywhere.'

Sandra and Pete clustered round Celina, who looked as if she was beginning to suspect that something was going on. From their vantage point at the highest part of the club, they looked in every shadowy alcove, behind every revelling punter, among drinkers and dancers alike, but he was nowhere to be seen. Growing more and more nervous as the evening wore on, the decibels increased as the beat became more insistent and the bass lines thundered in reply; all outdone, as the clock struck midnight, by a blood-curdling scream that saw all in the vicinity jump in unison. It was Celina who'd seen him first, drifting across the dance floor in staccato fashion as the strobe lighting exposed him first here, then there, then not at all; a brief but unmistakable vision of her worst fears.

'It was Emre!' she panted. 'I svear, I saw him.'

Robbie grabbed both her arms and held her tight until she stopped shaking. 'Now calm down,' he demanded. 'You stay here with Sandra, Pete and Barry; we'll sort him out, I promise.' A kiss on the lips and he was gone, with Stevie, Joey and Jimmy in close pursuit. Robbie had him in sight and weaved in and out of the crowd as he followed. He signalled for the others to spread out and a pincer movement was formed with almost military precision as they closed in on their prey. At last they had him cornered and, before he could turn, Stevie and Jimmy had an arm each and were bundling him down a corridor towards the toilets.

A shocked, sallow punter jumped as they all crashed through the door of the Gents and Robbie declared. 'This one's out of order, pal; you'll have to use the bog on the first floor.'

'N-no problem,' he replied.

'And you haven't seen anything, right?'

'N-not a thing, no.' He retreated, terrified, tripped in his haste and didn't look back.

Robbie shouted to Joey. 'Have you put the "out of order" sign on the door?'

'Yeah, and I'll make sure no-one comes in. But don't be too long, right. I'm bursting for a piss myself.'

Emre struggled and protested, but he was no match for the combined strength of Stevie and Jimmy One-Note. 'You will regret this,' he snarled. 'Do you know who you are dealing with? You will not live to tell of the day that you crossed Emre.'

'Ha, we're really scared,' replied Stevie. 'You're on our patch now and you don't make the rules around here. My friend here has been telling us what a lowlife and a bully you are and it will be an absolute pleasure to teach you a lesson you'll never forget. If you can walk when we've finished with you, then you will leave here and return to Holland. If we ever see you again, or I hear about you intimidating *any* of my friends, then we won't be so gentle next time. Do I make myself clear?'

Emre spat derisively in his face and attempted once more to wriggle free. 'Fight like a man, you English scum, one against one. I will bet that you are not so brave without your gang to hold me down. Humph.'

He doubled-up as Robbie landed a well-aimed punch to his abdomen. 'Should we be as brave as you,' he asked, 'when you and your dead brother beat-up Kim-Ly? And what about all the other girls you've ruled through fear? What chance did you give them to fight back?'

'Robbie, stop this now.' The assertive female voice from behind prevented the second blow from landing. He turned to see Celina glaring proudly down at the pathetic figure of Emre.

'I tried to stop her,' shouted Joey. 'I told her there's a "Ladies" on the other side, but she insisted on coming in.'

Surprised at the interruption, Stevie and Jimmy momentarily loosened their grip and in a split-second Emre was upon Celina, his hands tightening around her throat. She gasped as his thumbs pressed firm upon her windpipe, his frenzy and hatred accentuating the pressure. Despite their collective might, Stevie, Jimmy and Robbie struggled to loosen his manic grip and he left Celina gasping for air before they wrestled him to the ground and resumed their assault.

'Vait!' rasped Celina, on her knees and taking deep, deep breaths. Robbie knelt beside her and held her tight until she was able to stand and regain her composure and dignity. She placed her hands gently on her neck and felt the tender flesh where Emre's callous hands had been. Her face hardened in an expression of distaste as she stared down at the wretched pimp before her. She took in more rancid air and, eventually, addressed Robbie in measured tones. 'And vhat vill happen vhen you have finished vith him? Do you think he vill simply disappear and leave us in peace? No, this coward vill find us and shoot us in the head vhen ve are not ready or he vill vait until me or Kim-Ly are alone and find a new vay to torture us.'

'Then what do you suggest?' asked Robbie.

'I think I may have a better idea,' answered Celina. Rummaging in her bag, her hand emerged with a large syringe and she looked Emre in the eye as he cowered in fear. 'This is how you took away my life, how you controlled us all and stole our free vill. Perhaps now it is your turn to feel vhat it is like to be a slave to heroin.'

Emre summoned all his strength and battled against the iron grip of his captors, but to no avail. 'Please, no!' he pleaded. 'Do not let that crazy woman near me. Can you not see the evil in her eyes? Please, have some mercy.'

Robbie turned angrily to Celina. 'Where did you get that? You promised you were clean and Timmy the Bouncer searched your bag on the way in.'

'It is not hard to score in a place like this,' replied a contrite Celina. 'I am so sorry, Robbie, but it is not that easy to stop. Look, I have enough here to finish the job and better it course through that bastard's veins than mine. Vhat do you say? In the morning they vill find another dead junkie in a sleazy nightclub toilet, with an empty syringe by his side. It happens every day; no-one vill suspect anything and ve are free of him forever.'

'No,' begged Emre. 'Please, you are all men. Have you never been with a prostitute? It is men like me who provide the service and it is girls like her who provide your pleasure. It is the way of the world.'

'Well, it's not the way of our world,' said Stevie. 'We're no fucking angels, but we do have some standards. What do you think, Robbie?'

Robbie shook his head, his face etched with panic as he took in Celina's expression; cold-blooded hatred as she stared at the pitiful, trembling Emre, begging for his life.

'Jesus, I hadn't planned for this,' gulped Robbie. 'I don't know.'

'Then turn the other vay,' said Celina. 'It vill be over in minutes.'

A shiver came over Robbie, as if there was a ghost in the room; and he quaked as he saw the cold and steely resolve in Celina's eyes. Without answering, he walked towards the door and joined a curious Joey. 'What's going on in there?' he asked.

'You don't want to know,' answered an ashen-faced Robbie, as the muffled screams of Emre faded to silence.

25.

One year had passed before Terry felt able to sit back down at his PC and complete the catharsis. Every piece of writing should have a conclusion, he thought. His journalism training had taught him thus; but life was a different beast entirely. As one episode closes, then another begins, interwoven with the unsynchronised chapters of those you meet along the way. Who knows how things would have panned out had he pulled the covers up around his ears and shut out the screams of the girl downstairs; who knows where they would all be now?

So, what happened to those disparate characters, thrown together by that single act of impetuous folly? Well, for all but the tragi-comic Van Otterloo, and the ne'er-do-well Emre and his brothers, mortal life went on.

Following advice from the hospital, Bomkamp spent another week with the professor and Bunty, during which time he made himself known to the British police. He told them how he and Van Otterloo had been in pursuit of a drugs and prostitution boss who had fled Holland. He assisted the police in identifying the body of Emre, confirming that he was indeed the man they were looking for and that he was almost certainly the one who'd murdered his colleague. He advised them of Emre's known next-of-kin and, after some indignant comments about a lack of international co-operation, the Met had closed the case and sent him on his way.

With relief, he returned to his wife and family, who welcomed him with open arms and nursed him back to health. Once the dust had settled, he resumed work and, with a certain amount of imperceptible spectral assistance, he was being spoken of as the next Commissaris.

Surprisingly, Sandra settled into the Grand Union lifestyle with little fuss and was often seen happily creating inspirational canal-influenced art; while Pete pottered perpetually with an enduring air of contentment. They both eschewed luxury and learnt to share confined spaces without too many arguments.

Celina and Robbie registered their charity, aptly named *Fallen Angels*, which boasted Professor Nutt and Bunty as generous benefactors and trustees. Sandra and Pete offered occasional refuge for some of the fleeing girls, while Bunty insisted on doing her bit by offering temporary accommodation, in spite of the professor's reservations.

Kim-Ly boarded that plane home to Vietnam, despite Terry's Hollywood-style last-minute dash to the airport. He'd begged and badgered Professor Nutt and Bunty, until they finally gave in on the day of the flight and told him that she was boarding Vietnam Airlines 503 at 18.00. At first she didn't recognise the shaven-headed maniac jumping up and down and desperately calling her name. With a tear in her eye, she hesitated, torn between two worlds, between love and duty. With a barely perceivable sob, she blew Terry a farewell kiss; and then she was gone, back to the bosom of her family. It was where she belonged; far away from the West that had caused her so much misery and far away from the broken man who thought he could offer salvation.

Terry had returned devastated to his empty flat and there he'd stayed until financial necessity dictated that he do some work. With the anonymous assistance of Professor Nutt, he'd delivered his piece exposing the corruption of Sir Nigel Shelby, thereby earning a temporary stay of execution on cutbacks to the education budget. He knew it would not be long, however, before the government employed someone else to do their dirty work and the battle would start anew. Terry's reputation ensured that he was never short of takers for his freelance work and, whenever he needed pictorial accompaniment to his articles, he'd call on Barry.

Terry and Pete never did get to write that sitcom as life had gotten far too serious recently, but if they ever get round to it then Bomkamp and Van-Otterloo will surely land the leading roles. To disguise his new lack-of-hair-style, Terry grew accustomed to donning an array of stylish pork-pie hats, similar to those favoured by best-selling author Joe Stamford. Even Robbie thought he looked cool.

Terry didn't hear a word from Gemma, nor did he feel he had the right to contact her. Reports from Robbie hinted that she was in a relationship and that it might be best if he stayed away. Hadn't he caused her enough heartbreak already?

And what of the girl downstairs? Kim-Ly fulfilled her promise to write to Professor Nutt and Bunty, telling of her poignant return home. Destiny dictated that she realise her dream to become a schoolteacher and, under her tutelage, the village school was thriving. All of the children were learning English and she would often tell them the tale of a tall, gangling hero who looked a bit like Elvis.

And perhaps that's the end. Terry's fingers hovered undecided, between the 'save' and 'delete' buttons on his keyboard, while he stared sadly at the screen with the title *The Girl Downstairs* glaring back at him. One hour later, he contacted his prospective publisher to inform him of his decision.

The Epilogue

A holiday, that's what the doctor ordered. 'Take a break and get some sea air,' he'd said. 'I could give you some pills, but you will simply become reliant on them; and I'm sure you'd rather walk out of here with the determination to beat this unaided. If Cornwall doesn't work, then come and see me again.'

And hence Terry found himself on the beach, with only his iPod, Steinbeck's *East of Eden* and a cacophony of seabirds for company. He felt hollow, as if his insides had been scooped out and fed to the vultures of lost love. Somehow he'd conspired to lose both of the girls he loved and, along with them, the ability or will to permit any hope for the future.

He stared wistfully as a distant ship hugged the horizon and wondered as to its destination. Maybe he should leave for pastures new, start again somewhere else: Australia, New Zealand, America? Yeah, why not; what did he have to lose? He turned up the volume, closed his eyes and let the music wash over him as the sun beat down and shed warmth upon his battered soul; until a shadow rudely blocked the rays. He opened his eyes, expecting to see an inconsiderate cloud, and squinted as a silhouette stood above him, hands on hips in a defiant pose.

'Are you OK?' asked the silhouette.

'Been better, but I'll survive. How did you find me?'

'Your Uncle Tony told me you'd be here; said you were

depressed and needed to get away for a while. He was worried about you.'

'Ah, yes, Uncle Tony, the amateur psychologist. He was telling me about the therapeutic qualities of listening to *Quadrophenia* on the beach at very high volume.'

'And is it working?'

'No, not really. What about you? The last I heard you were having an affair with some guy from work.'

'Oh, you know; the same old story. When it came to the crunch he wouldn't leave his wife and the guilt was destroying me. I guess we've both been through the mill recently, most of it self-inflicted.'

'You could say that, yeah. How did it ever come to this, Gemma? We made a good team, didn't we?'

As his eyes became accustomed to the light, he saw the hint of a smile on Gemma's lips. 'We sure did. You remember that note you threw across the classroom – "meet me outside after school"? It seems a world away from what we've both become.'

'Are we really that different?' asked Terry. 'Life just got in the way. We're still the same people if we dig deep enough.'

'You think so?'

'Absolutely. I'd throw paper at you any time.'

'I once thought that you'd never throw paper at anyone else,' said Gemma. 'Have you heard from Kim-Ly?'

Terry looked pensive. 'Only through the professor. It seems she's doing OK.'

'It wasn't a bad thing you did, you know. You set her free. She and Celina would still be there if not for you; and Emre and his cronies would still be making their lives a misery.'

'Yeah, I guess you're right. You always were a glass-half-full person.'

'So were you, once,' said Gemma; then an awkward silence prevailed until she asked in tentative tones, 'Terry Logan, will you marry me?'

Terry gasped. 'What, are you serious? You'd take me back after all I did?'

'Yes, I think so; but this really is your last chance.'

Terry spent a short while in thought, milking the moment and taking Gemma to the edge of infuriation. 'Yes,' he said at last, 'on one condition.'

'What condition? You're not in a position to be making conditions.'

'That we start making babies.'

'What, now?'

Terry looked up and down the beach, completely deserted apart from a few disinterested seagulls. 'Yeah, why not?'

And, through the discarded headphones, *Love, Reign O'er Me* reached its dramatic climax, as the waves crashed upon the shore.

Lightning Source UK Ltd.
Milton Keynes UK
UKOW02f1026171114

241724UK00001B/2/P